OSLG

W9-CFZ-084

MAY 10 2001

The Angel and the Jabberwocky Murders

An Augusta Goodnight Mystery
(with heavenly recipes)

**Center Point
Large Print**

**This Large Print Book carries the
Seal of Approval of N.A.V.H.**

The Angel and the Jabberwocky Murders

An Augusta Goodnight Mystery
(with heavenly recipes)

MIGNON F. BALLARD

CENTER POINT PUBLISHING
THORNDIKE, MAINE

This Center Point Large Print edition
is published in the year 2007 by arrangement with
St. Martin's Press.

Copyright © 2006 by Mignon F. Ballard.

All rights reserved.

The text of this Large Print edition is unabridged. In other
aspects, this book may vary from the original edition. Printed in
Thailand. Set in 16-point Times New Roman type.

ISBN-10: 1-58547-922-5
ISBN-13: 978-1-58547-922-1

Library of Congress Cataloging-in-Publication Data

Ballard, Mignon Franklin.
   The Angel and the jabberwocky murders : an Augusta Goodnight mystery
(with heavenly recipes) / Mignon F. Ballard.--Center Point large print ed.
      p. cm.
   ISBN-13: 978-1-58547-922-1 (lib. bdg. : alk. paper)
      1. Goodnight, Augusta (Fictitious character)--Fiction. 2. Guardian angels--Fiction.
   3. Women college students--Crimes against--Fiction. 4. South Carolina--Fiction.
   5. Large type books. I. Title.

PS3552.A466A83 2007
813'.54--dc22

2006029161

For my sister, Sue Marie Lewis, my "almost" sister and brother, Tommye Johnston and Jim Lay, and for Pam Rivers and Lizann Lutz, Augusta's best friends, with love and thanks

Mystery
Ballard, Mignon Franklin.
The angel and the Jabberwocky
murders [large print] : an

Acknowledgments

Sincere appreciation to my agent, Laura Langlie, and my editor, Hope Dellon, masters of the craft.

Chapter One

*O*h, I wish I were a little bar of soap! I wish I were a little bar of soap! I'd slippy and I'd slidy over everybody's hidey. Oh, I wish I were a little bar of soap . . ."

Sighing, I flipped over in bed for the umpteenth time and buried my head under the pillow. Teddy, my six-year-old grandson, had plagued me with that ridiculous ditty all afternoon and now I couldn't get the silly song out of my head, so when thunder rattled the windows and lightning exploded like a flashbulb just outside my bedroom, I welcomed the diversion.

Clementine, however, did not. My dog awoke from her favorite sleeping spot on the kitchen rug and began to bark frantically, toenails scratching as she dashed back and forth on the hardwood floors. I was reaching for my robe to go and calm her when I heard her enormous paws pounding up the stairs to Augusta, her guardian angel. And mine.

It had been Augusta who had taken the puppy under her wing, so to speak, the year before, and now Clementine not only claimed what had been my grandmother's rag rug in the kitchen, but my favorite chair, the run of the house—and my heart.

"Hush now, it's all right." Augusta spoke from the top of the stairs and the dog immediately stopped barking to huddle at the angel's feet. "I think this calls for some spiced cider," she said, gathering a voluminous cloudlike shawl about her trembling shoulders. Augusta has suffered from bouts of the shivers since that long-ago Christmas at Valley Forge, she tells me. She sat on the stairs and took the big dog's head into her lap, drawing the animal closer until they both stopped trembling, then followed me into the sitting room, where I poked futilely at the embers in the fireplace.

With an inconspicuous wave of her hand, Augusta soon had amber flames licking what had once been a limb from a black-walnut tree that had come close to crashing into the house during a late-August storm.

"Do-law! Another two inches and that thing would've slammed right into your roof," my next-door neighbor, Nettie McGinnis, had announced, observing the sodden debris. "I'll swear, Lucy Nan, you must have a guardian angel!"

I smiled and agreed. She was right, of course, but except for me, no one was aware of Augusta's presence but my friend Ellis Saxon. A year ago, when she came to my door in response to my advertisement for a room to rent, Augusta had announced that during that particular period in her life Ellis needed a bit of divine intervention as well, and it wasn't long before her prediction proved to be true.

Warmth from the fire had taken the chill from the room when I returned from the kitchen with two steaming mugs of cider and a doggie treat for Clementine, whom I rudely dislodged from my chair. Augusta curled up with a lap robe on a corner of the sofa and the two of us sipped in companionable silence, listening to rain pounding against the house and the rhythmic thump of Clementine's tail. Another peaceful evening in Stone's Throw, South Carolina, I thought.

Of course it didn't last.

"I'm kind of worried about Claudia," my neighbor Nettie said the next day as we attempted to clear a pathway through soggy leaves and twigs from the sidewalk out front.

Acorns crunched underfoot as I sidestepped a puddle. "What's the matter with Claudia?" I asked. Claudia Pharr was the youngest and most recent member of Stone Throw's oldest book club, the Thursday Morning Literary Society (commonly referred to as The Thursdays), which now meets on Monday afternoons.

"Money—or the lack of it—would be my guess. Seems depressed. You knew her husband had to take a cut in pay when they downsized his company last year, and their oldest boy's just about ready for college." Nettie attacked the sidewalk with accelerated strokes of her broom as she neared the end of her stretch. "Plus, I think she's bored. Needs something to do."

"She has been unusually quiet," I said. "But then Claudia was never much of a talker."

My neighbor laughed. "Never had a chance with the rest of us yakkety-yakking all the time!"

"I knew she was looking for a job," I said. "Worked for some big corporation in Charlotte before she decided to stay at home with the boys. Remember? Claudia has great organizational skills—think of all her volunteer work. Why, half the groups in town would fall apart without her."

"That's all well and good, but it doesn't put food on the table." Nettie pushed up the sleeves of her baggy brown cardigan and paused to survey the results of our efforts. "Enough of this. I made some pumpkin muffins this morning. Come on in and I'll give you a cup of coffee. We've earned a break."

She shaded her eyes and squinted through foggy bifocals at the lanky figure crossing the lawn on the other side of the street, mailbag strapped to his sloping shoulder. "I'll swear, Bun gets later every day. Must be after three."

"Probably takes him that long to feel his way around town," I said. "Blind as a bat! I don't see how he reads the addresses."

"Sometimes he doesn't." Nettie rested on her broom. "Look at him—see how he bends the envelope to try and make out the name. Just about every piece of mail I get is delivered in a permanent curl, and you know how he's always mixing ours up."

I propped my broom against the low stone wall that borders our lawns as I watched the tall figure shuffling across the street at the corner. "Poor Bun. If he held those letters any closer they'd be at the back of his head."

"Well, he never says no to a mid-afternoon snack. Tell him to wait up and I'll grab him a couple of muffins," Nettie said, hurrying inside.

She was back with two napkin-wrapped muffins on a paper plate by the time Bun Varnadore turned in at the walk. "Thought you might like a little something for your sweet tooth," Nettie called, meeting the letter carrier at the foot of the steps. "And you might as well give Lucy Nan her mail, too. Spare yourself another stop."

I joined her and greeted him, holding out my hand for the letters. It wasn't until Bun had continued on his way that I noticed one of the dog-eared envelopes hand-delivered to me was addressed to the neighbors who live two houses down. Nettie smiled when she saw it. "Wait until Bun's out of sight and then drop it in their mailbox," she whispered, and I agreed. We wouldn't hurt his feelings for the world.

"Nettie thinks Claudia might be having financial problems," I confided to Ellis when she dropped by later that day. Like Nettie, Claudia, and me, along with several others, Ellis Saxon is a member of The Thursdays, and what concerns one of us, usually concerns us all.

My friend nodded. "I think she's right. Unfortunately, there's not much opportunity for employment here in Stone's Throw."

"What about the college, Lucy Nan?" Augusta asked. "Since you'll be teaching a course at Sarah

Bedford this quarter, you might be in a position to hear if something becomes available."

"I'll keep my eyes and ears open," I said, "but I'm only there a few days a week and it's just the one course."

"We might ask Jo Nell's friend if she knows of any opportunities," Ellis suggested. "What's her name, Lucy Nan? You know—that mousy little woman who's in charge of food services at the college."

"Willene Benson? She's a nutritionist, I think—oversees the cafeteria." I shrugged. "It won't hurt to ask her."

Augusta and I sat at the kitchen table wrapping cheese dough around pimento-stuffed olives. "Wash your hands, pull up a chair, and throw in," she said to Ellis, who grinned and raised a brow at me, knowing the angel meant "pitch" in.

"At least you didn't ask me to *throw up!*" Ellis said, dutifully following Augusta's instructions. "And why, might I ask, are we making all these olive-cheese balls?"

"Jo Nell's hosting The Thursdays next week and I promised I'd help with refreshments since her arthritis is acting up again," I explained. It was peculiar how my cousin's ailments seemed to worsen when there was work to be done, but she'd always been there for me during life's darker days, so I didn't mind lending a hand. Besides, with Augusta's help, making them really wasn't that much of a chore.

Now Ellis examined the rows of unbaked pastries

lining the cookie sheet. After they were frozen they would be transferred to a freezer bag and later baked by my cousin just before her guests arrived. A Stone's Throw favorite, the appetizers were delicious at any temperature, but when served warm they were, as my daddy used to say, "just too blamed good for most folks!"

"Would you look at that!" Ellis pointed out. "Augusta's olive-cheese balls are all exactly the same size! And how do you make them so fast?"

Augusta smiled. Today, I noticed, her eyes were exactly the same aquamarine as the dazzling necklace she wore. "You forget I have a few hundred years' experience on you," she reminded us.

"Tell us, what's it like to be a professor?" Ellis asked me as she pinched off a wad of golden dough.

I laughed. *"Professor!* I don't think so! Teaching one class a few days a week hardly qualifies me for that title—and I had to bargain with Bellawood's board of directors to get them to agree with that arrangement."

In my part-time position as public relations director at the restored plantation of Pentecost Pitts, one of South Carolina's early governors, I edited the monthly newsletter, *Past Times,* sent out news releases about upcoming events, and was often called upon to speak to organizations about the facilities there, stressing the benefits, of course, of membership and financial support. When I was approached by the local college to teach a hands-on history class on the skills of daily pioneer living, I snatched at the opportunity to spread the word. The board at Bellawood, however, had reservations.

"I should think it would be in their interest," Augusta said.

"You'd think," I said, "but they had a picky little point."

"Like what?" Ellis asked.

"Like I don't know how to do all that stuff," I told them.

Ellis made a face. "I did wonder about that, but I wasn't going to say anything."

"Well, that's a first!" I said. Ellis Saxon and I had been best friends since we ate out of the same paste jar in Miss Jan Smith's nursery school class at Stone's Throw Presbyterian and we rarely hold anything back.

"So how do you plan to get around that little hitch?" she asked.

"By bringing in experts, naturally. The class and I will learn at the same time." I fished the last olive from the jar and ate it. "I already have them all lined up, and I met with Joy Ellen Harper yesterday. She's the history professor I'll be working with."

"And?" Ellis slid the sheet of pastries into the freezer.

I shrugged. "And I got the distinct impression my course had been thrust upon her." A small-framed woman who looked to be in her mid-forties, Joy Ellen dressed in sort of a threadbare elegance and had very little to say to me.

"She'll get over it," Ellis assured me. "When's your first class?"

"Monday, and I'll be getting a little help with my lesson plans over the weekend." I smiled at Augusta, who raised her coffee cup to me in acknowledgment.

"Good. You can tell us all about it at The Thursdays that afternoon," Ellis said, slinging a sweater about her shoulders. "And don't forget to put out the word for Claudia."

"I won't," I promised.

But when I arrived at the campus the following Monday, all thoughts of Claudia Pharr vanished from my mind.

The knot of girls whispering in the hallway outside my classroom fell silent as I approached. I recognized one of them as Celeste Mungo, the younger sister of Weigelia Jones, whom I had tutored in the literacy program a few years before. "What's up?" I asked, unlocking the classroom door.

"It's D.C.," Celeste explained. "She's disappeared, and nobody seems to know where she is."

"D.C. who?" The room smelled of chalk and of more than a century's accumulation of dust and grime, in spite of the freshly painted walls, and I sniffed as I dumped an armload of reference books on the desk at the front of the room and wrote my name on the board behind it.

"D.C. Hunter," another girl explained. "Nobody's seen her all weekend."

"Oh, she'll come dragging in when she's good and

ready," someone muttered from the back of the room. "It's just like her to make everybody worry over nothing!"

"Who's worried?" Celeste's comment made everybody giggle.

When everyone was seated I handed out the syllabus and explained the course of study, and the whereabouts of D.C. Hunter took a backseat for a while to the practical basics of what we were about to undertake. "You might want to put your nice clothing in the back of the closet when you come to the class from now on," I warned them, "because we're going to get down and dirty!" I explained we would be sharing a firsthand experience in cooking over an open fireplace, soap-making, creating natural dyes and other handicrafts our ancestors practiced out of necessity. When Joy Ellen Harper quietly entered the room at the end of the period, I was relieved that she found the class in an enthusiastic discussion on the pros and cons of herbal remedies.

"Ms. Harper, have they heard anything from D.C. yet?" a student asked her as the class filed out.

She shook her head. "I don't believe so, Paula. If they have, I haven't heard anything about it.

"I'm sorry I missed your class today," she said, addressing me. "I had a conference with one of my students, but I do plan to sit in as often as I can from now on."

I told her I would look forward to that, although to tell the truth, she made me feel a little uneasy. I was gathering up my teaching materials prior to leaving when I remembered to ask about a possible job opening for Claudia.

"I haven't heard of one, but you might check with administration." The professor paused. "And about this girl who's supposedly missing . . . I hope you won't mention it off campus. Sometimes it doesn't take much for these students to get all worked up, and I'm sure the Hunter girl will show up soon if she isn't back already." She gave me a stiff attempt at a smile. "I imagine the college would prefer this not to be spread all over town."

I gave her an even stiffer smile in return. "Believe me, I have no intention of spreading unfounded rumors," I said.

But of course, it was too late. Apparently, Joy Ellen Harper wasn't acquainted with The Thursdays.

"Well, it's happening again," Idonia Mae Culpepper said, looking around to see if anybody was listening.

"What's happening again?" Nettie McGinnis leaned forward to set aside her coffee cup and the rustic porch chair creaked under the strain.

Members of the Thursday Morning Literary Society (which now meets on Monday afternoons) were taking advantage of the mild October weather by holding their meeting on my cousin Jo Nell's large screened porch, where a ceiling fan circled lazily, stirring the open leaves of Jane Austen's *Pride and Prejudice*, our current undertaking.

19

"Something's not right over at the college. Sounds like another girl's disappeared." Idonia scraped the last smidgen of damson pie from her plate and blotted bright pink lipstick on Jo Nell's monogrammed tea napkin.

My cousin pretended not to notice, but the vein in her temple throbbed double-time. "What do you mean, *disappeared?*" She turned to me. "Lucy Nan, you're teaching a course over at the college this quarter, aren't you? Do you know anything about this?"

I shrugged. "No more than you do, but I'm sure it's just a rumor."

"Are you certain about this?" Ellis asked Idonia, who was sometimes known to exaggerate. "I haven't heard anything about it."

"No, and you won't if the college has its way," Idonia said. "I found out from Kim this morning when I had my hair done." She gave one flaming curl a twist. "I have a standing appointment on Mondays, you know."

Several of the ladies nodded impatiently. A few of them had their hair washed and set on a weekly basis at the Total Perfection Beauty Salon across from the Stone's Throw Post Office, and they shared a similar style. Kim knew a good thing when she saw it.

"Maybe she just took a long weekend," Zee St. Clair suggested. "Went off somewhere with her boyfriend. They don't think a thing in the world about doing that now, you know."

20

"Hasn't anyone contacted the girl's parents?" Ellis asked.

"Kim says her grandparents are the ones who raised her. They live up in Virginia somewhere and haven't the least idea where she is," Idonia chimed in. "And she didn't say anything to her roommate about it, either."

Zee groaned. "Well, for heaven's sake, who is this girl? Doesn't anybody know her name?"

Willene Benson spoke up. "D.C. Hunter. And I think you're all hard up for something to worry about."

The college nutritionist had come as a guest of the hostess, and she now screwed up her pale thin lips as if she struggled to stanch her opinions. It didn't work. "I know this girl," she said, "and it wouldn't surprise me a bit if she weren't just staying out of sight to create a sensation."

"Why would she do that?" Jo Nell asked.

Willene rolled her eyes. "Drama major—went to school in England a couple of years and used to doing pretty much as she pleases. Reckon she must have a first name, but everybody just calls her D.C."

I passed around what was left of the olive-cheese balls. "How did she end up at Sarah Bedford?" I asked.

"I wondered about that, too," Willene said, taking two. "Somebody told me her grandparents wanted her closer to home and thought a small school might be good for her. A relative went here once, I believe."

"Sarah Bedford always had a good drama department," Zee said, "and from what I hear, everyone seems to like the new head."

"We try to see all their productions," Jo Nell said, "as long as they don't run around naked onstage!"

"Really?" Zee cocked her head and laughed. "I try not to miss it when they do."

"I think they're doing *Dracula* this month," Willene said. "Fully clothed, I assume. Opens the week before Halloween. The Hunter girl's supposed to play one of the leads, but I hear she's missed two rehearsals already."

"Now that doesn't sound right to me. And it hasn't been long since that Isaacs girl drowned in the Old Lake." Jo Nell leaned down to feed a crumb of pastry to her obnoxious terrier, Bojo, and I cringed as the moth-eaten little animal wormed underneath my chair and slobbered on my shoe. He had nipped me twice and I held my fork like a bayonet, waiting for revenge.

"It's been four years this month," Zee reminded her. "And she didn't just drown, she was murdered."

"Never came close to finding out who did it, either," Nettie said. "Or why." She looked down at the small dog with distaste and prodded him ever so slightly with the toe of her shoe. "Just think of that poor girl's parents—not ever knowing . . ."

"I wonder if it's the same person this time." Idonia folded her napkin and gave her mouth another swipe. "No telling who could be next!"

"Oh, for heaven's sake, Idonia!" Ellis said. "We

22

don't even know if the girl's dead. She's probably off partying somewhere."

"If anything *has* happened to her, it's going to hurt the college," Jo Nell said as she stacked dishes on a tray.

"Can't help the town, either," Zee said. "That college is about all there is to Stone's Throw. If Sarah Bedford goes, there won't be anything left."

It grew cool in the shade of the wisteria vine that crisscrossed my cousin's wide porch, and spoons rattled against fragile china cups as the group came to terms with that last comment.

"Claudia was supposed to lead the discussion today," Zee announced, flipping through the pages of her book, "but she had a job interview in Columbia, so I guess you're stuck with me."

"Columbia? Isn't that a little far?" Ellis asked.

"She'd prefer something closer—especially with her younger son still in middle school," Zee said, "but Claudia thought it worth looking into. I do wish she could find something at the college."

Willene nodded. "Told me she applied there. If you ask me, it's past time some of those people retired!"

Although it's usually warm in the piedmont of South Carolina in early October, I was glad I wore a lightweight blazer as shadows crept across the lawn. A brief gust of wind rustled burgundy leaves that clung to the oak by the front walk, and a few houses away a dog yapped as if the whole world depended on its frantic warning. Bojo, hearing the summons, joined in.

"Do you think there's anything to all that talk about a missing girl?" I asked Ellis as we walked home together.

She frowned. "I hope not. Sounds to me like this D.C. person just likes to do her own thing."

"What about the girl who drowned in the Old Lake—the Isaacs girl—how do they know that wasn't an accident?" I asked.

Ellis frowned. "Don't you remember? It was in all the papers. They said she'd been hit over the head, but they never found the weapon, *and* she was fully dressed. She certainly wouldn't have been going for a swim."

"I hope this girl turns up soon," I said. "Did you notice that Nettie was unusually quiet this afternoon? Her niece's daughter, Leslie, started as a freshman at Sarah Bedford this year."

"That little girl who used to visit here in the summers? The one with the freckles and bangs? You've gotta be kidding. She can't be more than ten!"

"She spoke to me in the quad today. Had to tell me who she was. Must've grown a foot since I last saw her. And you remember Weigelia Jones? Her sister Celeste is a sophomore there, and she'll be taking my class. Both girls live on campus."

"Well, I wouldn't worry too much about what Idonia said," Ellis assured me as we parted at the corner. "You know how she carries on."

I hoped she was right.

24

Across the broad oak-lined street a neighbor waved as he raked leaves into crisp brown hills, and a bright orange pumpkin sat on the steps of the house next door. I inhaled the tingling smell of dry leaves; somewhere nearby somebody was baking a ham for supper.

In spite of the chill in the air a warm, snug feeling crept over me, beginning somewhere in my middle. It was a familiar sensation I often experienced while walking the streets of Stone's Throw. I was born here, belonged here. The town had nurtured me through good times and bad, and until recently it had been a quiet town. I wanted to keep it that way. Idonia's grim announcement, I thought, was nothing but idle beauty-parlor chatter, and wouldn't her face be as red as her hair when the missing girl turned up safe and sound tomorrow?

Yet something . . . *something* small and pesky nagged and nipped at the back of my mind. Something Augusta had said when she decided to stay in Stone's Throw after helping The Thursdays clear up a nasty chain of murders the year before. There were other secrets here, she had confided, that could use her attention as well.

But what other secrets? I hurried up our worn brick walkway, shaded now by a large magnolia on one side of the yard and a towering spruce on the other, loving the way the gentle yellow light from the fan-shaped window above the door made a pattern on the porch. Inside I could hear an authoritative voice barking, "Stretch! Right! Left! Reach higher! *Higher!* Step . . .

25

step . . . step!" Augusta Goodnight, my resident guardian angel, was working out with her aerobics video, and I knew better than to interrupt.

The savory aroma of vegetable soup greeted me in the hallway, along with Clementine, our lovable dog with the world's largest feet. Whatever I had to ask Augusta, I decided, could wait until after supper.

Chapter Two

I had hoped Augusta would dismiss all the hoopla over the missing girl with a flutter of her elegant fingers, but she did just the opposite. "Exactly how long has she been gone?" she asked with the tiniest hint of a line between her brows that in her case passes for a frown. "Who was the last person to see her? Did she have her cell phone with her?"

I shook my head. I hadn't thought to ask, I admitted. After supper I stacked soup bowls in the dishwasher and scrubbed the pot while Augusta painted at the kitchen table. She had recently taken up painting and was presently working on a pastoral scene of a man and woman picnicking on strawberries beside a shallow stream. Augusta manages to include straw-berries in most of her pieces, I've noticed. A reminder, I expect, of her time in the strawberry fields of heaven. "Can you imagine heaven without them?" she explains.

Tonight her honey-gold hair was caught up with a green ribbon at the top of her head and her face was still flushed from exercising. Augusta's hair always looks good with very little help from her, no matter what she does, and she never, never perspires. Angels don't sweat, she tells me. When she first came to my door a year ago, claiming to be my guardian angel, I had my doubts, of course. Well, after all, who wouldn't? In fact, I came close to asking my friend Ed Tillman, who happens to be a policeman, to send for the men in the white coats. But there was an essence of calmness about her, something so right, so good, I couldn't bring myself to do it. Smelling of honeysuckle, she had produced a basket of warm strawberry muffins and soon had me sitting at my own kitchen table heaping my myriad of problems onto her angelic shoulders.

Now Augusta was quiet as I sat at the table across from her going over my plans for the next day, making notes as I thumbed through material on natural dyes. "You think something's really happened to that student, don't you?" I asked, glancing at her pensive expression.

She added a swirl of green to her painting and leaned back to study the result. Her lustrous necklace, which hung to her waist, winked at me in colors of a stormy sea. "I'd rather not go off the steep side," she said, which, in Augusta terminology, I took to mean the deep end. "I don't know the girl or the circumstances, of course, but I would certainly be concerned if they don't hear something from her soon." She swished her brush in water and dabbed on a blob of brown. "I suppose it wouldn't hurt to take a look around the campus."

"Fine," I said, trying to discourage Clementine from climbing into my lap. "Just don't suddenly appear in my classroom tomorrow. I'm jittery enough getting used to the job without being distracted by somebody no one else can see."

"We'll see," Augusta said. Which meant, I knew, that wild horses couldn't keep her away. "Meanwhile, let's hope the missing girl turns up."

But when I walked into my classroom at Sarah Bedford the next day, I didn't have to be told that D.C. Hunter was still missing. In spite of the students' eagerness to begin a new project, I sensed a restless, uneasy atmosphere in the room. I expected Augusta might suddenly decide to "pop in" on my class at any minute, but she must have remembered my request because she didn't show up. I was almost sure, however, that she was somewhere not too far away.

"Sally thinks the worst has happened," Celeste Mungo said as I walked with her and her roommate to their dorm after class. She wanted to send home some of her lighter clothing now that the weather had turned cooler, and since she didn't have a car, I had offered to deliver them for her.

"Sally who?" I asked.

"Sally Wooten, D.C. Hunter's roommate." Celeste tossed her notebook onto a low stone wall and stretched into a light denim jacket. Wind ruffled the hickory above us and sent golden leaves sashaying to the ground. "Says she just knows she's not coming back," she added.

"Sounds too good to be true," Celeste's roommate Debra said. "Why, D.C. could be over in England with some of her ritzy school friends. It probably wouldn't occur to her that somebody might worry."

"Not one of your favorite people?" I glanced at her as we walked.

She shrugged. "If you lined up all the people at Sarah Bedford D.C. Hunter has insulted, they would circle the campus. Deep Chill—that's what everybody calls her."

"And she's only been here a little over a month." Celeste nudged her roommate and grinned. "Of course the fact that D.C. got the lead in the play doesn't make you like her any better."

"Well . . . I might've locked her in a closet if I thought it would help me get that role, but I draw the line at kidnapping." Debra tugged open the massive oak door to Emma P. Harris Hall and a wave of stale heat engulfed us. "Go pick on Katy Jacobs," she said as the door slammed behind us. "She's her understudy."

I sat on Celeste's bed as she stood on a chair and searched her closet for the box of clothing. Since the dormitory was built in the 1920s, the rooms were larger than most, and the girls had used bright rugs, spreads, and curtains to make it theirs. A microwave and small refrigerator sat in one corner and a television and stereo took up one large shelf. All the comforts of home, I thought, remembering my own college days, when we had to hide the hot plate from the hall monitor.

Both dressers were cluttered with framed photographs and I noticed a smiling picture of Celeste's older sister on hers. I had tutored Weigelia Jones through the literacy program a few years before and was pleased that she was currently studying for her GED. Celeste planned to major in political science and hoped eventually to get into law school, and I knew her sister was cleaning other people's houses to help pay for her education.

"What about boyfriends?" I asked Celeste as she stuffed another pair of shorts into the box. "Is D.C. seeing anybody?"

"Not that I know of. She went out a couple of times with one of the locals, I think, but there was nobody special. Let's face it, Sarah Bedford has only six male students and there's not a whole lot to pick from here in Stone's Throw. We have to import them."

"Like from Clemson!" Debra giggled. Weigelia had told me her sister was dating Stone's Throw's all-star quarterback, Delray Lyons, who now played for the nearby university.

"I think she's been seeing somebody on the sly," Debra said. "Haven't you noticed her dragging in here late—or maybe I should say, *early*—with that smug look on her face? You don't get a smile like that from going out with the girls."

"Surely there must be somebody who likes her," I said.

"I've never heard her roommate say anything bad about her," Celeste said, "but I wouldn't say she and Sally were friends exactly."

I jumped at the pounding of what sounded like enormous feet on the stairs, followed by a curiously sweet male tenor belting out "In the Sweet By and By."

Footsteps clomped past our closed door and turned a corner in the hallway, but the singing continued . . . "We shall meet on that bee-yoo-tee-ful shore . . ."

"Londus," Debra explained, smiling at my puzzled expression. "From maintenance. That's how he lets us know there's a man on the hall."

Celeste laughed as she added another pair of shoes to her stack. "Seriously, though, if anybody would know about D.C.'s love life, it would be Londus Clack. He sees everything that goes on around here."

Lugging a sack of soiled laundry she'd decided to send home, I followed Celeste into the hall. I could guess how her sister would be spending her spare time. It hadn't been too long, I remembered, since my own daughter, Julie, had done the same to me.

About midway down a dim passageway I saw a handyman in blue coveralls on a stepladder replacing a lightbulb. He had started another verse.

Celeste nodded in his direction. "D.C.'s room's down there. End of the hall on the right."

As we reached the main floor, a tall dark-haired girl who obviously had just come in from outside shrugged out of her heavy sweater in the hallway.

"Sally . . ." Celeste paused at the door. "Have you . . . have they heard anything yet?"

Sally Wooten nodded slightly as Celeste introduced us. "If they have, nobody's told me, but it doesn't look good. Her grandparents are flying in tomorrow, and the police were here earlier asking questions. You must've just missed them."

Celeste's dark eyes were somber as she shifted the heavy box of clothing in her arms. "You don't really think anything's happened to her, do you? Don't you have *any* idea where she might be?"

"D.C. doesn't confide in me," Sally said, "but it's definitely time to worry. She couldn't have gone very far. They found her car way back in that parking lot behind the gym, and the keys were right here in her desk."

"Then she must've been here all the time," I said.

But D.C.'s roommate shook her head. "That car wasn't there Friday night. I know it wasn't because I went out with a group from the dorm that night and when we got back at a little after midnight, that parking lot was empty. It was dark there, too, and kind of secluded, so we found a place to park on main campus closer to the dorm."

"But if it was dark, couldn't you have missed it?" I asked.

Sally turned to go upstairs. "Not that car. D.C.'s car is yellow—canary-yellow. You'd have to be blind not to see it."

I remembered what Augusta had mentioned earlier. "What about her cell phone?" I asked.

Sally shrugged. "The police asked me that, too. She must've taken it with her. We haven't been able to find it."

Celeste and I didn't speak as we crossed the campus to my car and I kept a watchful eye out for Augusta, as I had a feeling she must be "casing the joint," as she says. Lately, Augusta has taken to reading old detective novels, and I'm finding it difficult to keep her supplied.

Sarah Bedford College had been built in the 1880s and it had its share of ivy. The buildings of aged brick, some so dark they resembled brownstone, reflected the period with towers, turrets, and marble trim. Present-day students in short skirts and jeans seemed out of place on this broad shady campus where girls in long dresses once played croquet. Now, gentled by the late-afternoon sun, it looked like a place where nothing bad could ever happen.

A shedding sycamore had littered my windshield with curled yellow leaves, and I stopped to brush them away, giving Celeste the key to my trunk.

"Miss Lucy, if you don't mind I wish you wouldn't mention this to Weigelia—about D.C.'s being missing, I mean." She slammed the lid shut on her belongings and walked with me to the driver's side. "You know how my sister is. She'll drive us both crazy, and for all we know, that girl could show up in class tomorrow."

"Celeste, I can't promise you that. Besides, Weigelia probably knows about it already. It's all over town by now, and Sally said the police had been here earlier. Don't you-all have a cousin on the force?"

"You mean Kemper? Shoot, he won't tell us a thing! Acts like such a big shot, you'd think he was Double-O-Seven or something!" She sighed. "So if she mentions it, just pretend it's business as usual, okay?"

"We'll see," I told her, waving as I drove away.

"But it isn't, is it?"

I jumped as a voice spoke beside me. Augusta!

"I wish you'd quit doing that," I said, frowning. "One of these days you're going to make me drive straight into a tree! Isn't *what?*"

"Isn't business as usual—not when a young woman disappears."

"You've heard something, haven't you? Tell me."

"Only that the girl wasn't well liked and didn't seem to have any close friends. No one seems to know very much about her—or, sadly, to care."

"I know she's made enemies," I said, "but I can't imagine anybody taking it to that extreme."

"The police were there today asking questions, looking around the campus." Augusta's face clouded. "I hope they're not too late."

I had several calls on my answering machine when I got home. The first was from Ben Maxwell confirming dinner plans for Saturday. Ben and I became friends when I met him last year at

Bellawood, where he was restoring antique furniture for the plantation. My husband, Charlie, had died in an accident three years before, and the idea of seeing someone else took some getting used to after having been married for thirty years to the man I thought would be my one and only love. As for Ben and me, we're still in the "circling" stage of our relationship, but the circles are getting smaller.

Jo Nell and Idonia had both left messages to *please* let them know if I'd heard any more about the missing girl, and my next-door neighbor Nettie McGinnis had called to ask if I'd seen her niece that day. The last message was from Weigelia: *"Lucy, what's going on over at Sarah Bedford? Is Celeste all right? I've near 'bout worried myself half to death over that young 'un. How about giving me a call when you got a minute?"*

She sounded desperate, so I phoned her first, but her line was busy, so I returned Nettie's call.

"Do a favor for me, will you, please, Lucy Nan?" My neighbor spoke slowly and plainly, so I knew she must be wearing her teeth. "I don't want Leslie to think I'm butting in, but I don't like what I'm hearing about this girl who seems to have just up and vanished. Would you look her up sometime tomorrow—when you get a chance, of course? I've baked some of those snickerdoodle cookies she used to like, and I thought maybe you might take them to her for me."

"Of course I will, and try not to worry, Nettie. I'm sure Leslie's fine, and from what I've heard about D.C. Hunter, she might have just decided Sarah

Bedford wasn't for her."

"The cookies are cooling now, and as soon as I can get them boxed up, I'll bring them over."

I was about to tell Nettie I would be glad to come by for the cookies myself when my doorbell rang.

Weigelia Jones stood on my porch, looking kind of like a wilted hydrangea in her baggy blue sweater and flower-splashed dress.

"Now how did I know it would be you?" I said, ushering her inside. "Come in and have some coffee." Augusta usually keeps a pot on, and there was a plate of fresh brownies on the table, although I don't know when she'd had time to make them.

Weigelia plopped her ample self on one kitchen chair, her large purple purse on another, and helped herself. "Did you see Celeste? She's okay, isn't she? She told me she's taking your class."

"Not only is she all right, but I'm delivering her dirty laundry, which you'll find in the trunk of my car along with some of her summer clothes."

"And what's all this about a girl disappearing over there? It sure don't sound good to me."

"Celeste is fine," I told her. "She doesn't even know this girl well. Nobody seems to. Heck, Weigelia, you probably know more than I do. I know you hear everything that goes on in Stone's Throw—and don't tell me different! The police were over there asking questions a good part of the day. Didn't your cousin tell you anything?"

"Kemper says Chief Harris don't want any of that

36

stuff to get out, so he ain't talkin' much," she muttered. "Bossy, thick-headed thing probably don't know enough to talk about!"

As much as Weigelia bad-mouthed her cousin Kemper, I knew she was proud of him, so I just let that pass. Besides, in my book, Chief Harris is a Jackass with a capital *J.* but I didn't share my opinion with Weigelia, and I could tell by her expression she wasn't sharing everything with me, either. "You've heard *something,* though, haven't you? What is it? Tell me."

It was like prying up chewing gum, but she finally gave in. "Kemper says somebody on that girl's— what's her name, B.C.? Sounds like a headache powder."

"D.C.," I said.

"Anyway, somebody on D.C.'s hall thought she heard her door slam Saturday morning. Woke her up, she said. Then it sounded like somebody was crying."

"Where was her roommate?" I asked.

She shrugged. "That's all I know, and I ain't supposed to know that. I reckon she wasn't there that night." Weigelia pushed aside her coffee mug and frowned. "Wasn't some girl killed there not too long ago? Found her body in the Old Lake?"

"Four years ago, to be exact. Girl from somewhere in Florida, but I don't see how the two can be related. Besides, D.C. Hunter isn't dead . . . at least we hope she isn't."

"You will keep an eye out, though, won't you?" she said on her way out. "The good Lord ain't seen fit to give me and Roy no babies, and Celeste, she's my only little sister—but that girl—she ain't tellin' me nothin'!"

I put my arm around her as I walked her to the door. "Try not to worry. If anything has happened to this girl, they'll have to beef up campus security big-time and be on the lookout for strangers."

Weigelia turned to look at me from underneath her squashy violet hat. "And how do they know it's a stranger?" she said.

Chapter Three

The pale thin girl with shoulder-length brown hair sat alone in the college cafeteria, a book propped in front of her. Her lunch tray, I noticed, was pushed to the side and contained a bowl of chicken noodle soup with skim on top, some broken crackers, and a pear with a few bites out of it. She didn't look up as I approached.

I had come early to deliver cookies to my neighbor's niece. Leslie Monroe had been having some emotional problems, Nettie said. Something to do with her father's remarriage, and she had been concerned about her even before the D.C. Hunter dilemma.

"I come bearing gifts," I said and put the box of cookies on the table in front of her. "Snickerdoodles. Your aunt sent them." From the looks of her, she could use them.

Her smile was sudden and sweet and I noticed that

she had the kind of plain, no-frills good looks that would last, if only she weren't so skinny.

"Oh, great! My favorites. Thanks." Leslie moved a stack of books from the chair beside her and offered me a seat. "Two major tests tomorrow," she explained.

"I honestly didn't recognize you when I saw you on campus the other day," I admitted. "You've changed quite a bit since you used to visit next door."

Leslie groaned. "And I'll bet Aunt Nettie sent you to check up on me. Dad's already called like three times this week."

"Not so. I happen to be working here with a class this quarter—Hands-on History. I'm only an errand girl, although I would accept a commission." I gazed longingly at the cookies until she finally caught on and offered me some.

"Oh, I've heard of your class. Wish I could take it, but they didn't offer it to freshmen." Leslie glanced at the cookies but didn't take one. I started on my second.

"I've been smelling these all the way over here," I said, dusting crumbs from my hands. "Had to get them to you right away or there might not have been any left."

"Please thank Aunt Nettie for me . . . and tell her I'm still present and accounted for."

I promised her I would. "I don't suppose they've heard any more about the missing girl?" I refused another cookie, feeling extremely self-righteous.

"No, but the police have been here like all morning.

It's pretty grim around here." Leslie pointed to a man with a scraggly-looking beard toying with his lunch at a table in the corner. He frowned at whatever he was reading in a folded newspaper. "Some people think she's been seeing Dr. Hornsby like outside of class—if you know what I mean."

"Why? Has anybody seen them together?"

She shrugged. "I don't think so, but you know how rumors get started. She's in his lit class—sort of an unofficial assistant, I guess. Helps grade papers and stuff. I've seen them together a couple of times in the library. He's writing a book, you know, and I heard it's already been accepted. Anyway, you could tell she like had the hots for him just from the way she acted."

The mysterious Dr. Hornsby slathered butter on a square of cornbread and chewed slowly, washing it down with coffee, apparently unaware of our attention.

"A little old for her, isn't he?" I said. "Must be close to forty."

"Has a flock of kids, too. Four, I think. Wife's kinda weird. Won't wear makeup and gets all her clothes like from the Salvation Army—at least that's what I've heard. She's not real friendly. We don't see her around much."

I glanced again at the professor as he shoved aside a half-eaten dish of pudding. His tie was crooked, his eyes red-rimmed, and his beard was long overdue for a trim. Who knows what he might look like on a good day, but this wasn't one of them.

"Somebody said they thought they heard D.C. come back to her room early Saturday," I said.

Leslie slammed her book shut. "Yeah, she was there—for a while, anyway. I just try to stay out of her way. Had to play basketball with her in PE last week and she told me I moved like a slug."

On my way out of the cafeteria I looked around for my son, Roger, who teaches in the History Department there, but I wasn't surprised not to see him. When he's not raiding my refrigerator at lunchtime he's usually indulging in a cheeseburger or a Reuben sandwich over at As You Like It, a nearby sandwich shop catering to the student body and faculty alike. Roger's wife, Jessica—bless her heart—chose my son to love— which, in itself, makes her okay in my book—and together they have given me six-year-old Teddy, the future catcher for the Atlanta Braves; but to Jessica, consuming meat and sweets is in the same category as running with scissors.

If something had happened to D.C. Hunter, I thought on my way to class, there wouldn't be a run on the florists here in town, and from the discussion I overheard before class that day, it seemed that even her roommate wasn't sure how long she'd been missing.

"Sally left D.C. brushing her teeth when she went to breakfast last Friday," one girl said, "but she never showed up for any of her classes."

"Didn't make it to rehearsals, either," another

reminded us. "I hear the director's already replaced her with the understudy." She spoke softly and looked around as if one of the others might be next to disappear.

A classmate nodded solemnly. "They've tried calling her cell phone but can't get through. She must've turned it off."

"Or somebody did," Paula Shoemaker said. "A girl on her hall said she thought she heard D.C. crying in her room sometime early Saturday morning, but I don't know if anybody actually saw her."

"Where was Sally all this time?" I asked. "Wouldn't she hear her come in?"

But D.C.'s roommate, I was told, had bunked in with friends on the first floor Friday night.

"Sally said she found a damp towel in their bathroom later that Saturday," Celeste said, "but she isn't sure it wasn't there the day before."

"And what about her mail?" The girl they called "Troll" plopped her books on the table. Her name, I learned, was Joanette, but she happened to have the distinction of living in the room under the stairs in Emma P. Harris Hall. "Sally's been collecting it from the school post office since Friday. It's on her way to class, so she usually picks it up for both of them. Somebody said it's still sitting there on D.C.'s desk—hasn't even been opened."

"I don't know why I let you talk me into this," Ellis said later, picking beggar lice from her mud-streaked jeans. "Augusta's had firsthand experience with natural dyes, and she's been around a lot longer than I have. Why me?"

"She'll turn up sooner or later," I said, "but it makes it a little awkward when we're the only ones who can see her. Besides," I reminded her, "Papa Zeke taught you all about things like this. Remember how he used to whittle us whistles out of slippery elm, and those little water wheels we put in the creek?" Back in our Scouting days, Ellis's granddaddy had taught us how to identify all kinds of wildlife and once made pink lemonade from sumac berries—not the poison kind, of course.

The girls in my class were on a field trip after class that day to gather the materials we would later use for dyes, and I glanced warily at the sky as I walked. The day had begun brisk and sunny, but now the blue was almost obliterated by a gray watercolor sky, and it seemed to be getting darker by the minute.

The wine-red roots and berries of the pokeweed that sprouted tall in scraggly undergrowth dyed up anywhere from red to purple, and the outside hulls of black walnuts from a tree at the far end of the back campus produced shades of black and brown. We collected the pokeweed first, pulling the plants from the ground with a few forceful tugs. I wanted to keep the roots and berries separate to see if it would make a difference in color, and each student had brought along bags for that purpose.

Ellis stopped to dig up a couple of tiny red cedars

that dotted the field around us. The roots were supposed to dye up purple, and several of the girls were
collecting the flowers of goldenrod for a particular
shade of yellow.

"I see the professor is keeping her distance," Ellis
whispered as Joy Ellen Harper and some of the others
plunged ahead of us through broom sedge and bram-
bles to the remote part of the campus that had once
been a popular recreation spot.

"At least she had the good sense to wear boots," I
said, extracting my sneaker-clad foot from a clump of
muddy goo. Joy Ellen seemed resigned to my being
assigned to her, but I got the distinct impression that
she wasn't happy about joining us today. Well, she
had insisted on coming along!

"Wasn't the old stable somewhere about here?" Ellis
asked, and I nodded, although I barely remembered
the building. The trails were long overgrown, and only
a faint circle remained of the riding ring where indus-
trious joggers sometimes ran. The Old Lake, once a
favorite swimming place, had been drained since the
death of that student several years before.

"Something tells me we'd better make it quick."
Celeste, who trudged along beside us, glanced up as
the first drops fell. We had spread out over several
acres to gather as much and as quickly as we could. A
couple of girls collected handfuls of acorns from a
gnarled red oak at the edge of the field, while a little
farther away three of their classmates knelt to scoop
up fallen black walnuts and throw them into bags. The

three of us hurried to join them, staining our finger-nails yellowish-brown from the hard green hulls. The acrid smell was almost suffocating. A red spatter of pokeberry juice stained the front of my shirt, and my hands looked as if I'd dipped them in blood.

"This is enough. We'd better start back," I said as water plopped on my face and trickled under my collar. A loud clap of thunder seemed to shake the ground and I called to the others to hurry back to the main campus and shelter. Through a scattering of pine saplings I glimpsed Joy Ellen's red-and-black-checkered jacket and heard her call out. She shouted again, and this time I detected what I thought was a little more than concern in her voice.

"You go with the others," I told Ellis, who wasn't the least inclined to argue. "I'll see what Joy Ellen's yelling about."

Great, I thought, as a dripping pine branch slung water in my face and thistles tore into my ankles, all we need now is to lose another girl!

Joy Ellen stood herding a group of students in front of her at the rim of what used to be the Old Lake and I could hardly see her for the rain. Sloshing through terra-cotta puddles, I called out to her. "Is this every-body?" I didn't want to leave any students behind, especially if the college had a killer-in-residence.

"All but two." Joy Ellen rubbed a wet sleeve across her forehead and still managed to look neat. "Paula and Miriam went over there on the other side of the lake bed for broom straw—said you told them it's supposed to make a yellow dye."

My fault, of course. I nodded, wishing I had left the broom sedge for another day.

Joy Ellen squinted into the distance, shielding her eyes from the rain. "I guess they're all right. Must've taken shelter somewhere, but I don't want to go off and leave them."

Like I would. "Then let's go find them," I said, and sending the others back to main campus, the two of us started around the mounded edge of the Old Lake bed.

And then we heard the screams.

They weren't "Hurry, we're getting soaked and I'm afraid of lightning" screams but were as cold and basic as fear itself. The horrible high-pitched shrieking went straight to the nerve like a nightmare dentist's drill, and it didn't stop.

The horror of that sound gripped my middle with a very real pain that worked its way to my chest, then my throat, until it rode my breath out in a groan. I found myself running without even realizing it and Joy Ellen sprinted along beside me, her fingers digging into my arm. We saw the old shed before we saw the girls. A sturdy square building of gray stone, it sat entwined in a network of vines behind a screen of cedars. One of the double doors stood open, and a few feet away Paula Shoemaker crouched and vomited in the tall grass. Beside her, Miriam Platt grasped her knees and cried, rocking back and forth in the mud.

Even from a distance, the stench from whatever was inside the shed made me want to be violently sick. Joy

Ellen had turned almost as gray as the sky and clutched her mouth as she gagged.

"Cover your nose," I said, "and try not to breathe. We've got to get them away from here." I pulled the wet bandanna from my hair and tied it around the lower part of my face, glad of the cold cleansing rain on my bare head.

Paula stared at us with wide glazed eyes and moved like a mechanical wind-up toy as I led her away, but Miriam shook so, it took the two of us to hold her, and gulped air in ragged, sobbing gasps.

"Go ahead, I'll catch up," I told Joy Ellen after we had led the girls a distance away. "I'm going back to close that door." Neither of us wanted to say it, but we knew what would happen if an animal wandered inside. Joy Ellen nodded mutely and started back the way we had come, with a shivering girl on either arm.

I took a deep breath of rain-washed air and ran back to the building, pressing my bandanna against my face. I didn't have to look inside to know what I would find, but in the few seconds before the thick wooden door slammed shut I glimpsed the discolored, bloated thing that had once been D.C. Hunter.

Halfway across the soggy field, Joy Ellen paused and called my name, a question in her voice. I hurried toward her, the rain mingling with my tears. Only when I turned to look back at the shed did I see Augusta standing there, her face as bleak as the sky.

Chapter Four

$\mathcal{T}$he rain had stopped by the time we sloshed back to the main campus, but it had also turned colder and I shivered in my wet clothing. The girls were quiet now. Head down, Paula stumbled along beside me, hugging herself for warmth. Miriam clung to Joy Ellen, crying silently. The two seemed to have aged ten years in the last hour, and their faces were a sickly pale, their lips a purplish blue.

I knew enough about hypothermia to realize the danger, and apparently so did Joy Ellen. She looked at me over her shoulder and I could tell by her expression that she was as scared as I was. "Let's get them inside to Blythe," she said. "She'll know what to do."

"Blythe?" A happy name. I liked the sound of it.

"Blythe Cornelius, Dean Holland's secretary—has an apartment right here in the dorm. We can call the police from there."

Blythe Cornelius was sort of an unofficial house-mother, Joy Ellen explained. Many of the girls called her Aunt Shug because of her frequent use of the affectionate term and would sometimes come to her for advice. A calming influence, she said. She sounded good to me.

"Hey! What took you so long? The others are all safely back in the nest, so I thought I'd see what was holding the rest of you up." Ellis hurried toward us with a huge black umbrella, then stopped abruptly, seeing our faces. "What's wrong? Are you all right? Is somebody hurt?"

At that, Paula burst into tears again and I drew Ellis aside to explain what had happened.

"Oh, dear God, not that! Not that!" Ellis shut her eyes, her jaw clinched tight, and for a few seconds I thought she was going to break down, too. I should have known better. My friend Ellis Saxon is made of sterner stuff. "I don't suppose anybody has called the police?" she asked.

With a dazed expression, Joy Ellen took a cell phone from her jacket pocket. "I had this with me all along . . . why didn't I use it?"

"We had more important things to do," I told her. "Like getting these girls back safely, not to mention warm and dry." I began to walk faster. "Come on, let's get them inside."

Blythe Cornelius's apartment was on the main floor of Emma P. Harris Hall and Joy Ellen didn't even take the time to ring the bell, but pounded on the secretary's door and called out her name.

"Hold on a minute! I'm coming, I'm coming!" Blythe's vexed expression vanished when she saw us standing there and Miriam immediately threw herself into the woman's arms. "What on earth has happened here?" Her question was directed at Joy Ellen as she drew us into the room. "Miriam? Paula? What's wrong? Why, sugar, you look as pale as a ghost! Are you all right?"

Blythe Cornelius looked to be about my age, which

is fifty-six, or maybe a little older. It was difficult to tell because she has that fine bone structure and smooth complexion that would probably keep her looking youthful for years to come, but she had made no attempt to disguise the gray hair that covered her head in a mass of short curls.

A gray cat that had been curled asleep in the armchair suddenly leaped to the floor and darted underneath the sofa. "Here, sugar, let's get off those wet shoes first," Blythe commanded, trying to straighten the bifocals Miriam had knocked awry, "then tell me what's going on."

And so we did. Ellis spread out a stack of newspapers where she piled soggy shoes and socks in a heap while I collected the wet jackets and stood wondering what to do with them. Joy Ellen waved her hand for quiet and turned away from the noise and confusion to speak calmly with the police. The students slumped side by side on Blythe's blue-sprigged chintz sofa, making two large wet spots, no doubt, while the rest of us dripped on her soft gray carpet.

If that bothered Blythe Cornelius, she didn't let on. "I can't believe this is happening," she said with a tremor in her voice. "That poor child! Who in the world . . . ? And right here at our own Sarah Bedford." For a few seconds she stood there looking about the small living room as if she wanted to drink in its comfort: the mahogany writing desk, corner bookshelves filled to overflowing, family photographs that cluttered every surface. And apparently it gave her strength because she quickly drew an afghan around the two girls, straightened, and started for the kitchen. "Our duty now is to tend to the living. First a warm shower, then you'll want something hot to drink. I'll put on the kettle."

"Let me, please," I said, tired of feeling useless, and was glad when she agreed. In the tiny kitchen, I arranged the dripping coats on the first chair I saw and started to fill the kettle. That's when I heard someone gasp.

For the first time I noticed Willene Benson seated at the small maple table in the breakfast nook with a Scrabble board in front of her, along with two china cups and a plate of Oreos. She looked up with a frown. "Lucy Nan! What's going on? I thought I heard a commotion in the living room."

"We found the missing student," I said, trying to play down the grizzly details. "She's been dead for some time and I'm afraid it's taken an emotional toll on all of us, especially the girls who found her. Joy Ellen has phoned the police."

Willene's hand went to her mouth. "Oh dear! In that case, I'd better go," she said, rising.

"No, please! We really could use your help. Blankets—as many as you can find, and something hot to drink: canned soup—anything." In spite of the warm kitchen, my teeth were beginning to chatter and I knew I had to get into dry clothing soon.

In the hallway off the kitchen I found Blythe Cornelius herding the two girls into her bathroom, and soon heard a shower running. Ellis, who was relatively dry, offered to run home for dry clothes, but Joy Ellen had already phoned her teenaged daughter to bring us something to wear, and Blythe sent a message to Miriam's roommate to hurry with warm clothing for the girls.

Joy Ellen and I eagerly snatched the towels and robes Blythe offered and headed for the girls' shower at the end of the hall. When we returned a few minutes later, we found Willene ladling hot tomato soup into Paula and Miriam, who huddled beneath blankets on the sofa. Two policemen stood outside the door and I recognized the younger one as Duff Acree, the sergeant who had searched my yard for missing jewelry the year before—but that's another story. Joy Ellen and I had to explain to the two why we needed to go inside before they'd let us into Blythe's apartment.

"Those policemen aren't setting a foot inside this door," Blythe told us, "until these two girls have warmed up and calmed down. If the Hunter girl is dead like you say, she isn't going anywhere, and neither are we."

But apparently that rule didn't apply to her employer, Dean Holland, who sat in an armchair by the window with a grim look on his face and a coffee mug in his hand. Willene had obviously taken her assignment seriously, as everyone seemed to have been supplied with something hot to drink, and almost as soon as I stepped into the room a cup of something that smelled like lemon tea was thrust in front of me. I gulped it gratefully.

The dean looked frail and ill, and when I went over to speak to him he merely shook his head from side to side and mumbled a groan. Partly, I knew, because he couldn't hear a word I'd said. Deaf as a roastin' ear, as my granddaddy used to say, but I could see the poor man was genuinely distressed at the turn of events on his campus. And he had good reason to be. If D.C. Hunter had been murdered, as it certainly seemed she had, it wasn't going to bode well for Sarah Bedford, especially after the drowning death of that other student several years before.

"One of the policemen told me they're waiting for Captain Hardy," Ellis whispered aside to me. "He said two men have already been sent out to the shed where you found the Hunter girl."

Having completed her duties, Willene Benson slipped into her raincoat, wrapped a shawl around her neck, and started out the door for home, only to be told by one of the uniformed men to wait until the officer in charge arrived. I thought the poor woman was going to break down and cry.

The officer in charge, I was relieved to learn, was not that doofus police chief, Elmer Harris, but someone new to the force, Captain Alonzo Hardy, who looked to be somewhere in his mid-forties. By the time Captain Hardy arrived, our clothes had been delivered and I was glad of something to wear, although Joy Ellen's warm-up pants were a little snug

53

in areas I won't mention. The captain had jack-o'-lantern hair and a good-neighbor kind of face, but I doubted if much would get past his observant green eyes.

The first thing the captain did was get rid of the college bigwigs who had accumulated as if by magic and disperse the collection of curious students gathered in the hallway around Blythe Cornelius's door. Willene and Ellis were allowed to leave, but the captain asked Joy Ellen and me to wait while they interviewed the two students separately. Blythe excused herself from the room, but since we didn't know where else to go, Joy Ellen and I remained and tried to make ourselves as inconspicuous as possible. The captain didn't object and I think it put the girls a little more at ease to have us there.

My hands were still cold in spite of the hot shower and I wrapped them around the warm cup, sipping the tea slowly and wishing Augusta were there. I had never seen her look as despondent as when I saw her last, and I knew she wouldn't be able to put what had happened behind her until the person responsible was brought to justice.

The sergeant, who looked to be about twenty-eight or -nine, talked with Paula in the breakfast room. He had a clean-cut college-boy appearance and she didn't seem intimidated, although I did hear her giggle nervously once or twice. Captain Hardy sat on the flowered sofa with Miriam and advised her just to take her time—even close her eyes if it helped—and tell him how they had happened to go inside the old stone shed.

"I don't want to close my eyes," Miriam said, kneading a ruffle-trimmed pillow in her lap. "I don't want to ever see it again, but I know I will. I'll never be able to forget it as long as I live."

She and Paula had run for the stone building when it started lightning, she said. "I'd forgotten the old place was there, it's buried so far back in the vines, but Paula remembered seeing it last winter when she went out to the back campus to jog."

Miriam clutched the pillow to her chest. "We should've known something awful was wrong by the smell as soon as we pulled open that door, but I thought it was . . . you know, a dead rat or a possum or something. We were soaking wet, and just then it sounded like the lightning struck something really close. I'm scared to death of lightning!"

Captain Hardy nodded. "Do you remember who opened the door? You or your friend?"

"Paula. Paula did, and then we started to go inside." Miriam covered her face. "We didn't get very far."

"I know this is difficult for you, but we have to know. Tell me exactly what you saw, every detail you can remember." The captain reminded me of Dr. Beasley the time I fell off Ellis's garage roof and broke my arm when I was ten. He prodded softly but with words.

Miriam grabbed a tissue and continued. "It—she was lying there on her back, kind of like she'd fallen from those steps, only it looked like she'd been cut."

He frowned. "What steps?"

"There were steps to a loft or something. It was too dark to see, and we didn't stick around."

"Why do you think she'd been cut?"

"Because there was a gash. Well, it looked like a gash . . . oh, God! And there was all this dark stuff—blood, I guess, and that curved blade farmers used to use to cut grain. You know, that thing that's on the old Russian flag."

"You mean a sickle? The girl had been cut with a sickle?"

Miriam tucked sock-clad feet beneath her and nodded. Her shiver shook the cushion where she sat. "I'm not sure, but it looked like it, and it was lying right there beside her on the floor. It looked rusty." She swallowed. "Or maybe it wasn't rust."

Eventually Miriam remembered that D.C. had worn a jogging suit—blue, she thought—and that there had been a large metal drum and an assortment of old tools against the wall near the door.

It was more than I remembered, but I did see what appeared to be a small plastic container of breath mints by the steps when I ran back to close the door. I guess the only reason I remembered it was because it seemed so out of place: breath mints in that dark, putrid shed.

"Do you recall seeing anything else out of the ordinary?" Captain Hardy asked when I told him what I'd seen, and I admitted I hadn't spent much time looking around. Blythe's gray-striped cat that had been hiding under the sofa finally came out and jumped up into my lap. She looked as if she meant to stay and I was glad of the company and the warmth.

The detective held a brief conference with the policemen in the hallway, then spoke with Blythe, who had returned from the kitchen where she had gone to make coffee. "I understand the Hunter girl has a roommate, but she's not in her room right now. Does anyone know where we might find her?"

"Sally? I think she has a lab this afternoon," Paula said, "or she could be at the library."

"Would either of you know if D.C. Hunter received any unusual communication in the last week or so?" he asked the two girls.

"You mean like a letter?" Paula glanced at Miriam, who shook her head.

Miriam shrugged. "D.C. doesn't—didn't have a lot to do with most of us, but I guess she e-mailed like everybody else. I don't know anybody who uses snail mail much anymore, but if she did get any letters, Sally would probably know about it. She usually collects their mail if there is any."

"What about boyfriends?" he asked. "Do you know if she's been seeing anyone—anyone in particular?"

The room grew so quiet I could hear the coffee percolating. "It's just rumor," Miriam said finally. "You know how people talk. I wouldn't want to hurt an innocent person."

"If he's innocent, he has nothing to worry about," the captain reminded her.

Paula flushed, and I was glad to see color come into her face for whatever reason. "Well . . . some people have been saying she was seeing Dr. Hornsby."

Captain Hardy looked at Blythe. "Dr. Hornsby?"

"English Department," she explained. "D.C. had him for English Literature this quarter . . . but I really don't think he could possibly have had anything to do—"

"I'd like to talk with him just the same. Would he be in class now?" Frowning, he started for the door, where he almost collided with Sally Wooten and an armload of books.

"Is it true?" she asked. "Have they really found D.C.?" With her blond hair pulled back into a pony-tail, she looked about twelve years old. "They said she's been out in some old storage building all this time." Her lip trembled as she looked at Blythe Cornelius. "Aunt Shug, what was she doing out there? Who would do this to her?"

Blythe put her arms around Sally and gave the policemen a warning look. "That's what we want to find out, sugar. Now, you sit down here and get your thoughts together so we can help these people find some answers."

D.C. had received a few pieces of mail during the past week, Sally told them, but she didn't know what they were. "I think there's a letter from her grand-mother. She writes almost every week, and it seems like there was a bill from a credit-card company. I don't remember the other stuff, but it's all up there on her desk. That's where I always put it."

"Would you mind going along while Sergeant Acree takes a look at those?" the captain said with a nod to the younger policeman. "We'll need your permission, of course, to enter your room, and we'll want to see her other things as well."

Joy Ellen had left a few minutes earlier, and I was squishing my wet clothes into a grocery sack before starting for home when Sergeant Acree put in a breathless appearance at Blythe's door with what appeared to be four or five envelopes in a plastic bag. "Looks like another one," he said in what I'm sure was meant to be a low voice. "Just like that other girl got."

Another *what?* What other girl? I knew they wouldn't tell me if I asked, but if I could manage to sort of blend in with the background, maybe the captain and his sidekick would forget I was there—at least long enough for me to eavesdrop a little.

But that was not to be.

"Where is she? Where's our granddaughter?" From outside in the hallway, the woman's words caught at my heart. There was still hope in her voice. She hadn't been officially informed of D.C.'s death, and for a few flimsy seconds she could cling to the possibility that everything would be all right. But she knew. The ugly, stark knowledge of it overrode her words, and it hurt, hurt, hurt.

The captain stepped outside at the commotion and I heard him speak softly. "Please, ma'am, let's go in here where you can sit down. I wish there were some kinder way to tell you . . ."

I stood aside to make room for them: the trim, matronly woman in what looked to be a designer dress, and beside her, a tall graying man who cried silently. "Now, we don't know, honey. We don't know," he said. His hand shook on her arm. He knew. I had seen those same expressions on the television news, on the front page of the newspaper wherever tragedy and disaster pointed a grim finger.

What if it had been Julie? My Julie? My own daughter wasn't much older than the young girl we had found that day. How could I bear it? How could they?

Nobody noticed when I slipped outside and hurried to my car and home. I wanted Ben to hold me, and I wanted Augusta to tell me everything was going to be all right.

Chapter Five

I'll have to admit, I'm not a bit surprised. I just had a feeling something awful had happened to that girl," my neighbor Nettie McGinnis said the next day when I dropped by to reassure her about her niece.

"You had a *feeling* the first time you flew on a plane, too," I reminded her. "Remember when you went to your cousin's wedding in Richmond? Made out your will and everything." I laughed, hoping my teasing would prod her out of her doldrums.

It didn't work. "And what's all this I hear about that English teacher? The one who's written that book. I always did think that man was peculiar. Leslie doesn't have him for any of her classes, does she?"

"You mean Dr. Hornsby? I doubt it. I think he only teaches upperclassmen."

"That's the one, all right—the one with the dowdy wife. Sour-faced as a dish of clabber, and about as appealing." Nettie flapped across the kitchen in her pink fuzzy bedroom slippers and removed a pile of needlework from a cane-bottom chair, gesturing for me to sit. "Know what that woman told Willene?"

Sitting obediently, I shook my head.

"Said she'd just as soon live in the backwoods as to be stuck here in Stone's Throw!" She lowered her voice. "It's all over town her husband and that poor little Hunter girl were *carrying on*."

I said I'd heard. "I'm sure the police plan to question him," I told her.

"Humph! They'll have to find him first. Nobody's seen him since his last class yesterday."

I frowned. "How do you know?" Since I wasn't due at Sarah Bedford until later that day, I hadn't been to the campus.

"You know Kim—does my hair at the Total Perfection—well, her daughter Belinda sits for them some, and she says he didn't come home last night at all." Nettie shook her head. "Can you imagine? And him with all those little children, too! Well, the police will round him up in short order."

Round him up? It sounded as though the missing professor was divided into numerous little pieces that the authorities would scoop together like bits of clay. I remembered watching the man calmly reading his paper in the cafeteria only the day before. Had he been planning his getaway even then?

My neighbor put a hand on my arm as I was leaving. "And by the way, what's the deal with that boarder you took in last year? The woman who's staying in Charlie's old office? I see her light from time to time, so how come I never see *her?*"

"Augusta? Oh, I think you'd like her, Nettie. She's simply an angel." I slipped through the door before she could pursue the subject. It's funny, but if you tell people the truth, I've found, they seldom ever believe you.

"Joy Ellen says D.C. probably was killed early Saturday morning," I told Augusta and Ellis over supper that night. The history teacher still wasn't thrilled about my being there, but at least she wasn't hostile when we met for a planning session that afternoon.

Augusta had discovered the slow cooker and planned the week's meals around it. Tonight it was chicken stew. Ellis, whose husband Bennett had some kind of dinner meeting that night, contributed her "homemade" biscuits (out of the freezer case at Harris Teeter) and I had stirred up a dessert.

Augusta broke open a steaming biscuit and slathered it with some of her strawberry jam. "How does she know that?" she asked.

"Heard one of the policemen talking about it. Said it looked like the Hunter girl died from a blow to her head, possibly from a fall. That old shed has a stone floor, but you probably wouldn't notice it for all the dirt that's accumulated there."

"I think it used to be a stable," Ellis said. "And after that, the college stored lawn tools there, things like that."

I nodded. "Joy Ellen said Londus Clack told her he remembers when it served as a concession stand back when students still swam in the Old Lake."

"When was that?" Augusta asked. "Ellis, you'll have to give me the recipe for these biscuits. They're simply delicious."

"Had to have been more than thirteen or fourteen years ago," I said. "Roger dated several girls at Sarah Bedford and I'm sure the lake was posted off limits even then."

Steam rose about her face as Augusta sipped her coffee. "Londus Clack? He's the maintenance person you spoke about, isn't he? The one who sings? Has he been with the school that long?"

"I'm not sure," Ellis said, "but Londus grew up here, you know. His father worked for the college."

"Then he must feel right at home there," I said.

Ellis ladled more stew into her bowl. "Maybe. Maybe not. The college let his father go. I remember Bennett talking about it. He was on the board of directors when it happened. Caused quite a stink at the time. Bennett never did believe he'd done it. Old

Dorsey Clack was as honest as the day is long, he said. Turned out later, he was right."

"What did they think he'd done?" Augusta asked.

"Some student accused him of stealing jewelry—a ring, I think. Said she'd seen him in her room." Ellis shook her head, her face stormy. "Of course he was in her room. They'd called him to fix the radiator. Months later they found the girl's ring behind the commode. She'd set it on top of the tank while she took a shower—but by then the damage had been done."

"What do you mean, *damage?*" I spooned up bowls of lemon mystery for everyone. It's really lemon pudding cake, but Mama always called it lemon mystery—makes it sound sort of exotic.

"Ruined his health, that's what. Poor thing fretted so, he went downhill like ice on a hot slide," Ellis said. "I don't think Dorsey Clack lived a year after that."

So the singing janitor had reason to have a grudge against the college, but would he go so far as to take it out in murder?

Ellis must've had the same thought. "Londus just doesn't seem the sort to go around doing in young women."

I thought of all those interviews I'd read where neighbors claimed *what a nice, sweet boy he was . . . why, they couldn't imagine him doing an awful thing like that!* "Maybe not," I said, "but he certainly had the opportunity."

I cleared away the dishes after supper while Augusta

helped Ellis with the cross-stitch she was attempting for her soon-to-be new grandson. Her daughter Susan was expecting in January and Ellis had brought over her snarled efforts and appealed to Augusta's angelic nature. "I'll give you the secret recipe for my biscuits," she promised. When Clementine began barking at footsteps on the back porch, I assumed Roger had come to take advantage of dessert, but it was my cousin Jo Nell who stuck her head in the doorway. "I meant to give this back to you after our meeting Monday," she said, presenting me with our great-grandmother's china platter wrapped in layers of newspaper. Our ancestor had hand-painted it with a dainty scattering of violets and it had a special place in my dining room. Jo Nell borrows it as often as possible, but the platter had been left to me and I mean to keep it.

"There's no rush, you know," I said, thanking her. "I could've picked it up later, but since you're here, how about some dessert and a cup of coffee?" I knew my cousin had come because she wanted to pump me about what was going on at Sarah Bedford.

"I can't stay long, but . . . is that lemon mystery? Well, maybe just a little . . . ." My cousin sat in the chair next to Augusta's, but of course she couldn't see her. "I suppose you've heard about all the awful goings-on with that Hornsby fellow—meeting in that old shed with that young girl. Willene Benson told me they'd found all sorts of things in that loft. A regular love nest, she said."

My stomach did a somersault as I watched her spoon up another mouthful of dessert, and I wished I hadn't eaten so much stew.

"I know how these girls talk—thought you might've heard more about it. The sooner they catch up with that one, the better!"

I nodded in agreement. "Sounds like you know more about it than I do," I said, and began drying dishes at the sink so I wouldn't have to watch her eat. The conversation had taken a revolting turn and I was ready to change the subject.

"Can't help but feel sorry for Blythe Cornelius," she continued mournfully. "Willene says she feels responsible."

Ellis tugged at a thread. "Why is that?"

"She wasn't in the dorm for most of the night. One of the girls came down with a really bad virus and Blythe sat up with her in the infirmary. That old nurse they've got over there is so lazy she wouldn't bring you water if she was sittin' next to the sink, and she must be near about as old as I am."

"But Blythe isn't a housemother," I said. "It shouldn't be her business to look after these girls just because she lives in the dorm."

"I know, but she babies those girls something awful. Should've had about ten of her own," Jo Nell said. "Anyway, Willene said Blythe came back to the dorm sometime before dawn to get the sick girl some fresh pajamas, and one of the students at Emma Harris had left a note on her door about the Hunter girl."

Ellis muttered something that sounded like "shit" and threw her stitching aside. "What about her?" she snarled.

"Somebody thought they'd heard her crying and wanted Blythe to check on her, but by then the girl's room was quiet, so naturally Blythe didn't want to wake her. Besides, the sick one was over in the infirmary with soiled pajamas and a temperature of a hundred and two." My cousin eyed Ellis's wadded-up needlework with a look of dismay. "A person can't be in two places at once," she said.

I said I guessed they couldn't and put away the last pan. "Why does Blythe Cornelius live in the dorm?" I asked.

"Couldn't find a place to rent when she started to work there and the college had it available. I don't think she pays much for it," Jo Nell said. "And it is convenient. A lot of the staff at Sarah Bedford live in faculty housing. That whole block across from the campus belongs to the college, you know, and then there's a couple of apartment units as well."

"Is that where Willene Benson lives?" Ellis asked.

"Oh, no. Willene lives right on campus in that little brick building behind administration. Used to be a garage. She and Blythe kind of keep one another company, I think. Blythe came from a big family, but most of her relatives are scattered now. And Willene . . . well, there's something a little sad about her. Can't quite put my finger on it."

I told her how Willene had acted when the police

came. "Couldn't get out of there fast enough. I thought she was going to have a nervous breakdown."

"High-strung," Jo Nell said. "And timid as a mouse."

Ellis scowled as she examined the finger she'd stuck with a needle. "If Willene Benson had lived a hundred years ago," she said, "she'd probably have the vapors."

Having had her fill of the local gossip and lemon mystery, my cousin prepared to leave. "You just be careful on that campus, Lucy Nan Pilgrim! No tellin' who's lurking around over there. Until they find that professor or whoever's responsible for that girl's murder, nobody's safe anymore."

But if Professor Hornsby was responsible for killing D.C. Hunter, why did he wait so long to leave? I wondered.

"Maybe he didn't think he'd get caught," Celeste suggested the next day as we measured walnut hulls into an iron pot and added water and salt to set the dye. One of the women who demonstrated spinning at Bellawood had donated skeins of wool for our experiment, only we cheated, using the gas stoves in the Home Economics Department instead of an open fire. When the water was dark enough, we would simmer the yarn until it turned a rich brown.

Looking thoughtful, Debra, Celeste's roommate, stirred the potent brew. "Wonder when Paula and Miriam will come back to class. I heard they were so shook up they've been excused for the next few days.

Just think—it could've been one of us. It could've been me!"

"You saw her, didn't you, Miss Lucy?" Celeste wanted to know. "Did he really . . . you know . . . cut her with a *sickle?*"

I closed my eyes against the thought. "I didn't see any sickle. It was enough to know she was dead." But I had noticed the plastic container of breath mints that I later heard bore Professor Hornsby's fingerprints. However, both Paula and Miriam had reported seeing the dark-stained sickle beside the girl's body.

"I heard they'd been screwin' around—oops, sorry!" One of the girls flushed and grinned. "I mean getting it on out there for weeks. 'Horny' Hornsby, they call him. And all this time I've been sitting right there in his class. Gives me the creeps! I wonder what she saw in him."

"Or he in her," Celeste said. "But he didn't have to kill her."

"She was gone all day Friday, you know, and so was he. They must've met somewhere," Troll suggested. "Maybe he wanted to break it off and she threatened to tell his wife. That's probably why she was crying the next morning." Troll was one of a group tending simmering pokeberries at the next stove and she carelessly shoved hair from her face, leaving a dark red smear. Though the girls were swathed in huge aprons and wore rubber gloves almost to their elbows, it was impossible to protect every inch. My old once-white sneakers were spattered in yellowish-brown, and I knew I had painted my nose when I gave in to an itch.

"Wait just a minute," I said. "We don't know that he *did* kill her."

Celeste fanned away walnut fumes and made a face. "He's gone, isn't he?"

"Maybe he's just scared," I said.

She shrugged. "That makes two of us."

It occurred to me as I drove home that afternoon that not one person had mentioned the suspicious letter D.C. Hunter was supposed to have received in the mail, which must mean that only the police knew about it. "Just like that other girl got," the sergeant had said. But what other girl? The girl who was killed four years ago? If only I knew what had been inside that envelope!

"What envelope?" Augusta asked when I told her about it that night.

"Then they must be keeping it quiet for a reason," she said when I told her what I had heard at Blythe Cornelius's apartment. "And by the way, your cousin called and left a message just before you got home. Seems the professor turned himself in this afternoon."

"Where was he? Has he admitted anything?"

"Jo Nell said he showed up at the police station around four—been staying with a relative. Says he didn't do it." Augusta had laid a fire in the sitting room and now she gazed at the embers, absently stroking Clementine's black-and-white head. "I wonder how long he's been at the college. Could he have had anything to do with the other girl's death?"

"I'm sure Captain Hardy's looking into that," I said. "He seems to know what he's doing. Do you think there might be a connection?"

Augusta's amber necklace reflected the flickering blaze on the hearth. "It might be a good idea," she said, "to look into some of the old newspaper files. You never can tell what might turn up."

"But don't you think the police have already done that?"

The angel turned her gray-green gaze on me. "That's just the point, Lucy Nan. You'll be looking at this with an open mind. You just might catch something that went right past them. Something so ordinary they wouldn't think it was important."

I frowned. "You mean like mysterious letters?"

"I mean, you'll know it when you see it," she said.

Chapter Six

I wasn't so sure about that, so I convinced Augusta to come along with me. It didn't take a lot of persuading.

Stone's Throw's weekly newspaper, *The Messenger* (Ellis calls it *The Mess* because she claims there's a typo on every other line), shares a yellow brick building facing the town park with Petal Pushers, the new florist ("We sell every blooming thing!") and McBride's Pharmacy.

The receptionist put her telephone conversation on

hold long enough to point out the small room where back issues were kept on microfilm, and Augusta, fascinated by the whole procedure, hovered over my shoulder as I scanned several weeks of news. "Imagine getting all that information on that little piece of film!" she said as the pages rolled past. I didn't bother to explain that technology had developed an even more advanced technique used by most contemporary publishers.

Rachel Isaacs's murder took up most of the front page of the October 5 issue that year. Londus Clack had discovered the girl's submerged body caught on debris just beneath the surface of the water as he trimmed the tall grass around the lake. She had been stunned or knocked unconscious by a blow to the head, then apparently was shoved into the water to drown.

" 'The victim could have stood if she had been able, as the water was only about four feet deep in the spot where she was found,' " Augusta read aloud. "That poor girl! What a cruel thing to do!" She sank onto the chair next to mine, her gray-green eyes filled with the horror of it.

"They just left her there—left her to drown," I said. Even though the girl had been killed several years before, reading the article made the tragedy seem fresh and new. "Who would do such a thing?"

"That's what we want to find out." Augusta nodded toward the screen in front of us. "Let's see what else it says."

Like D.C. Hunter, Rachel was fully dressed in shorts, T-shirt, and sneakers, and her roommate said she had gone to the Old Lake to jog. The weapon used to strike the girl was never found, I read, but a coroner's report didn't rule out the possibility it might have been a stout stick later camouflaged by others of its kind in the lake's murky waters.

Rachel Isaacs's smiling photograph looked out at us from the front page of *The Messenger*. It was made the week before her death, the article said, for a college annual she would never see. She was a freshman and looked it: pretty, heart-shaped face, bright smile, short dark hair that appeared to be naturally curly. And the expression in her eyes gave the impression she had just heard a really good joke and couldn't wait to tell it.

Friends planned to dedicate a sundial in her memory in the campus garden, I read, and the girl's roommate was so distraught she was under a doctor's care.

Augusta shook her head. "It seems as if she had absolutely nothing in common with D.C. Hunter, yet the two were killed near the same place at approximately the same time of year."

"There has to be some kind of mad reasoning behind all this," I said, "but I can't imagine what it might be."

"The article doesn't mention the Isaacs girl receiving any kind of note or letter," Augusta said, scanning the story again. She glanced at the office across the hall. "Do you suppose the editor might remember anything about it, or has she not been with the paper that long?"

Josie Kiker had been editor of the tiny weekly for over twenty years, and it didn't look as if her desk had been cleared since she'd started. When I poked my head in the doorway she looked up from her computer and stretched, shoving a mop of gray-streaked red hair from her forehead. "Did you bring me a scoop or you just out slumming?" With a sudden kick, she sent a straight chair sliding in my direction. "Have a seat. I need a break anyway—back's rebelling." Josie pushed up her glasses and rubbed the bridge of her nose. "What can I do for you?"

I told her what I had overheard the policeman say about D.C. Hunter supposedly receiving some kind of mysterious letter. "Just like that other girl got."

She reached for a pot of what looked like liquid coal that simmered on top of the filing cabinet. "Coffee?"

I thanked her but declined. I try not to drink anything you might have to scoop out with a shovel. I told her how the girls in my class had discovered D.C.'s body and how the police had examined her mail. "We—I—thought you might remember something like that happening when Rachel Isaacs was killed," I said.

Josie tossed down her brew like it was a shot of bourbon. "Seems like I did hear there was a message of some kind, but the police were real closemouthed about it. Never gave out so much as a hint. When nothing ever came out about it, I just assumed it was one of those rumors that circulate through the gossip mill." Shoving her coffee mug aside, the editor leaned

74

across her desk. "Did you actually *see* these letters? How do you know they were meant for the Hunter girl?"

"That's what Sally, her roommate, told police. She'd been collecting the mail and leaving it on D.C.'s desk. I was there when they asked her for permission to enter the room and take them."

She frowned. "How many letters were there?"

"Oh, I don't know. Four or five, maybe, but the attention seemed focused on one," I told her.

"I don't suppose you know what it said?" She tilted her head to look at me. I didn't even have to answer.

Josie Kiker had the look of a bloodhound in her eyes and I wouldn't have been too surprised if she had dropped to the floor and begun to sniff. Instead she leaned back in her chair. "Wonder if it held some kind of threat?"

I shrugged. "Your guess is as good as mine, but it sounds as if it might be something that would tie the two murders together."

The smell of scorched coffee filled the small room, and Augusta, standing behind the editor, wrinkled her nose at the sight of the stained pot, which looked as if it hadn't been scrubbed in this decade.

I turned away to hide my smile, but thankfully Josie didn't notice. "They'll say Claymore Hornsby did it," she said, studying a spot on the ceiling, "but I just can't see it."

"Was he here when the other girl was killed?" I asked.

"Oh, yes, Clay's been at the college for seven or eight years now and had a roving eye for as many, but I never thought he'd actually *do* anything about it. You've seen his wife, I suppose?"

I shook my head. "Not that I can remember."

"Well, as the old fellow says, 'She ain't got nary turn for inticin'.' Plain as a rag mop, Monica is—but then he knew that when he married her, didn't he?"

I said I reckon he did and tried to signal Augusta it was time to go. I wouldn't put it past her to go into a cleaning frenzy right then and there. "I just hope they'll soon find out who did it," I told her. "Two unsolved murders in less than five years isn't going to look good for Sarah Bedford."

Josie Kiker made a noise that was somewhere between a shish and a grunt. "Two is all they admit to, but I've wondered since about that other girl." She nudged her glasses into place and frowned at the computer screen.

"What other girl? You mean there was a murder before Rachel Isaacs's?"

"Accident, they *said*. Fell from the Tree House. You know, that circular platform around the big oak on the front campus. They use it mostly on Class Day."

I sat back down. "I don't remember that. When did it happen?"

" 'Bout nine years ago, I think. I can look it up. Seems it was a girl from somewhere in upstate New York."

Josie bustled out of the room, bypassed the microfilm, and went to a narrow alcove where I heard her shifting through bulky bound copies. Her glasses had slid midway down her nose when she returned dusting off her hands a few minutes later. "Martinez," she announced. "Carla Martinez." She looked at me across her rat's nest of a desk. "Happened in early October—just like the other two."

Nine years ago in October. That was about the time our daughter Julie, still in high school, had been hospitalized with a severe bout of flu that developed into pneumonia. I had been so preoccupied with worry I hadn't kept up with what was going on at the college—or anywhere else in town. If there was a connection with the three girls' deaths, that would mean a gap of five years between the first two, yet it was hard to believe it was coincidence. I also considered the fact that Stone's Throw was usually a slow news town and that Josie Kiker rarely had a chance to unearth a good story. Her hands paused now over the keyboard, aching back apparently forgotten in her eagerness to dig up old bones. "And guess who discovered the body?" she said.

I frowned. "Not Londus Clack?" I darted a look at Augusta, who was making her way to the door with a look of purposeful intent, and I knew she was headed for the bound copies.

"The very same. Found her early in the morning as he was setting out mums—always plants that pretty purple kind along the flagstone walk there. Everybody seemed to think she'd fallen the night before. Died of a broken neck. Doc Worley—he was coroner then—said she'd been dead about six or seven hours."

"What was she doing in the Tree House that late at night?" I asked.

"Who knows. Some of the girls in her dorm said she'd gone over to the practice rooms like she always did after supper—she was a piano student, you know—and she was wearing the skirt and sweater she'd worn to class the day before." The editor nodded toward the door behind me. "I left that issue out if you want to see it, but I doubt you'll learn much there."

Carla Martinez had large dark eyes and long straight hair that could have been light brown. She wasn't smiling in the picture and looked as if she might be the studious type. In fact, the article revealed she had come to Sarah Bedford on a partial scholarship and planned to major in music. She was a freshman.

I looked up at Augusta, who stood waiting. "What now?" I asked. She didn't answer, but as she fingered her glowing necklace the stones turned from brilliant sapphire to the mesmerizing cobalt of deep, deep water.

"Brendon Worthington—he was dean of the School of Music then—said Carla was one of the most promising pianists he'd ever taught," Joy Ellen Harper told me a few days later. "It just tore him up when that happened. She was only seventeen, you know."

"What do you think happened?" I asked. "She doesn't sound like the type to be hanging out in a tree house in the middle of the night."

"Could've been a prank, I guess. Underclassmen aren't supposed to go up there. The Tree House is off limits to everybody but seniors, although I doubt if any of them give a hoot about it. The college makes a big deal out of it on Class Day." Joy Ellen shook her head and frowned at the blue book she was grading. "What in the world's gotten into that girl? Didn't even try to answer half these questions." She slashed a red F on the inside cover and tossed the book aside.

"I really didn't know the Martinez girl," she continued. "She wasn't in any of my classes, but you're right, she didn't seem the type for midnight stunts. Kind of a shy little thing. We all just assumed she fell."

I glanced at the name on the failed exam. *Leslie Monroe*. I knew she had studied. I'd seen her cramming with a stack of books the day I'd brought the cookies from her aunt. She had seemed worried even then. Poor Leslie! She wasn't going to take this well at all.

"Where can I find Dean Worthington?" I asked. "Is he still around?"

"No, Brendon retired soon after that. He died a couple of years ago."

I sat on one of the desktops. "What about Dr. Hornsby?"

Joy Ellen let the blue book drop. "Claymore Hornsby? Uh-uh. Clay came here after old Amos Crockett died. Good English teacher, Professor Crockett, but a bit on the eccentric side. Died during midterms and they had to find a replacement fast. No, Clay couldn't have had anything to do with that girl's death."

She turned the red pencil in her fingers. "You know, I'd almost forgotten that incident. That's awful, isn't it? But it happened soon after classes started that year. The girl hadn't been on campus long."

Joy Ellen tossed aside her pencil and leaned back in her chair. "Hornsby's admitted he had a fling with D.C. Hunter, but he swears he broke it off that Friday night and didn't see her again."

"That was the night before she died . . . how do you *know* this?"

I must have had a strange expression because Joy Ellen laughed. "Campus grapevine. And it was in this morning's paper. I'm surprised you didn't see it."

"Haven't had a chance," I said. "But I did stop by *The Messenger* over the weekend to look through some old issues. Did you know that Londus Clack was the one who discovered the Isaacs girl *and* the girl who was supposed to have fallen from the Tree House?"

"Well, that makes sense. He's always up earlier than everybody else, and his work takes him all over the campus." Joy Ellen thought for a minute, then shrugged. "Nah! Londus is scared of his shadow. Besides, I can't see him getting that riled at anybody."

I told her what had happened to his father. "I've always heard it's the calm ones you have to watch out for," I said. "The ones who hold it in."

"Could be, but if the police thought Londus was guilty, they would've arrested him by now—unless he's a lot slyer than I think."

I resisted the impulse to look behind me. Were we dealing with two different murderers? "What about the professor?"

"I can't believe Clay Hornsby would let himself get mixed up in a thing like this—especially since his novel was accepted last summer. They've been playing it up big in the English Department." Joy Ellen's eyebrows went up. "But . . . a waitress in Columbia says she served Clay and a young woman that Friday before D.C. disappeared and that the girl looked like she'd been crying. Said she recognized them when she saw their pictures on the television news. Sounds like the two of them were together all that day." She marked another book. "And then there's that box of breath mints with his prints on it, and of course they were all over that shed, too, I hear."

"What does he say about that?" I asked.

"What can he say? They were his, all right. That old shed was their secret meeting place, but he swears he didn't see her after that night. Says they had a long talk, then D.C. drove back to the campus, or at least that's what he assumed she did. Clay drove over to Table Rock Mountain and rented a cabin for a couple of nights." Joy Ellen made a face and shook her head. "Needed time to think! Anyway, he got home late Sunday and didn't find out D.C. was missing until the next day . . . or so he says."

"That would explain why somebody heard her crying," I said. "And her roommate swears her car wasn't there when she got in that Friday night, so D.C. must've come in later. But wouldn't the people who rented the cabin to Clay Hornsby remember if he was there?"

"It seems so, but of course I don't know the details. The last I heard, the police were letting him go," Joy Ellen said. "Frankly, I think the only thing Claymore Hornsby is guilty of is poor judgment and a bad tailor."

The weather was almost summerlike as I walked across campus after class that day. Students in shirt-sleeves strolled past and several gathered by the fountain in the sunny commons area. Sarah Bedford seemed a different place from the cold bleak campus where we had found D.C. Hunter's body the week before.

The professor's story of a cabin at Table Rock Mountain must have checked out or he wouldn't have been released, I thought. But Table Rock State Park was only a couple of hours away. Clay Hornsby could have come back to the campus, killed his young lover, and been snug in his mountain cabin before dawn, and nobody would be the wiser. Unless they saw him here.

The students' light voices blended with the trickle of the fountain as I walked past the commons, and for a minute I almost forgot a girl recently had been murdered here. Two of the girls in my class called to me and I waved back. They walked in pairs now, or clusters. The students at Sarah Bedford were afraid to walk alone. Several, I heard, had already left the college.

In a far corner of the campus I saw the empty Tree House in the dark shade of the huge oak whose limbs almost touched the ground. Its leaves were beginning to turn the same color as the red earth that nourished it, and it looked like a picture you might find in a coffee-table book. I started to hurry past when I noticed a movement near the top of the twisting steps and glimpsed the swirl of a lavender gossamer skirt that shimmered as if it had been sprinkled with stardust. Augusta.

She hurried to meet me at the base of the tree and paused briefly to glance back at the platform above us. "There's only one way someone could fall from that Tree House," she said, "and that's if they either stood on the railing or crawled under it."

"Or if they were pushed," I said.

Chapter Seven

*A*ugusta looked up from her latest Agatha Christie novel and lifted a brow. She had already finished most of the stack I'd brought from the library and was especially fond of what she called the English village mysteries. "You wouldn't be going over to the college, would you?" she asked.

"I don't have a class there today, but I thought I'd

see how Blythe is doing. Want me to stop by the library?"

She marked her place in *The Body in the Library* and laid it aside. "Later, perhaps, but I'd like to go along if you don't mind, maybe stroll about the campus a bit." Augusta looked at me with a perfectly straight face and said, "Sometimes, you know, it's difficult to see the thicket for all the oaks."

"I see," I said, and nodded, planning to decipher that later.

Augusta seemed lost in thought as we drove to the campus. Blythe Cornelius had been so helpful during our recent chaotic invasion, I stopped by the store for a pot of African violets which Augusta held on her lap, and maybe I imagined it, but the soft lavender of the flowers' petals seemed more vivid after the angel's touch. We had waited until mid-afternoon to go so that Blythe would have a chance to unwind after what must be a tiring day with the dean, and she seemed pleased when she greeted me at the door.

"Why, Lucy! You didn't have to bring me anything, but it's good to see you again." Blythe took the foil-wrapped pot from my hands and held it to the window light. "See how it matches my curtains . . . and isn't it odd?" she added, sniffing. "It smells a little like strawberries." She bent to stroke a yellow cat I hadn't seen before that rubbed against her legs. "It will be lovely right here in the window if my babies will just leave it alone. You be a good girl now, Miranda."

I glanced quickly at Augusta, but her back was

turned as she stooped to examine titles in a bookcase across the room, looking for mysteries, no doubt.

Willene Benson sat on the edge of a dainty Victorian chair with her ankles primly crossed and dabbed her nose with a handkerchief. "Allergy," she explained without looking up.

The woman seemed to have a perpetual smile, as if her teeth were too large for her mouth and she didn't know what to do with them, but in spite of her ever-present grin it was obvious she had been crying.

"I was just about to offer Willene some banana bread," Blythe said. "Not homemade, I'm afraid—the bakery has me beat. The water's about to boil. Won't you join us?"

She sounded as if she meant it, so I accepted, leaving Augusta to her own diversions. Also, I wanted to find out what Blythe Cornelius knew about the girl who had fallen from the Tree House.

Blythe obviously had been working on cross-stitch, as a half-finished design of a vase of flowers waited on one end of the sofa. "For my niece," she explained. "She's getting married in May."

I helped her bring in the tea tray and sat at the other end. We had to move an array of framed photographs to make room for the refreshments, and Blythe spoke to each one as though the person were present.

"Excuse me, Uncle Henry, I'm going to put you over here on the end table with Cousin Ella for a while . . . Aunt Mae, I'll leave the twins with you . . ."

I almost expected some long-dead ancestor to plop

down beside me and ask me to pass the sugar.

Willene managed a smile. "Don't mind her," she said. "She talks that way all the time."

Blythe nodded. "They keep me company," she said, offering me a cup of tea. She called my attention to an oval portrait in a silver filigree frame. A pretty girl of about twelve sat with a chubby toddler on her lap. "That's me with my little sister," Blythe explained. "She didn't want to sit still for the photographer."

I smiled, thinking of what a wiggleworm Teddy had been at that age. Blythe Cornelius had been a striking-looking child with her straight nose and firm chin, and she had grown into a handsome woman.

I finished my banana bread and set my cup aside, fumbling about in my mind for a way to bring up the subject of Carla Martinez. As it turned out, I didn't have to because Willene led into it for me.

"I suppose you've heard the police have let Clay Hornsby go," she said, folding her paper napkin and laying it aside as though Blythe might want to use it again. "One of the cooks in the cafeteria told me he was here at the college when that other girl was killed, too. Sure sounds peculiar to me. I don't mind telling you, I'm afraid to go out alone."

"A lot of us were here when that happened, Willene." Blythe slipped a large magnifying glass around her neck and took up her cross-stitch, frowning as she poked the needle in and out. "Claymore Hornsby's a first-class jackass, but he wouldn't hurt you or anyone else. Besides, both the victims were college girls."

86

"And there may have been a third," I said, and told them about Carla Martinez.

"But that was an accident, wasn't it?" Blythe paused in midstitch. "An awful thing! I remember how shocked we all were. But murder? I don't think they ever considered it anything other than an accident. I was led to believe she went up there on a dare, or maybe even to meet someone."

"Did you know the girl?" I asked, trying to find a spot for my empty plate.

"Stop that, Mabel!" Blythe gently untangled the gray cat from a network of thread. "No, not well, and I was out of town when it happened. I think that was the weekend my cousin Joyce's baby was baptized. They were living in Birmingham then."

"What about Clay Hornsby?" Willene asked.

"Clay took old Amos Crockett's place when he died a few years back. He wasn't even here then," Blythe said. "I don't know why anyone would think that girl's death is related to the other two. That Tree House is dark enough in the daylight. The girl had no business there at that time of night. She probably slipped and fell." Blythe gave her needle a final jerk and bit off the thread.

"Blythe, where are your scissors? You'll ruin your teeth doing that." Willene sounded just like Miss Harriet Middleton, who taught me home economics in the ninth grade.

"Must've mislaid them. Can't find 'em anywhere, and my thimble's gone, too." Blythe shook her head.

"Reckon I'm getting addlepated. Could've sworn I left them right here on this end table." She shrugged. "Guess they'll turn up sooner or later."

"I'd better be getting on home," Willene said, brushing a crumb from her lap. "And I don't care what you say, I'd feel a lot safer if they kept that man locked up." She set her cup aside and stood, and since she seemed to be waiting for me to say something, I looked at my watch and announced that it was time for me to go, too. Augusta, I noticed, had already taken her leave.

"I know you'll think I'm the biggest baby in the world," Willene said as we stepped outside, "but would you walk with me as far as my door? It's getting kind of late, and I don't like to cross this campus alone."

I said I'd be glad to. It was on the way to where I'd parked my car, but it wasn't even dark yet, and I didn't think we needed to worry about somebody jumping out at us with a sickle. Poor Willene reminded me of a child playing "Ain't no bugger bears out tonight," anticipating monsters behind every tree.

It was hard to believe Willene Benson's quarters had ever been a garage. Set snugly behind Main Hall, the worn brick had faded to pink, and long windows with dark green shutters flanked a polished oak door. A profusion of purple pansies nodded above twin window boxes.

Willene hesitated at the door. "I'm such a scaredy-cat, would you mind waiting while I look around inside? It will only take a minute."

I could hear her telephone ringing as she searched for her key, and by the time she had unlocked the door it had rung at least five times. She seemed in no hurry to answer.

I stood in her neat but shabby living room while Willene crept timidly through each room, ignoring the shrill noise. Was the woman deaf? "Aren't you going to answer the phone?" I asked when I couldn't stand it any longer.

She didn't answer but her face was vanilla-white, and there was no mistaking the fear in her eyes. Willene Benson was afraid to answer her telephone.

"Are you all right?" I steadied her with my arm and led her to a faded green sofa. Thank God the phone finally had stopped ringing.

"I—I think so . . . yes . . . I'm fine, really." She looked up at me and attempted a smile. "I'm afraid all this has just upset me. I'm sure I'll feel better after a good night's rest."

This was none of my business, but I've never let that stop me before. "Willene," I said, "have you considered getting caller ID? When somebody calls, their number appears on your phone, so you don't have to answer if you don't want to. In other words, it screens your calls."

She sighed. "Administration has been after me to get one of those answering machines, but I've been putting it off. Seems people would know that if I don't answer, I'm not here!" Willene laughed halfheartedly at her attempt at a joke. "The management people keep reminding me there are times when it's important for them to be able to leave a message, so I suppose I'll have to break down and get one just so they'll leave me alone."

She seemed calmer now, so I began to take my leave.

"Does that thing really work?" she asked, accompanying me to the door.

"What thing?"

"That caller ID thing. Can you really tell who's calling?"

I assured her that you could. "Why don't you talk to the phone company?" I said. "They can tell you more about it than I can."

"Why, yes, I believe I will . . . and thank you, Lucy, for being patient with me. I'm not . . . well, I wasn't always this way."

I waited outside while she double-latched the door and then waved to me from the window. Dusky shadows were blending as I crossed the courtyard to the parking lot and Augusta was nowhere in sight. I walked a little faster.

I barely had time to pick up shrimp from the market, shower, and change before Ben was due for dinner, so I didn't waste any time getting home. I sensed Augusta wasn't there as soon as I walked in the door. Whenever she's present, there's a certain awareness that makes colors seem brighter and troubles seem lighter, and I wondered where she could be, then smiled when I saw the note on the kitchen table.

Augusta's elegant handwriting resembles something you might find in an old manuscript, and it seemed oddly out of place on the back of a grocery list: *Gone to help Ellis with her needle work. Don't eat all the apple cobbler! Augusta*

Apple cobbler? What apple cobbler? I certainly hadn't had time to bake—but Augusta had, and there it sat on the counter basking in all its warm, spicy goodness. Ben would be delirious with joy, as it was his favorite. Augusta was aware of that, of course, which is why she made it. She would never admit it, but I suspect Augusta has a bit of a crush on Benjamin Maxwell!

I knew Ellis's husband was due to attend a session meeting at our church that night, which would allow Augusta time to help her with her embroidery project, but I also had an idea the angel deliberately made herself sparse so Ben and I could have the house to ourselves. Maybe that's part of being an angel.

Later, the two of us sat at the kitchen table eating Cajun spiced shrimp with corn on the cob and washing it down with beer. Messy eating, but Ben is the kind of person you can relax and be messy with, which is one of the reasons I like him—plus he makes me laugh.

Ben comes from this little crossroads town called Sweet Gum Valley, which is even smaller than Stone's Throw, and he probably makes up most of those tales, but that's part of who he is. And more and more, I'm kind of liking who he is!

When we first began seeing each other, I thought the man was about to launch a serious discussion when he managed to weave in one of his stories, which, if I remember correctly, involved a nineteenth-century farmer going into town to see his first train come through. Fearing the horse would be frightened, he tied the animal to a tree and got between the traces of his buggy to keep it from rolling away. "When he saw that train," Ben told me, "that fellow took off running, dragging that buggy behind him and turned up in a cloud of dust ten miles down the road!" Now I know more or less what to expect and can sometimes even predict when he's getting ready to "hark back to Sweet Gum Valley," as he says.

When we had finished dinner, Ben took our empty plates to the sink and poured more coffee for both of us. "I'd sure like some of that apple cobbler," he said, eyeing the dessert, "but I'd die before I'd ask for it."

As we lingered at the table after dessert, I told him about the eerie feeling I'd had that day after leaving Willene Benson, and how terrified she had seemed. "These murders are gnawing away at all of us," I said. "It's frustrating as well as frightening! I feel like I should be doing *something*."

The first thing I noticed about Ben Maxwell was his eyes: expressive, intelligent, and blue enough to bore holes through you—as they were doing then. A large, russet-bearded man who looks as if he should be wearing a kilt, he reached for my hand across the table. "Why do you think you have to find all the answers, Lucy Nan? It's not your job, and as you should know by now, it could be dangerous."

"Easy for you to say," I told him, still holding on to his work-callused hand. Ben is a furniture craftsman—a fine one, and his fingers are blunt and strong. "I have to see these people on a regular basis and this thing has turned the whole campus upside down. And now I've learned there may have been an earlier murder.

A freshman died from what everyone supposed was a fall from the Tree House nine years ago at about this same time of year."

"And what makes you think it wasn't a fall?" he asked.

"From all I've heard about her, she didn't seem the type to even be up there," I said. I didn't mention the mysterious letters the last two victims were rumored to have received.

Now Ben shook his head solemnly and I sensed he had a "harking" spell coming on. Turns out I was right. "Honey, you've gotta learn to relax, just let go . . . like old T. G. Talley."

I laughed. "Okay, I'll bite. Who's T. G. Talley?"

"T. G. Talley was this old fellow who belonged to the Rising Star Baptist Church way out on the edge of town . . ." Here Ben paused for dramatic effect and a long swallow of coffee. "When anything was bothering old T.G., he'd stand up in church and pray about it. 'Lord,' he'd say, 'this here's T. G. Talley from Sweet Gum Valley speaking . . .'"

I must have been laughing to myself when I thought about Ben's wild story during the Senior Citizen Singers Fall Fa-la-la Exhibition at the Baptist Church the next day because Opal Henshaw gave me a dirty look from the alto section. After the concert I went to dinner with Nettie and we had to stand in line at the Full Plate Cafeteria, whose sign advertises "All you care to eat!" I usually don't care to eat there at all, but Nettie likes it because she can get liver and onions. I try not look at her while she's eating it.

Naturally I had to give a report on Leslie, so I told her I had delivered the cookies, and hoped she wouldn't ask about her niece's scholastic accomplishments.

"Leslie went through some difficulties when her daddy remarried," Nettie told me as we moved through the serving line. She studied the desserts and added a piece of coconut cream pie to her tray. "And she's skinny as a string, but I reckon it's just getting adjusted to living away from home."

"That and not eating." I told her how Leslie had only nibbled at her lunch.

"Her daddy always treated her like a grown-up and expected her to act like one," Nettie said. "Leslie was only six when her mother died, and this new wife's never had children. The poor little thing never had much of a childhood, and frankly, I think they've pushed her too hard. Her daddy's worried about her, and so am I . . . and now another girl at Sarah Bedford's been killed. It's a wonder to me they aren't all nervous wrecks over there!" Dishes rattled as Nettie plunked down her tray. "I don't care what that Franklin Roosevelt said—there are *a lot* of things worse worrying about than just being scared!"

I took a long pull on my sweetened iced tea. If I didn't know better, I'd think my neighbor had been hanging out with Augusta.

Coffee sloshed into the saucer as Nettie sat down her cup. "If Leslie were mine, I'd jerk her home so fast you couldn't say scat. I hope you're keeping your car locked, Lucy Nan. That campus isn't safe anymore with that maniac going around slashing people with a sickle!"

But the next day the findings of the autopsy confirmed what the police had suspected. D.C. Hunter had died from a blow to the head. Apparently somebody had waited at the top of those dark stairs, then lashed out with the rusty sickle, causing her to fall and hit her head on the stone floor. The girl had gashes on her face, hands, and upper body as if she had tried to protect herself.

Chapter Eight

The Dulcimer Man came to my class the next day. His name is Andy Collins, but most people just call him the Dulcimer Man. When Augusta heard about it, a look that can only be described as blissful reverie crossed her face.

"Sophronia Lovelace," she said, pausing in her spasmodic aerobic exercise—which that day involved running up and down the stairs.

"I haven't heard one played as sweetly since she strummed 'Flow Gently, Sweet Afton' during a musical evening back in 1898 . . . or was it '99?" she said in answer to my unspoken question.

"Then by all means, come along," I told her. And since so many others wanted to hear him, we held class in one of the larger lecture rooms in Main Hall, where the musician played and sang, then demonstrated how the instrument was made. Augusta was serenely transported.

The Main Hall at Sarah Bedford has marble floors, mahogany banisters, and a ceiling that goes on forever. A large portrait of Sarah Bedford herself hangs in the place of honor above the staircase. It's one of those paintings that looks as if the subject is stepping out of a cloud of mist—or else she's just standing there while the house burns down around her.

We stayed until our guest had left and the last listener straggled away, so the building was relatively empty when Augusta and I started to leave. We were at the top of the stairs when she stopped me with a touch of her hand. "Listen . . ." she said, her head to one side.

I started to tell her I didn't hear a thing when I realized someone was singing what sounded like an old hymn and it seemed to be coming from a room down the hallway to our right. "It must be Londus," I said, "but is somebody with him?"

Augusta put a finger to her lips as we inched closer. It soon became obvious that the janitor wasn't singing alone, but was accompanied by a tinny mechanical voice that seemed to come from far away. The two of us stood outside the door labeled maintenance and eavesdropped shamelessly on the peculiar duet. Londus Clack was singing backup to *himself!*

When the roll,
When the roll is called up yonder, I'll be there.
When the roll,
When the roll is called up yonder, I'll be there.
When the r-o-o-o-l-l is called up yon-der,
When the roll is called up yonder, I'll be there!

Augusta, apparently having second thoughts about intruding, shook her head and turned away, beckoning me to follow. Having come this far, however, I resisted and held my hand to my mouth and my ear to the door until I couldn't stand it any longer. "Londus?" I tapped lightly. "Londus, is that you?"

Immediately the music stopped and the red-faced janitor opened the door. On a shelf behind him, between a can of floor wax and a bottle of glass cleaner, sat a huge stuffed teddy bear, the kind that has a tape player in its stomach.

Mop in hand, Londus stepped quickly into the

hallway, closing the door behind him. "I didn't think nobody was here," he said, wiping his pink face with a dingy handkerchief. "Singin' . . . well, it kinda makes the work go faster."

I agreed. "You sounded great—both of you—and I shouldn't have interrupted. I'm sorry."

Londus grinned and shook his head. "Ah, well, that's all right. One of my nieces gave me that old toy a few years back, said it would help me stay on key." He laughed. "Reckon she thought I needed it."

He turned as if he meant to go and I walked along beside him. "Wait, please. If you have a minute, maybe you can help me . . ." How could I word this diplomatically?

"You were here at Sarah Bedford when that girl fell from the Tree House, weren't you?"

Londus closed his eyes. "Lord, that were a long time ago."

"Not that long. About eight or nine years." I stopped at a water fountain. My mouth felt dry. I could be standing here talking with a murderer in this great hollow hall and my guardian angel seemed to have abandoned me.

"Your job takes you all over the campus, so you must have a pretty good idea of what goes on. Do you know if the girl who drowned and the one who fell from the Tree House had anything in common with D.C. Hunter?"

He shook his head. "I wouldn't know nothin' about that."

"What about boyfriends? Were Rachel Isaacs and the Martinez girl seeing anybody in particular?"

Londus frowned. "Martin who?"

I repeated the name. "The newspaper account said you found her body beneath the Tree House. Remember?"

He nodded, shoving his handkerchief in his back pocket. "She fell. That girl fell. Sure were a sad thing."

"Some people think she might've been meeting somebody that night—a boy, maybe. And what about the girl who drowned? A pretty girl like that must've had a boyfriend."

Londus clutched his mop with both hands. "I didn't pay no mind to them," he said. "But that girl they found in the shed—what's her name, B.C.?"

"D.C. Hunter."

"Yeah, her. I'm real sorry for what happened to her, but I seen what she was doin', and she weren't no better than she oughta be, sneakin' out and meetin' that man thataway. And he weren't neither."

I nodded solemnly. "I guess you must notice a lot that goes on here."

Londus cleared his throat and blew his nose as if he could get rid of all the bad things at Sarah Bedford College. "More than you'd think," he said. "More than you'd ever believe."

"I wonder what he meant by that," I said to Augusta, who waited on the stairs. I knew she'd overheard every word.

She paused briefly to glance at her reflection in the mirror that hung on the landing. "It seems to me that Londus Clack knows more than he's letting on," she said.

I repeated the question to Celeste and her roommate, Debra, later that afternoon, after telling them about my conversation with Londus. The weather was mild and the three of us sipped Cokes on the sunny steps of Emma P. Harris Hall.

"Londus doesn't miss much," Celeste said. "He not only sees who you go out with, he knows what time you get in, if you keep your room neat, or if you've sneaked beer into the dorm."

"Well, if he knows anything, he's not telling," I said. "Another student died several years ago, apparently from a fall from the Tree House, and Londus was the one who discovered the body. I asked him if the three girls had anything in common, but I couldn't get to first base with him. Claimed he didn't know anything about that."

Debra frowned. "I never knew there was another death. Do they know what caused her to fall?"

"Are they sure she *fell?*" Celeste wanted to know.

"That's what everybody thought—still do, I guess," I said. "The three girls who died were all new to the campus. Two of them were freshmen and D.C. was a junior, but she'd been to school in England until this year. That's the only thing I can see they had in common." I leaned against the brick pillar at the foot of the steps. "I realize D.C. was unpopular, but did she have any special enemies?"

Celeste grinned. "Do you have a phone book?"

"She and Leslie Monroe were having it out down in the laundry room one day not long ago," Debra said. "I thought they were going to start punching each other. Kinda freaked me out."

"What started it?" I asked.

"D.C. wanted to use the dryer, so she threw Leslie's clean clothes on the floor. Leslie had to wash them all over again."

Celeste turned the can of Coke in her hands as if studying the label. "I heard she pitched a hissy fit at rehearsal one night. Actually threw a script at Katy Jacobs."

Debra's eyes grew wide. "What happened?"

"D.C. was late, so Mrs. Treadwell—that's the director," Celeste told me, "put Katy in her role for the first scene. Katy was the understudy, you know, and D.C. had to wait until it was over to take her place. Made her mad enough to snag lightning, they said."

"When did that happen?" I asked.

"I think it was about a week before she disappeared," Celeste said. "Katy says she feels funny about playing that role now."

Debra drained her drink and scooted down a step into the sun. "That girl made more people cry than a bushel of onions. I don't see how her roommate could stand her."

"I guess she just got used to her," Celeste said.

Debra made a face. "Shoot! You could get used to hanging if it didn't kill you."

We were still laughing when somebody screamed.

"Oh, dear God, what's happened now?" Celeste jumped to her feet and started running toward the sound.

"Sounds like it's coming from the cafeteria," I said.

Debra looked at me and shrugged. "I *asked* Mrs. Benson not to serve that leftover spaghetti *again!*" And she took off after her roommate.

I hurried across the quad behind them as girls streamed out of dorms and classrooms, collecting on the leaf-strewn campus in a jittery chattering mass. Joy Ellen Harper rushed from her building, running toward the cafeteria faster than I would have thought possible, and I waded through a crowd of students to see what was going on. *Please, not another murder!* I thought, looking about frantically for Leslie Monroe. Across the campus, Blythe Cornelius stood on the steps of Main Hall with a bewildered-looking Dean Holland leaning on her arm.

"What's going on, Miss Lucy?" Paula Shoemaker worked her way over to me, remembering, no doubt, her own screams of only a few days ago. "Do you think there's been—"

I put an arm around her shoulders. "Let's hope not," I said, wishing Augusta were nearby. We could use her tranquil influence now.

"It's Pearl!" The girl they call Troll appeared beside

us. "You know—that lady who works in the cafeteria? The one who laughs a lot."

But Pearl wasn't laughing now, and when we reached the steps of the building I saw why.

Willene Benson stood in the doorway with her frail arms partway around a large hysterical woman. On the floor at their feet lay a big white apron like the ones we wore to boil pokeberries, only this one wasn't stained with berry juice. It was spattered with what looked a lot like blood.

If the scene in front of us hadn't been so frightening, it would have been funny. Pearl, who was at least six inches taller and about seventy pounds heavier than Willene, stood crying into the smaller woman's shoulder, and her sobs had now reached the hiccupping stage. To my surprise, Willene seemed to have overcome her customary skittishness and, at least for now, was holding her own. Still, her face was almost as white as the uniform she wore and her eyes held a dazed expression. "It's all right," she whispered to the other woman. "It's all right now, Pearl . . . it's all right."

It didn't look all right to me.

Pearl, I learned, had discovered the grisly apron at the bottom of a hamper of soiled towels and aprons used by the kitchen staff while gathering items for the laundry.

Joy Ellen had the presence of mind to summon the police and attempted to shoo away the curious onlookers, but it didn't do much good. I was relieved to see that one of them was Leslie.

The rest of us waited in the cafeteria while Pearl sat with her feet propped on a chair and sipped water. The cooks had been preparing chicken pot pie, and the smell of it made me feel queasy.

"What makes you think it's human blood?" I asked Willene, taking her aside. "Couldn't it be beef or chicken—something like that?"

She turned a shade paler and looked away. "Look at it, Lucy—the way it's spattered . . . it wouldn't be like . . . that."

I didn't want to look at the ghastly thing, but it was hard to look anywhere else. The stain dotted the apron from top to bottom like a big question mark.

"Lucy." Willene spoke softly as we watched the local police winding through the gathering outside. "I'm not feeling well at all. Would you mind staying here with Pearl?"

Before I could answer, she had scurried out the back way.

I recognized Captain Hardy, who was accompanied by Weigelia's cousin Kemper Mungo and Sheila Eastwood, two of Stone's Throw's finest. Pearl, more composed now, was able to show them where she had found the apron in the narrow room behind the kitchen where soiled laundry was collected.

"When I seen what was on there, I dropped it like it'd been a snake!" she told them. "Willene—she brought it out here so she could look at it in the light." Pearl mopped her eyes and braced herself on

Kemper's sturdy arm. "Do-law! I wouldn't touch that thing again for a million dollars!"

Wearing gloves, Sheila Eastwood carefully placed the apron in a large plastic bag. When she lifted it from where it had been spread on the floor, something fell out of a pocket and landed with a clank, while another, smaller object rolled against my foot.

Not thinking, I reached down to pick it up, and I would have if Kemper hadn't stopped me.

"Don't touch it!" Using a pen, he held the thimble up for us to see. It was hand-painted with tiny blue violets, and on the floor near where it had fallen was a pair of embroidery scissors.

Joy Ellen sank into a chair and looked up at me with shock-glazed eyes. We both knew the thimble and scissors belonged to Blythe Cornelius.

Chapter Nine

*T*he phone was ringing when I finally got home that afternoon. "Thank goodness I caught you!" My daughter-in-law Jessica sounded as if she'd been in one of her marathons—she runs at least three mornings a week and weighs about fifteen pounds soaking wet.

My heart jumped into a reggae beat. "What's wrong? Has something happened to—"

"No, no! Nothing like that. It's just that Roger and I were planning to take in dinner and a concert at the college tonight, and our sitter just canceled on us. I wondered if you'd mind keeping Teddy for a while?"

"Well, of course not! And you might as well plan to let him spend the night, since you're bound to be late getting home."

"I suppose you're right," Jessica said. "It is a school night, though, so he'll need to get to bed early—and if you would, he'll probably need some encouragement to finish his homework."

"Don't worry, I'll encourage," I told her.

"I hope it won't be an inconvenience . . ." Jessica hesitated. "I mean, I wouldn't want you to have to cook anything special." Meaning, I knew: "Don't feed my son any junk food!"

"Teddy is never an inconvenience," I told her. "And of course I'll give him something special." *Like the peppermint ice cream—my grandson's favorite—I keep hidden in the freezer*. I sniffed. Augusta was making her savory fish stew in the Crock-Pot and I knew Teddy wouldn't touch it, but that's what macaroni and cheese is for. He only likes the disgusting kind that comes in a box.

"I really appreciate this, Lucy, and I'll pick him up in plenty of time for school in the morning."

"There's no need, Jessica. The grammar school's only a few blocks away. I can walk him there in five minutes." Our two children had walked daily to the two-story red brick building, as had I, and I looked forward to it being a part of my grandson's growing-up experience as well.

"If you're sure it's okay . . . ?"

"I'm sure. Why not spoil yourself and sleep in tomorrow?" I suggested, although I knew she wouldn't. If the automobile industry could figure out how to harness one-tenth of my daughter-in-law's energy, we wouldn't have to depend on foreign oil.

"What's this?" Teddy frowned at the mysterious lumpy red mixture I had ladled into his bowl.

"It's stew. And it's good, just try it," I urged.

My grandson shoved the offending bowl away. "I don't like stew. It's all smushed together."

I broke off a piece of French bread and dipped it into mine. "Mmm . . . sure tastes good to me!" The macaroni and cheese waited out of sight on the stove, but he didn't know that yet.

Teddy drew his bowl a little closer and sniffed. Behind him, Augusta stood with her arms crossed, smiling.

"Smells good, too, don't you think?"

"It's okay." I could see he was weakening, so I broke off another piece of bread and gave it to him. "Dare you!" I said.

He made a face and dipped timidly into the stew . . . once . . . twice, then went at it with a spoon. "Hey, this *is* good!"

"There's some of that macaroni and cheese you like on the stove," I confessed finally.

"No, thanks," he said. I threw it in the garbage.

After ice cream we tackled the reading lesson, which went quickly since Teddy has always liked books and so have I. Math was another matter. I don't remember arithmetic being that complicated when his dad and aunt Julie were in the first grade.

Discouraged, Teddy put down his pencil. "I don't see why I have to learn all this stuff. Baseball players don't need to know math, do they?"

"Of course they do," I told him. "How else are you going to know how to add up all the money you're going to make?"

Teddy nodded solemnly. "Yeah, I guess you're right, Mama Lucy."

After assuring him I would be sleeping upstairs in the room next to his, we progressed through the familiar rituals of bath, pajamas, story time, bed and prayers, and I had just kissed him good night for about the third time when the telephone rang.

I knew it was Ellis on the other end. She's the only person I know who can make a telephone sound impatient. "I was about to give up on you!" she said. "Phone must've rung five times."

"Teddy's staying over tonight and I was just getting him tucked in. What's up?"

"What's all this I hear about Blythe Cornelius and a bloody apron? I just came from circle meeting and that's all anybody talked about."

"Circle meeting! I forgot all about it," I said.

"That's okay. We put you down to polish the brass for December."

"Thanks a bunch. Just for that, Ellis Saxon, I ought not even tell you what happened today!"

"Oh, simmer down. I signed up to polish with you," she said. "Did those things they found really belong to Blythe?"

I told her what I had seen. "Of course somebody else could have put them there."

"Mama Lucy . . . ?" Teddy stood at the top of the stairs.

"Teddy Pilgrim, you get back in that bed this minute. It's way past your bedtime. Ellis, I've got to go. If Teddy sleeps through school tomorrow we'll both be in big trouble."

"Okay, but I wanted to let you know I won't be at The Thursdays Monday. I'm going to the doctor with Susan to see her ultrasound."

"I'm serving Mimmer's banana pudding," I said, referring to my grandmother's recipe, "but I guess I can't compete with that."

"Tempting, but I'm on a diet," Ellis said.

"Since when?"

"Since I looked at myself naked in the mirror this morning."

"Mama Lucy!" Teddy called again. "I'm hungry. I think I'd like some of that macaroni and cheese after all."

"I still can't believe it," my cousin Jo Nell said. "Not Blythe Cornelius! Why, I'd just as soon suspect the preacher of stealing from the collection plate."

"Well, that's been known to happen," Zee said. "They haven't arrested her, have they, Lucy Nan?"

The meeting of the Thursday Morning Literary Society had come to order, and refreshments having been served and duly consumed, the members got right down to the business of the day, which, of course, was the discovery of the bloodied apron at the college.

"Not that I know of," I said, "but they did take her in for questioning. Had to, I guess, but it seemed so senseless. What a horrible thing for poor Blythe to have to go through! You should've seen her trying to assure those girls they had nothing to worry about, but I could see she was having a hard time holding back her own emotions."

Idonia shook her permed red curls. "Bless her heart! Wonder how those things did get in that apron pocket."

"I don't know, unless somebody put them there to make her look guilty," I said. "Blythe says she never saw that apron before, and I believe her. She was looking for those scissors when I was there just the other day."

"Why would anybody want to do that?" Zee asked.

Claudia Pharr spoke up. "Why, to throw the police off the trail, of course—and away from the real killer." Claudia watches every detective show on television, so I didn't argue with her. Besides, she had a point.

"I wish you'd get on another subject," Nettie said. "I can hardly sleep at night as it is for worrying about Leslie being over there." She helped herself to another cup of coffee from the pot on the sideboard. "Good coffee, Lucy Nan. Is this one of those special blends?"

"Nope, just added a few drops of vanilla." (A little trick I'd picked up from Augusta.)

"Then whoever planted those things there is a fool!" Idonia persisted. "Why in the world would anybody wear an apron to commit a murder, then leave incriminating evidence in the pocket? Give the woman credit for a little sense, for heaven's sake."

"But if Blythe didn't do it, who did?" I said. "You read the papers this morning. That was D.C. Hunter's blood on there. Whoever killed her was familiar enough with the college to know where the laundry was collected."

Zee St. Clair leaned forward. "It could be anybody," she said, speaking barely above a whisper. "One of the students, a member of the faculty—why, it might even be R.U. Earnest himself," she added, referring to the president of the college.

"Well, it couldn't have been Blythe who killed her. She was at the infirmary all night with that girl who was sick." I turned on a lamp in the living room window, making it seem even darker outside.

"And that no-good Professor Hornsby *says* he was at Table Rock Mountain," Nettie reminded us, "but how do we know either one of them was where they claimed to be the whole time?"

I took the opportunity to change the subject by asking Claudia about her recent interview in Columbia.

"I'd end up spending most of my paycheck for gas."

She shrugged. "Guess I'll be filling in as a substitute teacher until something better comes along."

"God bless you," Idonia said with a mournful shake of her head.

Jo Nell jumped as the bare branches of the quince bush scraped the shutters outside. "Looks like we've got a murderer running loose at Sarah Bedford, all right." She turned troubled eyes on me. "Do be careful, Lucy Nan. I wish you wouldn't go to that faculty reception tonight. A woman out alone after dark . . ."

I never knew what was supposed to happen to *a woman out alone after dark* because my cousin never finished her sentence. My guess is it was just too horrible to put into words. I patted her shoulder. "Then you'll be relieved to know that I won't be alone. Ben's going with me." I glanced at the clock in the hallway. "And, oh my gosh! I have twenty minutes to get ready!"

"You go ahead and get dressed, Lucy Nan," Jo Nell told me as the others began leaving. "I'll take care of these dishes. You wouldn't want your friend to walk in on this mess."

A man who works in wood shavings all day wouldn't notice a mess if it fell on his head, but I accepted my cousin's offer. I knew the only reason she wanted to stay was to get a better chance to size up Ben. She was still puttering about the kitchen when the doorbell rang, so the three of us left the house together.

"Good Lord, are we going to end up in Oz? What's the rush?" Ben asked as we drove away. "Your cousin was just telling me about the time you crawled under the stalls and locked the doors to all the toilets in the ladies' room at the Full Plate Cafeteria."

"I rest my case," I said. "Besides, I was only four."

It was an unwritten law that everyone who is connected with the faculty at Sarah Bedford is required to attend the annual reception at the president's residence, and cars lined the street in front of the Georgian-style house where every window gleamed with light. Someone was playing "Clair de Lune" on the piano and I could hear the rise and fall of sedate conversation as we walked up the long curved drive.

"How appropriate that I'm wearing black," I said to Ben. "I feel like we're going to a wake. Wonder if Blythe will be here."

President Earnest and his wife, Vivian, who wore more silver sequins than I ever knew existed, greeted us at the door and passed us along like a pail of water in a bucket brigade. By the time we had reached the end I had smiled so much, my cheeks hurt.

I saw Dean Holland gnawing on a chicken wing at the buffet table, but Blythe wasn't anywhere in sight. The dean looked kind of lost, so we wandered over to speak with him, or at least I wandered over. Ben grabbed a plate and got down to some serious eating.

"Dean Holland?" I stuck out my hand. "Lucy Nan Pilgrim. We met several days ago."

Nod. Smile. Chew. "Oh, yes . . ."

"I'm working with one of Ms. Harper's history classes this quarter."

"Ah, yes." Nod. Chew. Smile.

I looked around for backup, but my date had abandoned me for roast beef on rye.

"How is Mrs. Cornelius, Dean Holland? Will Blythe be here tonight?"

The dean added a bunch of grapes and a finger sandwich to his plate. "Yes. Yes, it is a lovely night."

I took a deep breath and plunged in once more. "When you see her, please tell Blythe I'm thinking about her," I said.

He patted my hand and smiled. "That's fine, just fine."

"Thinking about whom?" a voice said behind me, and I whirled around to see Blythe Cornelius standing there with a glass of wine in each hand. She handed one to Dean Holland and escorted him to an empty chair in the corner.

"You," I said as she joined me. "I've been thinking about you. Blythe, I'm so sorry you had to endure all that crap with the police. Surely there must have been a better way."

I could see she was trying hard to smile, and her eyes looked teary behind the thick bifocals. "Oh, well, I'll get through it somehow, but for the life of me I can't see why anybody would want to do this to me." She sipped her wine and looked away. "I must have done something terrible to somebody. Wish I knew what it was."

Thank heavens Ben joined us then because I didn't have a clue as to how to reply. I introduced the two of them and we chatted about the weather and the food and how we hoped we didn't spill anything on the expensive Oriental rug until I saw she had regained her composure.

"Oh, there you are." Joy Ellen Harper touched my shoulder. "Lucy, I'd like you to meet my husband . . .

"Blythe, how nice to see you!" I was glad when she put an arm around the older woman; still, I felt stiff and uncomfortable after all that had happened.

Later, when we worked our way to the dark-paneled library, I saw Willene Benson staring into the flames of the fireplace while nursing a cup of cider. The hem of her purple flowered dress drooped at the back, and she was wearing too much blush.

Ben and I were crossing the room to speak to her when one of the serving girls approached and whispered something in her ear. Willene turned around so suddenly, cider splashed down the front of her dress.

I grabbed a handful of cocktail napkins and tried to stem the flow while the girl turned back to see what had happened.

"Oh, my goodness, did I do that?" She set aside a tray of canapés to help me sponge Willene's splotched skirt.

"No, it's all right, really." Willene brushed us aside. "My fault entirely. I'm afraid I'm just clumsy tonight."

The girl, who was probably a student, gave Willene's dress a final swipe. "Don't you worry about it," she said. "If you like, I'll ask your friend on the phone for his number so you can call him back."

Willene warmed her hands at the fire, although it must have been eighty degrees in that room. "Yes, that would be good, thank you. Why don't you do that?"

"Are you going to be all right?" I asked after the girl moved away. The circles of blush on the woman's chalky face made her appear clownlike and she looked as if she might pass out at any second. I grabbed a fragile Victorian side chair and practically shoved her into it. "Why don't you let us give you a ride home? We can bring the car right to the door." Frankly, I would be glad of an excuse to leave. In the large gilt-framed mirror over the mantel I saw that Ben had been snared by two forty-something women whose intentions seemed less than honorable, and he was sending frantic "Save me!" signals with his eyes.

Willene clutched my arm with a cold hand. "Oh, would you mind? I hate to drag you away from the party, Lucy, but I'm afraid my nerves have gotten the better of me after finding that awful apron yesterday. I really shouldn't have come."

"Don't mention it," I told her, and rescued Ben on my way to the door. The girl who had given Willene the message about the phone call stopped her as we were leaving. "I asked the man who called for his phone number," she explained to Willene, "but he said you already knew it."

On our way out I saw Blythe Cornelius in a corner of the living room talking with Vivian Earnest and the PE instructor, and was reminded again of how difficult it must be for her to come here and pretend that everything was normal.

Claymore Hornsby, I noticed, didn't attend the president's reception. I heard later he had been dismissed from the faculty.

During the brief ride to her home, Willene Benson talked nonstop about everything from cookbooks to kittens, but avoided the subject of the mysterious phone call. She readily agreed to let us walk her to the door, but I was relieved when she didn't invite us in.

"What's all this about a phone call?" Ben asked as we drove home.

"I think somebody's been harassing her—in fact, I'm almost sure of it. The woman acts terrified every time the telephone rings, and whoever's responsible seems to know her every move—even phoned her at the party tonight."

"That's stalking, isn't it? She should report it."

"You're right, but Willene won't even talk about it, and she looks like she'd shatter if you said 'Boo'!"

"Do you think this might have something to do with that girl's murder?" he asked as we turned into the drive at 108 Heritage Avenue.

"I honestly don't know what to think anymore," I admitted.

The next day my class would spend the period planning a meal cooked over an open fire, and I had a lot of preparation to do, so we said good night at the door. Once inside, I stepped out of my heels and lingered in the foyer reliving the taste of Ben's lips on mine and the wonderful cedar smell of him. For three years after my husband Charlie died, I existed in some kind of lonely limbo. Then, on a brisk October day a year ago, Augusta whirled into my life, and before I knew it Ben Maxwell became a significant part of it as well. For a minute I closed my eyes. *Be happy for me, Charlie. Please!* Somehow I knew he was.

Clementine jolted me out of my reverie with a wet tongue from elbow to wrist and I followed her into the kitchen, where Augusta sat at the table putting the finishing touches on an autumn watercolor scene. "There's hot chocolate if you want some," she said, looking up when I came in.

I did. "How are you going to work strawberries into that?" I asked, glancing over her shoulder.

She laughed. "Already did. Look closer. Notice the little girl sitting on the tree stump in the left-hand corner . . ."

"Of course! She has a strawberry on her sweater." I poured the chocolate into a mug and tasted it. It wasn't too hot; it wasn't too bitter or too sweet—it was just right, as Augusta's chocolate always is. The weather had turned colder and a gust of wind rattled the windows and sent the screen door on the back porch banging. I joined Augusta at the table and told her about Willene's strange behavior and of Blythe's attending the reception. "It must have been miserable for her," I said. "I have to admire her courage."

Augusta swirled her paintbrush in water. "Isn't there

some kind of expression about riding the horse again? She would have to face the public sooner or later."

I admitted she was right.

"And didn't you tell me they found the blood on that apron to be the same type as the girl who was killed?"

"Right," I said, wondering where this was leading. I took another swallow of cocoa and waited.

"Then whoever killed D.C. Hunter must've worn the apron to protect their clothing from blood spatters—which means they *planned* to kill her." Augusta carefully put her paints away.

I nodded. "There were other stains on it, too. Looked like mustard, grease spots, things like that, so the murderer probably took the apron from the container of soiled laundry."

The angel's long necklace seemed to sparkle with all the colors in the paint box and she wound it around her fingers as she thought. Tonight she had tied her bright hair at the back of her neck with a vivid green ribbon—to keep it out of her way while she painted, I guessed—and she looked about seventeen.

"Willene Benson would know where the laundry is kept," she said finally.

"So would Blythe—and Londus. So do I."

"Have you considered that perhaps these murders *aren't* related?" Augusta suggested. "What do you know about Willene Benson? How long has she been at the college?"

"About three or four years, I think. And I don't know her well, but she seems terribly lonely. Jo Nell has invited her to The Thursdays a couple of times if we're discussing a book she thought she'd like. And she's big buddies with Blythe Cornelius. They eat Oreos and play Scrabble together."

Augusta shook her head solemnly but her eyes gleamed with laughter. "They sound like hardened criminals to me." She reached down to pat Clementine's tummy. "And . . . go on. What else?"

"Nothing else. That's about it. Her apartment is practically sterile. No pictures, no frills, just the bare essentials. And she disappears as fast as Superman changes his suit when the police come on the scene."

"Perhaps this Captain Hardy should have a word with her," she said.

"Willene Benson? Come on! Little timid Willene? Surely you don't think she killed D.C. Hunter."

"I wouldn't know about that, but if the woman's as jittery as she seems, she might have reason to believe she could be next on the list."

I put the chocolate-coated saucepan in the sink to soak. I hadn't thought of that. "I'll speak with her tomorrow," I promised. "Maybe I can get her to tell me what's going on."

But the next day Willene Benson had taken her few belongings and disappeared.

Chapter Ten

"*I knew* something was wrong," Blythe Cornelius said. "I should've insisted she talk to me about it. Now there's no telling where she is."

"Maybe she just took a day off," I said. "After all, Willene was pretty upset last night. Do you know where she's from? Somewhere down near Myrtle Beach, isn't it?"

"Orangeburg, I believe, but I don't think she'd go back there." Blythe shook her head. "It's not like Willene Benson to fail to show up for work, and she didn't say a word to anybody. Her car's gone, and Londus said he saw her early this morning putting a suitcase into the trunk."

"Maybe she left a note. Do you think somebody might let us into her apartment?"

"I have a key to Willene's place," Blythe said. "And she knows where I keep my spare—just in case of an emergency. I hate to be a snoop, but I guess this could be considered an emergency." She put a hand on my shoulder. "You'll come with me, won't you, Lucy? I'd rather not go in there alone."

As we walked the short distance to Willene's, I noticed the students made a point of speaking to Blythe, and the girls from her dorm had sent a huge arrangement of flowers that sat on her breakfast room table. Just about everybody at Sarah Bedford seemed to wish her well. But obviously there was one who didn't.

Willene Benson's apartment seemed even bleaker than it had the last time I saw it. The closets were empty, the bed stripped, and the kitchen looked as if it had never been used.

The only sign of habitation was the blinking light on the telephone answering machine. "I see she finally broke down and got one," I said, explaining Willene's reluctance to comply with the college hierarchy's request.

After staring at the red light for a minute, Blythe looked at me and shrugged. "Shall we?"

I nodded. "By all means."

The recorded message startled both of us. I don't know what I expected to hear, but it wasn't a man's grating voice singing a refrain from an old love song. It was one I remembered my mother singing at weddings.

Not for just an hour, not for just a day,
Not for just a year . . . but always.

I looked at Blythe and punched the "save" button. The police might be interested in hearing this. It was clear the verse hadn't been intended as a love song. I knew now why Willene Benson ran away. The taunting words were meant as a threat.

"It must be her former husband," Blythe confided. "They've been divorced for several years and she took back her maiden name. She's been afraid he would find her here. The poor woman's terrified of the man."

We searched the apartment for a note but couldn't

find one. "She probably left in such a hurry, it didn't even occur to her," Blythe said after we checked the empty rooms for a second time. After hearing that message, I didn't blame her.

Blythe had used up her lunch hour, and my class was due to begin in a few minutes, so we crossed the quad in such a hurry neither of us realized Sally Wooten was racing to catch up.

"Aunt Shug!" Waving and breathless, she ran up behind us and threw an arm around Blythe. "Don't you ever slow down? I thought I'd never catch you."

"What is it, Sally? Is anything wrong?" Blythe's smile was puzzled.

"No, as a matter of fact, something's right for a change." Sally held out a packet of photographs. "Look what I got back today." She laughed, thumbing through a stack of prints. "Now we can prove you didn't leave those things in that apron. Look."

The snapshot had been made in the lounge of Emma P. Harris Hall and showed a young woman in pajamas playing what looked like a harmonica among a group of laughing girls who were also dressed for bed. A little to the right of the performer sat Blythe Cornelius with an amused smile on her face.

"That's a good picture, sugar," Blythe said, squinting to see it better, "but I don't see how—"

"Look closer. What's in your lap?" Sally pointed at the photograph. "That cross-stitch you've been working on—and your scissors *are right there on the table beside you!* Now, look real close and you can see your

123

thimble . . . you can even make out the design—see?

"This was made the Saturday night *after* D.C. disappeared," she explained. "Only we didn't know that yet. That was the night we had ELEPHANTS, remember? There's Troll playing 'The Flight of the Bumblebee' on a comb."

I laughed. "You had *what?*"

"ELEPHANTS. The Extraordinarily Lousy Emma P. Harris Annual No-Talent Show," Sally said.

Blythe held the picture closer. "Well, I'll be. It is, isn't it? I knew I'd put those things on my little end table. It's where I always leave them."

"Then somebody must have come in and taken them," I said. "Who has access to your apartment? Can you think of anybody who had an opportunity to pick them up?"

Blythe Cornelius shook her head and laughed. "Only every girl in the dormitory, and practically half the faculty. Just about everybody knows I keep an extra key on a nail above my door."

"Looks like one of them wanted you blamed for D.C. Hunter's murder," I said.

"But why?" Blythe slipped the picture into her worn brown handbag. "Sally, do you mind if I borrow this? Maybe it will convince that redheaded policeman I don't go around killing my girls."

But somebody did kill them, and it seemed apparent that it was someone who was familiar with the campus.

That afternoon in class I found myself wondering if one of my own students had lured D.C. Hunter into that old shed for what she thought would be one last meeting with her lover.

Tomorrow the girls would meet at Bellawood to prepare a meal over an open fireplace, so we spent today's class period in planning. With our combined lack of knowledge about early American cooking, I had an idea tomorrow was going to be a very long day.

"You've got to help!" I had pleaded with Augusta the day before. "You've actually done all this, and all I've ever cooked over a fire were hot dogs and s'mores—and even then the marshmallows usually fell into the fire. What did people eat back then?"

"We'll plan a menu," Augusta said, putting aside her current whodunit. "Something simple." Later I was to wonder what it would have been like if she had suggested a *complicated* meal.

Nettie had asked me to look in on her niece after class that afternoon, so I dropped by Leslie's room before leaving for home.

I found her sitting in a lotus position at the foot of her bed with an open book in front of her, but her eyes were on something outside. She obviously hadn't heard me knock, so I opened the door and spoke her name. When she looked at me, I could see she had been crying.

"What's wrong, Leslie? Are you sick?" She looked as if she didn't want me to touch her, so I didn't.

"Yes, I'm sick. Sick of being me. I wish I were

125

somebody else—anybody else!" She snatched a pillow into her lap and socked it like a punching bag.

I sat on the empty bed across from her. "Why is that?"

"I'm a terrible person, that's why."

"What makes you think that? Your family worries about you, Leslie. I'm sure they must love you very much. I know how special you are to your aunt Nettie."

A tear slid down her cheek and the girl wiped it away with the back of her hand. "She wouldn't feel that way if she knew."

"Knew what?"

"Nobody would like me if they knew what I did."

I waited. If she wanted to tell me, she would, but I was almost afraid to ask.

"It's my fault D.C. Hunter was killed. I might as well have done it myself." And the crying started all over again.

"Oh, Leslie! Why in the world would you think that?" I reached out to her but she ignored my hand.

"Because . . . I was probably the last person to see her alive."

I passed her a box of tissues and she grabbed a few. "I don't have a roommate, you know, and there was like hardly anybody on our floor that Friday night," Leslie said. "I stayed up pretty late studying and had a hard time going to sleep. Then I heard D.C. come in and decided to go over there and get a book. Her roommate—you know Sally—has this novel I've

126

been wanting to read and she told me to just come over and get it anytime."

Leslie tossed the pillow aside and shoved lank hair from her face. "Well, I knocked but she didn't answer, so I just opened the door. D.C. was lying across her bed crying and she looked so like—you know—miserable, I felt totally sorry for her . . . for a minute. But when I asked her what was wrong, she screamed at me and told me to go away."

"And did you?"

"Yes, but not until I told her what I thought of her. I'd just held it in for so long I couldn't stand it anymore and it all came pouring out." Leslie swung long skinny legs to the floor and threw a wad of tissues at the wastebasket.

"I told her she was hateful and selfish and nobody liked her, and that she could cry her silly head off for all I cared, and then I left. She called to me to come back—called twice, but I was too furious to bother with her. If I had, well, maybe she'd still be alive." Leslie stared at the floor, avoiding my gaze. "Later, after I calmed down a little, I went down to ask Aunt Shug what to do, but she wasn't there so I put a note on her door asking her to like check on her, you know."

"So you had a temper fit! Most of us do at one time or another. But you cared enough to leave a note. Sounds to me like you were just reacting like a normal human being—one who might be dealing with some stress of her own—but if you like blaming yourself, there's nothing I can say that will make you feel any better.

"Is that why you're not eating?" I asked softly.

She looked up at me. "I eat."

"What do you eat? Tell me what you've had to eat today."

"Well, toast. I had raisin toast and juice for breakfast." Leslie examined her clasped hands in her lap. "And a salad for lunch."

She was watching her weight, she said. But if Leslie Monroe didn't get help soon, I thought, there wouldn't be any weight to watch.

"Try not to dwell on what happened to D.C. Hunter," I said. "She went to that shed because she was summoned there. Somebody either phoned her or left a message. Think about it, Leslie. Did you hear anything later that night?"

"Like what?" She smoothed her pink flowered bedspread and propped the pillow at the head.

"Like a telephone ringing, or voices. Footsteps. Her room is close enough to yours so you would probably hear if somebody visited or phoned, and she would have to pass by your door to get outside. Do you remember hearing her leave later that night?"

But Leslie was tired of talking about D.C. Hunter. She stood in front of the mirror and slowly brushed her hair. "I really can't remember," she said.

I wasn't so sure she was telling the truth.

My neighbor was in her backyard picking up limbs from the recent rain when I pulled into the driveway, and she came over as soon as she saw me and began to speak in unknown tongues. Fortunately, I had been around Nettie McGinnis long enough to be able to translate when she wasn't wearing her teeth.

"Yes, I had a long conversation with Leslie," I said, and told her about my visit with her niece. "And you're right to be concerned, Nettie. I don't know what's the matter with Leslie, but she needs help. I think you should speak with her father. She should be under a doctor's care."

She nodded solemnly. "I'll call him tonight," she told me. At least, that's what I thought she said.

Augusta greeted me at the back door with two glasses of wine and a tray of my favorite cheese-olive pastries hot from the oven. "What's the occasion?" I wanted to know, snatching a glass without waiting for an answer.

She smiled and clinked her glass with mine. "There's a message on that machine that answers the telephone for you," she said.

I greedily gobbled a couple of cheese balls. "Must be a cause to celebrate?" But Augusta only smiled.

The first message was from Jo Nell wanting to know what in God's name Willene Benson was thinking of running off like a bat out of hell without so much as a by-your-leave! The second was Claudia Pharr asking for the recipe for my grandmother's Mimmer's Lemon Mystery since she was hosting her bridge club next week. The third message was from my daughter, Julie.

"Mama, guess what? I'm moving up! I've been

offered a position as Lifestyles Editor at a much larger newspaper in Cedartown, Georgia, and I'm to begin in two weeks! I've found a cute little two-bedroom apartment not too far from the paper so there'll be room for you to come and visit. And, as you might guess, all contributions of household goods and furniture will be greatly appreciated. Call for details!"

I called. "Congratulations!" I said when my daughter answered. "That's fantastic! When will you and Buddy be moving?"

Julie has a live-in boyfriend I call Buddy-Boy Bubba whose main goal in life is to consume large quantities of beer, watch perpetual basketball, and complain that he can't find a job that fulfills him. I have swallowed my feelings about BBB so many times they are beginning to fester in my gut, but in the interest of mother-daughter relations I've learned to chomp down on a hard stick and keep my opinions to myself.

There was a moment of silence on the line. "I'm not sure, Mom," Julie said. "Buddy's looking around for a job there but he hasn't had much luck."

Imagine that, I thought and clenched my teeth to keep the words inside. "I'm sure something will turn up," I said. *Not!* "Now, tell me what you need and I'll take inventory in the kitchen. And what about that old rolltop desk in the upstairs hall? You always said you wanted it."

"What do you say to another glass of wine?" I asked Augusta when I got off the phone.

She had the bottle ready.

Chapter Eleven

*P*aula Shoemaker checked the cornbread baking in a Dutch oven on the hearth. "What a relief to get away from Sarah Bedford for a while! Seems the police are everywhere you look . . . uh-oh! I think this cornbread's baked long enough. It's getting really brown on top."

"Then take it off—hurry!" Debra watched as she moved it away from the ashes. "It smells wonderful!"

Celeste looked up from her churning. "Is it just me, or do the rest of you feel like people are eyeing you suspiciously? I'll swear, I'm getting paranoid!"

"I know what you mean," Paula said. "I wish they'd hurry and get to the bottom of all this. It's impossible to concentrate on anything else."

But as my hands-on history class bustled about the kitchen at Bellawood preparing a made-from-scratch dinner the old-fashioned way, they soon discovered they didn't have time to think of murder.

"Ouch!" Miriam Platt stuck a finger in her mouth. "I must've shredded half my knuckles with those sweet potatoes. Are you sure the pioneers didn't have food processors? This grated sweet potato pudding had better be worth all the blood I'm sacrificing." She stirred in eggs, milk, butter, and spices, spooned the concoction into a cast-iron pan, and gently shoved it into the coals.

"Don't worry, it'll blend in with the pink," Paula

assured her. "And it's yummy! My grandmother makes it, but you have to stir it a lot."

A thick soup of dried beans flavored with a ham bone bubbled in a large black pot that swung out over the flames where a smaller pot of dried apples simmered.

Celeste looked up from her churning in the corner. "My arms are killing me! I've been churning this stuff for ages. It's somebody else's turn."

Debra looked at her watch. "Five minutes—that's all you've churned since I spelled you the last time. I'll relieve you after ten and not a second sooner. Besides, I have to find a centerpiece for the table. It looks bare."

The class had arrived at Bellawood that morning in a body—well, maybe I shouldn't use that word—with skeins they had dyed earlier, and Mary Barton, the only person I know who can actually make cloth with that big monster of a loom in the downstairs bedroom, showed us how it was done. It wasn't easy.

By noon the girls had learned how to make a warp on a warping frame and thread a four-harness loom for a plain weave. When Mary left later, her eyes were crossed and she babbled incoherently, but each member of the class had had a turn at weaving a few inches of cloth.

After a bag lunch, we tackled the demanding particulars of cooking our dinner over an open fire, and for a while I felt safe there in another time where I could pretend the horrors of the past few weeks had happened somewhere else. The others seemed to relax, too, as they tended to the simple basic chores women performed hundreds of years ago—well, maybe except for Celeste, who decided she really didn't care for butter after all.

The weather had turned damp and cold, but we were warm—almost too warm—by the kitchen fire, where the apples and sweet potato pudding gave out warm spicy smells, and even the most troubled class member giggled over Celeste's comical battle with the butter churn.

We had all worked up an appetite by the time the food was ready, and bright-red berries from a hearts a burstin' bush in a brown earthenware jug gave the old pine table a festive look. What a shame, I thought, that Leslie Monroe wasn't in the class. If she had to work this hard for her dinner, maybe she would be hungry enough to eat.

The meal was delicious—including the sweet potato pudding—and Celeste and her fellow churners had even managed to produce enough butter to spread on the cornbread. Of course cleaning up was awful. We had to heat our dishwater over the fire, and the bottoms of the pots were black with carbon. When the girls left to drive back to Sarah Bedford, every one of them was smudged with soot and smelled of wood smoke.

I stayed behind to put a few things away, and was drying the last of the crockery when I heard a car outside and a familiar blast of a horn. Ellis.

Ellis Saxon and I have been best friends since we both wore lace-trimmed socks and smocked dresses, and I found out early on there wasn't much she was afraid of. She thought nothing of climbing the water tower behind the depot; jumped from our garage roof to the top of the apple tree that was so far away I couldn't even look; and was the only one of us who dared to snatch a rose from a bush in the cemetery during the dark of night on that scavenger hunt back in junior high. My brother Joel, who went on to become a scientist, always said Ellis had more energy than mc^2. When Ellis Saxon enters a room I almost expect curtains to billow in her wake. This time she was followed by a gust of cold air—and Augusta.

Holding out her hands, Augusta gravitated to the dying fire. "It's freezing out there," she said, wrapping herself in her voluminous green cape with the shimmering plum lining. "Is there anything hot to drink?"

"I think there's still some sassafras tea in the pot," I offered, pulling a chair closer to the fire. "Here, sit and take off the chill. I'll warm it up—might take a minute."

"I'll pass," Ellis said, watching me pour the pink liquid into an enamel mug and set it in the embers, "but I'd sure like some of whatever that is that smells so good." She sniffed at the dab of leftover pudding the girls had spooned into a plastic container brought for that purpose. Ellis frowned. "Looks strange. What is it?"

I told her. "The girls loved it—and it won't kill you. It's Augusta's recipe."

"Well, maybe just a taste . . ." Ellis dipped in with a spoon. "Hey, this is good!" She dipped again, and then again until she'd eaten it all.

"I thought you were on a diet," I reminded her. "What happened?"

"I've had about enough of that." Ellis struck a dramatic pose. "As God is my witness, I'll never be hungry again!"

"Haven't I heard that somewhere before?" Augusta asked. With a dish towel she removed her mug from the hearth and took a cautious sip. "Mm . . . nice. It's been a while since I've tasted this."

I banked the coals with ashes and hung the stubby fire shovel on its nail, dreading to leave the warmth of the room.

"What do you think about the latest development at the college?" Ellis asked.

"What development?" I asked.

"Haven't you heard about the letters?" she said. "No, I guess you haven't, being out here all day. This girl who was killed—D.C. Hunter, and the one before her, too, got some kind of weird note—a quote from Lewis Carroll's *Through the Looking-Glass*."

I glanced at Augusta and we said "aha" at the same time. "Where did you hear that?" I asked.

"It was in *The Mess* this morning. Josie Kiker found out about it somehow, and now the radio and TV people have picked it up. It'll be all over the Columbia paper tomorrow, wait and see." Ellis frowned. "What do you mean, 'aha'?"

"I suspected there must have been some kind of written message because of what Duff Acree said that day we found D.C.," I told her. "He discovered some letters in her room and said it looked like another one—'Just like that other girl got.'"

"I knew it was only a matter of time before that editor at the newspaper got to the bottom of that story," Augusta said. "You could see she was chomping at the ground and pawing the bit."

"She was at that," I said, trying not to look at Ellis, who was obviously trying not to look at me.

"Did both young women receive the same quote?" Augusta asked.

"It was from the same poem but a different verse," Ellis said. "Remember that silly rhyme about the Jabberwocky, Lucy Nan? Betsy Ann Overcash could say it by heart when we were in Mrs. Dixon's literature class."

"She always was a show-off," I said. "What did it say?"

"Do I look like Betsy Ann Overcash? Something about a blade. Decidedly graphic and to the point—if you'll excuse the expression."

"I think I've seen a copy of that book in the bookcase over at the main house," I said. "Just give me a minute to look."

"I'll go along," Augusta offered.

"And risk getting chilled all over again?" I said. "Stay warm. I'll be right back."

Although most of Bellawood is wired for electricity,

the kitchen house is not, so only the anemic glow of the lantern shone out as I crossed through the blustery dark to the back door and hurried to flip on a light. Darting a look over my shoulder, I wasn't surprised to see Augusta standing in the kitchen doorway watching after me.

I knew the tall glassed-in bookcase in the front parlor contained several volumes of its former owner's cloying verses, but there were other works there as well, and I finally found Lewis Carroll's book wedged between *Uncle Remus* and *Oliver Twist*.

Back in the kitchen we gathered at the long pine table where Ellis thumbed carefully through the brittle old pages. "Here it is!" She marked the passage with a finger. "Good Lord, it gives me the creeps. Listen, this is what Rachel Isaacs received the day before she drowned:

And, as in uffish thought he stood,
The Jabberwock, with eyes of flame,
Came whiffling through the tulgey wood,
And burbled as it came!

Ellis looked up, frowning. "Now what in the world could they have meant by that?"

"I suppose it could be some kind of warning," Augusta said, reading the lines over her shoulder. "The tulgey wood . . . She drowned in the college lake, and the lake was in the woods."

"What did she do about the note?" I asked Ellis.

"They didn't go into detail in the newspaper, but her roommate said she thought it was a joke."

"What about the other girl?" I asked. "What about D.C. Hunter?"

Ellis put the open book in my hands. "Gets a little gory."

One, two! One, two! And through and through
The vorpal blade went snicker-snack!
He left it dead, and with its head
He went galumphing back.

A sickening kind of shudder went through me. Back in the ninth grade we had laughed over Carroll's nonsensical verse. It wasn't funny now. This must have been what was in the letter the police found in the Hunter girl's room.

"Were the verses typed or handwritten?" Augusta asked. "I've read where they're sometimes able to trace—"

But Ellis shook her head. "Came from a book. Somebody made a copy of a page from the book and glued the verse to a piece of notepaper."

I looked at the poem again. "Wonder why they started in the middle?"

"The middle of what?" Ellis asked as she and Augusta followed me outside. I was glad for their company as I stood in the darkness to lock the heavy oak door.

"The middle of the poem. Didn't you notice? The

person who sent them only used the fourth and fifth verses. Do you think maybe he sent the first three to somebody else?"

"The girl who died in the fall from the Tree House might have received one," Augusta said, explaining to Ellis what we had learned from Josie Kiker. "And there're still more verses to go."

When I got home that night I found my old copy of *Through the Looking-Glass* and looked up the poem again.

"If the killer had sent them in order," Augusta pointed out, "Carla Martinez should've received this third verse before she fell—or was pushed—from the Tree House:

> *He took his vorpal blade in hand:*
> *Long time the manxome foe he sought—*
> *So rested he by the Tumtum tree,*
> *And stood awhile in thought.*

I wondered how long the murderer waited in the Tree House and contemplated shoving that girl to her death.

"Why Jabberwocky? What does that have to do with anything?" Weigelia asked the next day. She had dropped by to borrow my thirty-cup percolator for her upcoming family reunion and wanted to know what the fuss was all about.

"Beats me," I said. "I thought you might have some

inside information from your cousin Kemper, but if you think about it, it sort of fits the way these girls died." I told her about looking up the verses.

Weigelia shook her head and made what I call her "woebegone" face. Today she wore a bright red hat with shoes to match and her new black dress with the velvet collar for an afternoon meeting of the Blessed Sisters of Praise and Glory. "I don't know what's goin' on over at that school, but I don't like it one little bit! I told Celeste she should come home and stay until they catch that devil what's doin' all this, but she won't pay me no mind."

The weather had turned warm and sunny and I had dusted off the front porch chairs where we sat drinking some of Augusta's apricot tea. Ellis found us there a little later when she came by with a set of dishes Julie had always admired. "Thought she might be able to use these in her new kitchen," she explained. "Bennett's aunt Eunice gave them to us when we married, and you know I've never cared much for blue," she said, setting the box on the floor.

"I've been thinking about this Jabberwocky thing," she said, ignoring the offered chair to sit on the steps. "There has to be a connection. Assuming the Tree House death was a murder, too, what could be the common denominator?"

Weigelia put down her cup with a clatter. "What Tree House death? You tellin' me another one of them girls has done gone and got herself killed?"

"This happened about nine years ago," I told her,

"and we're not even sure it was a murder.

Ellis drained the rest of my tea. (She really didn't care for any, she'd said. She'd just have a little swallow of mine.) "All the girls were new to Sara Bedford . . . and they all came from out of state."

I nodded. "That's right. D.C. was raised in Virginia, Rachel came from Florida, and the other girl was from somewhere in New York."

"That other girl, did she get the same kind of note?" Weigelia asked.

"If she did, she must've thrown it away," I told her. "The newspaper didn't even mention her."

Ellis gave me back my empty cup. "What would you do if you got a letter like that—a silly verse pasted on a piece of paper? I'd figure some nut had too much time on his hands and toss it."

"Clay Hornsby was seeing the Hunter girl," I said. "And somebody told me the girl who drowned had a boyfriend back home in Florida. I don't know much about the girl from New York except that she was a music major."

"D.C. was interested in drama," Ellis added, and I don't guess anybody knows about the other girl's major."

"I think she was a freshman," I said, "so she probably hadn't decided yet."

Weigelia sighed a deep-down sigh. "Do-law! Them poor little things. They didn't get a chance to decide about nothin'!"

141

Chapter Twelve

I never thought I'd see Ellis Saxon at a quilting bee. Well, for that matter, I wasn't a likely participant, either, but there we sat cutting calico patches and sewing them into squares under Nettie's supervision.

The hands-on history class was making a friendship quilt with each quilter's name embroidered on a square of her own making. Nettie would then stitch the squares together and bring them back to class to be quilted by hand.

"This doesn't seem so hard," Ellis said, weaving her needle in and out. "I should be able to finish one like this for Susan in time for Christmas, don't you think, Nettie?"

My neighbor laughed. "We'll see, but you might want to start over on that square. You've sewn it to your skirt."

"Oh. Well, no problem. I've started over so many times already, this cloth is beginning to look like corduroy."

I laughed. Ellis had asked to sit in on the quilting sessions because she'd "always wanted to learn how." Just as she had always wanted to paint with oils, refinish furniture and play the guitar. And so what if her quilt ended up in the attic with a partially sanded dresser, an almost new guitar, and a still life of a purple geranium and two eggplants on steroids?

I was having problems of my own. I've always

wanted a quilt—especially the colorful patchwork kind, and I had good intentions of learning to make one, but I had stuck my finger so many times my name was embroidered in red. Although Nettie managed to maintain a calm demeanor as she collected our creations at the end of the class, I could swear her face blanched at Ellis's and mine.

"Who's getting this masterpiece, anyway?" Ellis asked as we swept up scraps of cloth.

"It's going to be raffled in December to help raise money for needy families," I said. "How many chances do you want?"

"If all the squares look like yours and mine, I'll gladly pay *not* to win," she said.

"I don't care how messy it looks," I said. "I'd love to have one just like it. Wouldn't it look perfect in Julie's old room?"

Nettie seemed somber as she gathered the finished squares and put them into her big canvas bag. She had been kind and patient with the novices in the class—which meant most of us—but my neighbor hadn't seemed her usual lighthearted self since I told her what I suspected of her niece.

"I've read about eating disorders," she had said earlier, "but I never thought of it affecting someone in my own family. Are you *sure* that's what's wrong with Leslie?"

"Good heavens, no! I'm not sure of anything, but she does seem a likely candidate. It certainly can't hurt her to see a doctor."

That was when Nettie decided to work in a visit to

her niece on the day she helped with my class. Now she crammed the last scrap into her bulging bag and straightened her shoulders. "You don't think she'll guess why I'm *really* here?"

"Why should she? I told her the other day you were coming. It's perfectly natural that you'd drop by to see her. And does it really matter if she does guess? She must know you're concerned about her."

"You're right, of course." Nettie smoothed her gray hair back into a bun. "And I have to find out what's going on so I can prepare her father. Should've called him earlier, I know. Guess I just kept hoping this would pass."

I put an arm around her plump, solid shoulders. It was like my neighbor to have problems understanding why anybody would deliberately pass up good food. I have trouble with it myself.

"Let me put that heavy bag in the car for you," I told her. "Ellis and I will meet you at Leslie's dorm in about an hour."

"This is a kind of day they write poetry about," Ellis said as we left the parking lot. "Remember 'October's Bright Blue Weather'? Mrs. Strain made us memorize it in the sixth grade.

" 'O suns and skies and clouds of June, and flowers of June together, ye cannot rival for one hour October's bright blue weather,' " a familiar voice chanted behind us. Augusta. Today she wore a coral crepe with a multitiered skirt that fluttered behind her as she walked. Her hair, the color of maple leaves, escaped from a trailing turquoise scarf.

"Did you have Mrs. Strain in the sixth grade, too?" Ellis asked, apparently not at all surprised by the angel's abrupt appearance.

Augusta laughed, twirling among the bright oak leaves as they zigzagged to the ground. "I learned that from a lady named Mary Emma Howard," she said. "She had a lovely soul, and I was fortunate to be assigned to her toward the end. Her eyesight wasn't good and she loved being read to—especially poetry. That was one of her favorites." Augusta smiled as a leaf caught in her hair. "I like to think it helped to ease her over."

Ellis and I stood in silence. "Augusta, what a beautiful thought," I said finally. "And I agree with Mary Emma—October's the most brilliant month of all. Makes me feel like striking out on a wooded trail with a pack upon my back."

"'There is something in October sets the gypsy blood astir,'" the angel quoted as we waded through papery leaves.

"There's sort of a trail down by the Old Lake," Ellis said. "Will that do?"

Augusta hesitated. "The Old Lake? Isn't that where you found the Hunter girl?"

"Near there," I said, but we can walk here on main campus if you'd rather." I hadn't been near that old shed since that awful day, and I didn't care if I never saw it again.

"There's a path that follows the hills above town," Augusta said. "A bit of a climb, but I could probably use the exercise after that barbecue I had for lunch." She had made a large batch in the Crock-Pot the week before and frozen most of it in meal-size portions.

"I have to be back in an hour to meet Nettie," I explained. "I'm afraid that would take too long, but if you really want to take the hill path, go ahead. Who knows what the weather might bring tomorrow."

"And Bennett's taking me to dinner tonight," Ellis said, "so I need to get home early." She smiled. "We're shopping for the new baby afterward. There's a big sale in Charlotte, I hear."

"I hope you're not disappointed," I said to Augusta. "Maybe we can explore it together another day."

But she was already trailing across the leaf-strewn campus with a jaunty wave of her hand, her vivid scarf fluttering behind her.

"I know you and Augusta didn't want to go near there, but frankly I'm curious about that old shed," Ellis said. "Did those two really have a tryst in that old place? Not that I'd want to go inside or anything."

"Good, because it's probably padlocked. I doubt if the college wants anybody going in there," I said, reluctantly following her lead.

But as we drew closer to the stone building I noticed one of the doors ajar.

Ellis touched my arm and looked at me. "Let's."

"Let's not," I said. I could almost smell the odor of death.

146

"We might never get the chance again," she said. "Come on, Lucy Nan. I don't want to go in there by myself."

I had heard this before when, against my better judgment, I followed her up the fire tower when we were eight, and again at ten when she dared me to climb on top of the arched stone entrance to the Confederate Cemetery. The fire department had to come and get me down. And in the ninth grade didn't I help her put that bottle of gin in Miss Edna Barnhardt's desk drawer? Our math teacher belonged to the Reach of Love Church of the Comforting Arms and didn't even wear makeup.

Okay, I'll have to admit, sometimes I like taking chances. It's kind of like jumping into a hot tub after a cool swim. It makes my skin tingle. It was tingling now, but more in dread than excitement. *You're getting too old for this, Lucy Nan Pilgrim!* I told myself. The sun scalloped the woods in yellow patches. A squirrel skittered up a hickory and disappeared beneath leaves that looked like old gold. Close by a lingering robin sang just for the glory of it. I wish I could.

Snicker-snack, snicker-snack . . . the vorpal blade went snickersnack! Like an evil nursery rhyme, the words went back and forth, back and forth. The stone shed. The cold gray rain. The putrid smell. Desolation. "I can't," I said. "If you want to go inside, go ahead. I'll wait here."

I watched as Ellis walked slowly, quietly to the door.

Did she think somebody was going to hear her? She stood there for a minute, then put her head inside, and finally the rest of her.

Augusta, how I wish you were here—or that I weren't! I waited. Ellis had only been in the shed a few seconds when she stepped out again with a warning finger to her lips and motioned for me to join her. I came halfway.

Urging me to hurry, Ellis pointed to the shed with all the drama she could muster. Why didn't she just speak up? But when I got close enough to see the look in her eyes, I knew something was wrong.

"There's somebody up there," she whispered, latching onto my arm.

"Are you sure? I don't hear anything."

"Of course I'm sure! They're in the loft."

I wasn't convinced, but I let her drag me along. Hardly daring to breathe, we stopped to listen at the open door. A mouse, I thought. The shed would be full of them—rats, too. Or a squirrel could be nesting in the rafters, I told myself.

But an animal doesn't have a heavy tread like the one I was hearing now. Footsteps. Human footsteps thudded in the loft, then paused as if whoever was up there was listening, too. Did they know we were there?

Well, one thing was certain—we shouldn't be there. I looked around. We couldn't run fast enough to get away, but underbrush surrounded the building and I hurried behind it for cover, hoping Ellis would follow. She quickly squiggled out of sight behind a clump of

148

cedars, and I hugged the rough back wall of the shed, along with the Virginia creeper and whatever else grew there. My right ankle burned and I looked down to see a red jagged tear, probably from a blackberry bush; there were scratches on my hands as well. I doubted if the sun ever reached this side of the building. In spite of the clear October day, my hiding place smelled damp and earthy.

I heard the door of the shed bang shut and wondered what had become of the lock, as I was sure the police hadn't left the scene accessible to the public. So how did they get in, and who could it be? I remembered that old adage about a murderer always returning to the scene of the crime. If so, I wished this one had picked another time to return. My stomach was none too happy and it was hard to breathe past the knot in my throat. A few feet away I saw the bright yellow sleeve of Ellis's blouse as she crouched in hiding. If whoever had been in the shed looked in her direction, he would see it, too. He wasn't even trying to be quiet. Leaves rustled in the woods to my right and I took a chance to get a glimpse of his face.

But it wasn't a man walking away from the building. It was a woman. Tall, of indiscriminate age, she wore khaki pants and a navy-blue windbreaker, and her dishwater-blond hair was coiled in a braid at the back. I had never seen her before but she had been described to me often. *Monica Hornsby.* I was almost sure of it. But what was "Horny" Hornsby's wife looking for in that shed?

"What do you suppose she was doing in there?" Ellis asked as we hurried back to main campus.

"Looking for something, I guess."

"Wonder if she found it."

"I don't know," I said. "I couldn't tell if she had anything with her, could you? Besides, I'd think if there was anything to find, the police would've already found it."

Ellis glanced behind us as she walked. "Should we tell somebody? About what we've seen, I mean."

"I don't know . . . not yet, anyway. What would we tell them? She wasn't breaking the law. Maybe she was just curious."

I was glad when we came into the clearing and made our way past the familiar campus buildings. Nearby a girl shrieked as two others threatened to throw her into the fountain, and both Ellis and I jumped at the sound.

"I think I just lost a year of my life," Ellis said. "We're getting too old for this, Lucy Nan. I don't know why I let you drag me into these things.

"Do you think the Hornsbys are still living together?" she asked before I could protest. "I can't believe she'd take him back."

"Maybe she's used to him," I said. "Or maybe she just doesn't care. Who knows? Could be she's out for revenge."

"And could be she's already had it," Ellis said.

Chapter Thirteen

*W*e found Nettie having tea in Blythe Cornelius's snug living room while her niece hung around in the doorway looking like she'd rather be someplace else. Leslie scooped up Blythe's big orange tabby and stroked it until it squirmed free. Some of the tension was gone from my neighbor's face, so I guessed her visit with Leslie had gone better than she expected.

Nettie stood when she saw us. "Do-law, has it been an hour already?"

"Time flies when you're having fun," I said with an insinuating glance at Ellis. "I hate to drag you away from good company, but Ellis here has a hot date tonight."

"Then I'd better get a move on," Nettie said, setting aside her cup, "but I'm glad Blythe and I had a chance to visit. It's a comfort to see some things don't change. My niece—Leslie's mother," she explained to Blythe, "lived right here in Emma Harris back when she was in school, only her room was in the other wing. Many's the time I've gone up and down those stairs helping to move her in or out." Nettie smiled at her grand niece. "The old place looks pretty much the same."

"There are several old yearbooks in that bookcase in the lounge," Blythe said. "Maybe your mother's in one of them, Leslie. Do you remember when she was here?"

"Why, it's been at least thirty years." Nettie seemed

surprised at her own words. "Margaret started at Sarah Bedford the year they built the new gymnasium, and that part of the campus stayed in a mess. Naturally, the girls tracked in a lot of mud and the housemother was a regular old dragon about it! I believe she lived in this very apartment, Blythe. The girls were terrified of her."

"Wouldn't it be fun if we could find your mother's picture, Leslie?" Blythe said, gathering up the empty cups. "What was her maiden name, sugar?"

"Oh, we have one of her annuals around somewhere—from her freshman year, I think." Leslie stooped to pet the gray cat. "She never did graduate, though. Mom married right after her sophomore year."

"Married Doug Dixon when she was barely twenty," Nettie explained. "Lost one baby before it came to term, and another was stillborn. Then Doug was killed in an automobile accident right soon after that."

"Oh dear!" Blythe shook her head.

"Margaret was in her early thirties when she married George Monroe and had Leslie," Nettie said.

Leslie shrugged. "That must've been a surprise."

"But a nice one." Nettie put an arm around the girl's shoulders. "My niece died when Leslie was only six," she explained to Blythe. "And her father's always expected her to be a straight-A student and act like a grown woman."

I saw the look that passed between Nettie and Blythe Cornelius. *No wonder this child has an eating disorder.*

Leslie walked with us to the car, where her great

aunt gave her a cushiony hug. "It's all right to relax and have fun, you know. You don't have to be perfect, honey," Nettie told her. She held Leslie by the shoulders and looked into her face. "Now I want you to promise you'll follow through. Remember what we talked about? Don't put it off."

The girl nodded and watched as her aunt climbed into the car. "Aunt Nettie . . ."

"What, honey?"

Leslie shook her head and shrugged. "Nothing." Shoulders sagging, she turned and walked back toward the dormitory.

Nettie frowned. "Now what was that all about, I wonder."

"Did you talk with her about not eating?" I asked.

Nettie buckled her seat belt and took a deep breath. "Yes, and she denied it at first. I finally got her to agree to see somebody about it, and she promised to call home tonight to see if they can make an appointment with their family doctor. I guess he'll know where to go from there. Bless her heart, she's always tried so hard to please her daddy, and now she thinks she has to compete with his wife!"

"I don't blame you for worrying," Ellis said. "She's awfully thin."

"And white as Sunday slippers," Nettie said. "Acts like she's afraid of something to me. Can't say I blame her, with young girls being murdered left and right."

"Have you heard any more about those Jabberwocky notes?" Ellis asked me as we started home.

153

"Not much," I said. "Joy Ellen Harper says they only have two: D.C.'s and the one sent to the girl who drowned. Of course D.C. never opened hers because she rarely checked her mail. Her roommate said it had been sitting on her desk for a couple of days. Weigelia told me her cousin Kemper said the police think the two were killed by the same person, and D.C.'s must have been hand-delivered because there was no name on the envelope."

"So it didn't go through the regular mail." Nettie frowned. Then somebody must have slipped it into her box. This is getting too close to home."

"I don't suppose they ever found one to the girl who fell from the Tree House." Ellis's eyes met mine in the rearview mirror.

"But that doesn't mean she didn't get one," I said.

Nettie clicked her upper plate. "I wish Leslie would go somewhere else for a while. She doesn't need all this worry on top of everything else."

"Fall Fest is coming up this weekend," I reminded her. "Maybe that'll help take her mind off it."

"I'd almost forgotten about that," Ellis said. "I think they've been having Fall Fest at Sarah Bedford forever. Susan always loved to go when she was a child."

"I'd like to take Teddy, but I have to oversee our class project," I said. "The girls are making hand-pulled taffy and popcorn balls to sell, and there'll be a cake walk and fortune-telling—even a haunted garden. It gives the campus organizations a chance to earn money."

"Sounds like you're going to be busy," Nettie predicted.

"Not really. I just plan to enjoy it. Jo Nell and Idonia always come—haven't missed one in years—so it should be fun, and the girls in my class are taking turns with the booth," I said. "I shouldn't have to do a thing."

"That'll be fifty cents for the popcorn ball and a quarter for the taffy." I took a mangled dollar bill from a small boy in a pirate outfit and gave him back a sticky quarter. Where *was* that girl? Troll had asked me to relieve her for ten minutes so she could go to the bathroom, only it seemed she'd been gone an hour.

Across the lawn I saw my cousin Jo Nell having her palm read by a student wearing a red turban and about fifty pounds of jewelry. On closer scrutiny the gypsy looked slightly familiar under all that makeup. Sally Wooten, D.C. Hunter's roommate. It was good to see her loosen up after all that had happened lately.

Idonia had bypassed our booth for candied apples, then wandered off to watch the jugglers. On my right the college tennis team sold funnel cakes, while the Science Club grilled hot dogs and onions in the booth to my left. I felt like the inside of a junk food sandwich, but this wasn't going to be a calorie-counting night. I took one long happy sniff and told my skinny little conscience to go to hell.

Someone waved to me from across the quad and I wasn't surprised to see Augusta strolling happily among the food booths. "Isn't the sense of smell a wonderful thing?" she said as she approached—then winked. "Of course the sense of taste is even better."

Taking the hint, when my replacement finally returned I bought the two of us hot dogs with everything on them which we ate on the steps of the science building while watching a puppet show. The night smelled like hot grease and dry leaves, and children called to one another, racing in and out among the booths. I had just finished my supper and was trying to decide between a funnel cake or ice cream for dessert when a blue-faced dwarf barreled into me, almost bringing me to my knees.

"Teddy!" I stooped to hug my grandson, who gave me a sticky kiss while happily devouring the last of his indigo-tinged cotton candy.

"Don't tell Jessica!" my son Roger whispered as Teddy dragged him off to discover other forbidden delights. I hoped he would remember to scrub his son's face before returning home.

The evening had turned crisp and cool as darkness settled in, and I was glad of my comfortable jeans and the baggy sweatshirt that said, "This is my Halloween costume!"

The usually sedate little college looked almost gaudy in its effort to forget, if only for a while, the gruesome thing that had happened there. Earlier I had seen Ed Tillman and his partner, Sheila Eastwood, from the local police attempting to blend in with the crowd, while Weigelia's cousin Kemper strolled about the fringes, observing the activities from a distance. I was glad to know they weren't far away. It was difficult not to watch the faces of the Sarah Bedford students as they went about the business of playing, and of trying not to be afraid. Some succeeded, I think, but I wasn't sure about the others. I wasn't sure about me, and I certainly wasn't looking forward to staying on campus overnight.

Nettie had phoned earlier that evening with a peculiar request. "I know you're going to think I'm neurotic, Lucy Nan, but I'm really concerned about Leslie. They've made an appointment for her with their family doctor early next week, but her dad's not able to come for her until Sunday. Frankly, I don't think the child's sleeping any better than she's eating." She paused. "Is there any way you could make some excuse to stay with her Saturday night, since you'll be there for the festival anyway? I'd do it myself, but it would be too obvious. There's an extra bed in her room, you know. The girl who was to room with her got homesick and went home after a couple of weeks."

"I guess I could tell her I'll be working late after the festival and need a place to crash, but do you really think she would want me?"

"I think she'll jump at the chance to have someone in the room with her," Nettie said. "I honestly believe part of Leslie's problem is being in that room alone—especially after what happened to that other girl."

"Okay, I'll see how she reacts when I mention it," I

told her, "but I'll bet she'll come up with a string of excuses why I shouldn't stay."

"Oh, that would be great!" Leslie said when I asked her. "I'll make up the other bed with my extra set of sheets." And she showed such animation I felt ashamed for not wanting to stay. Now and again during the festivities I caught sight of her with some of the other girls, and each time she smiled and waved. Tonight she didn't have to dread being alone.

With Jo Nell and Idonia, I bought a chance at the cake walk and came away empty-handed, but Jo Nell won a sour-cream pound cake with cream-cheese icing.

"I can't walk around with a pound cake all night," she said. "Will you go with me to put it in my car, Lucy Nan?"

"There's no use in both of us going," I said, reaching for the cake. "Here, I'll take it."

"And trust you alone with a sour-cream pound cake? Not in this lifetime!" my cousin said. "Besides, you're not walking across this campus by yourself with a murderer lurking about, and that parking lot's dark as a bat cave. We'll both go." Jo Nell marched resolutely ahead, holding her cake like a trophy, and I trailed obligingly along behind. Idonia, I noticed, had been waylaid to decorate a pumpkin. She never can resist a chance to smear paint on something—usually it's an unspoiled and unsuspecting canvas.

Blythe Cornelius hollered as we passed her table.

"Guess how many beans are in the jar and win a prize!" She pointed to a huge panda wearing a vest in Sarah Bedford's colors of gold and white. "Come on, ladies—only ten cents a guess!"

I shoved a dollar her way. "We're on the way to the car with this cake. Catch you when I get back." Sadly, Teddy had recently decided he was too old for stuffed animals.

"Lucy, do me a favor, would you, please? Since you'll be going right past there anyway . . . ." Blythe took off her glasses and polished them on the sleeve of her shirt. "I cleaned out Willene's refrigerator this afternoon and unplugged it, but I can't remember if I left the door open. It'll smell something awful if it's left closed. Would you run in and check it for me? Shouldn't take a minute."

"Sure." I waited while she fished the door key from her purse. Jo Nell stopped trying to count the beans and looked up at her. "You've heard from Willene?"

Blythe placed the key in my hand and smiled. "She's fine—just taking a few weeks' leave of absence to get her life in order. Wouldn't tell me where she was, though."

I could tell Jo Nell was restless to go on, so we didn't linger. My cousin has legs as long as cornstalks and doesn't waste any time getting where she's going. I stopped to buy a double-dip chocolate-chip ice cream cone and had to run to catch up with her. "Poor Willene! I do believe she's outweirded herself this time!" she said. "Why doesn't the woman *do* something about that horrible man?"

"She was probably too frightened," I said, and told her about the telephone message. "Couldn't get away fast enough. Sounds to me like her ex has a screw loose."

Willene's small apartment was dark except for a faint light from the street, and we paused to unlock her front door. "Here, hold this a minute, would you?" I shoved my half-eaten ice cream at Jo Nell and she set her cake box down to take it, then waited while I went inside. Blythe had been right to be concerned. The refrigerator door was closed and I propped it open with a kitchen chair, thinking how sad it was that the place didn't look less lived in with Willene Benson gone than it did when she was here.

The rooms seemed hollow, and even with the lights on I could imagine someone hiding here. I couldn't wait to get outside and hurried to lock the door behind me. Willene's converted garage was far removed from the crowd. And it was quiet. The kind of quiet that makes me jumpy.

Snicker-snack . . . snicker-snack . . . The vorpal blade went snickersnack!

My hand shook so, I dropped the key and had to scratch around in dead leaves to find it. A falling acorn pinged in the black-dark area beside the building where a huge oak stretched skeleton limbs . . . and I thought I heard something else there. Maybe not. I stumbled over a root in my rush to get away.

Jo Nell sighed impatiently and held my melting ice

cream at arm's length. "Hurry and take this thing, it's dripping all over me."

I relieved her of the messy cone and looked for a place to get rid of it, but there wasn't a trash can in sight. We had started to the parking lot when I either sensed or saw movement behind us to my left and a figure stepped out of the shadows.

"Hurry!" I whispered, grabbing my cousin's elbow.

"Quit shoving me, Lucy Nan! It's dark out here."

Too dark. The lamps beside Willene Benson's door weren't lit and the large oaks screened the lights from main campus.

"Where is she?" Someone spoke behind me. A man. "Where's my wife?"

I tried to move away, but his hand gripped my arm. "I don't know where she is," I said. "Leave me alone."

Jo Nell stepped closer and put an arm through mine. "And we wouldn't tell you if we did," she said. "Now, I'll thank you to get out of our way."

Please, Jo Nell, not now! Don't say any more! The man's fingers dug into my wrist. He was so close I could smell his sour breath, see the dark stubble on his chin. Willene Benson's ex-husband. The nearness of him made me want to be sick.

Jo Nell locked on to my arm and tried to wrench me away, but the man stepped between us. My voice hid somewhere deep inside and I had to reach for it. When the words came they sounded as if they needed to be dusted. "Look," I croaked, "I can't tell you anything. Now please, let us go."

161

He gave me a sudden shake and shoved his pasty face into mine. "You're lying! I saw you come out of her place. You know where she is, and you damn well better tell me!"

A cold wind zapped me in the face, yet I felt uncomfortably warm—even hot. Every sound seemed magnified: Jo Nell's fast breathing, the crunch of an acorn. This man was unstable. He might have a knife, a gun. My cousin was too old to run fast, and I was no track star either. I had to do something.

And then I saw her standing there—Augusta—and she seemed to bask in a calming blue aura. Think blue, Augusta always advised me whenever my emotions got the better of me. Take a deep breath and think blue. And I did. For a brief second I was only aware of the ice cream trickling down my hand.

Ice cream. I pulled free of Jo Nell's grip and smushed the melting confection right between the man's eyes, screaming as loud as I could while little streams of chocolaty liquid oozed down his face. For a few seconds he wore what was left of the cone like a unicorn's horn in the middle of his forehead. And then he ran.

Panting the whole way, Jo Nell and I pushed and pulled each other toward the lights, toward the voices and activity. My sweatshirt seemed to weigh a ton, and my heart drummed so, I felt it might make a hole in my chest. Apparently no one had heard me scream over the hubbub of the festival.

Just ahead on the flagstone walk Dean Holland tried

to make a decision on a painted pumpkin the art students were peddling. He looked even more puzzled than usual when I grabbed him by the arm.

"A man!" I yelled. "A man just threatened us back there! Willene Benson's husband—he's crazy and he's running loose right here at Sarah Bedford."

The dean smiled as he patted my hand. "Well, that's fine. Just fine. I'm crazy about Sarah Bedford, too."

Chapter Fourteen

*T*hat sounds like Riley Herman," Blythe said when I told her what had happened. I could tell she was trying not to laugh. "And you hit him with *what?*"

"What was left of my chocolate-chip cone. It was the only weapon I had, and a waste of good ice cream, too." I didn't think it was so funny.

"But you had to think about it," Jo Nell reminded me. "Seems like you stood there for at least five minutes before you came to parting terms with it."

"I didn't see you parting with that pound cake," I told her.

Blythe was serious again. "You did report this, didn't you, Lucy?"

I nodded. "As soon as I had the breath to speak. If he's still on campus, the police shouldn't have any trouble finding him."

"Now you see what Willene had to put up with," she said. "Can you blame her for trying to hide?"

"But aren't they divorced?" I asked. "Isn't there a

163

law against that sort of thing?"

"Can't make it stick. I don't know how many times Willene has taken out a restraining order against that man." Blythe rattled her bean jar at a passerby. "But this time she thought maybe she'd lost him for good."

"Well, he gives me the creeps," I said. "He's not right, not normal. No wonder she's afraid of him."

Blythe zipped up her jacket and tucked soft gray curls under a blue knitted cap. "Let's hope campus security will turn that one over to the police . . . if they can find him."

I heard the jangle of bracelets behind me and turned to see Sally Wooten. "Find who?" she said.

"Never you mind, sugar," Blythe told her. "Just be sure you don't wander off alone. A drunk frightened Miss Lucy near the parking lot a while ago, so keep your eyes open."

Sally made a face. "It wasn't that Londus, was it?"

"Londus Clack? *Drunk?* Surely you must be joking, Sally," Blythe said, "Why, he'd as soon drink drain cleaner than touch a drop of liquor. What makes you say a thing like that?"

Sally looked at me and shrugged. "I don't know. He's been acting kind of funny lately. Follows us sometimes, and sort of hangs around like he wants to say something." She rolled her eyes. "Weird!"

Blythe frowned. "Follows who? Where?"

"I guess he's trailed after just about everybody at one time or another. Celeste and Debra said he walked a few paces behind them when they went to the library

164

the other night, only when they turned around he pretended to tie his shoe; and Paula said he was watching while she swam laps in the pool yesterday. He's always prowling around our hall."

"How long has this been going on?" Blythe asked.

"I don't know. Couple of weeks, maybe longer." Sally dug two quarters from her pocket and wrote down five guesses for the bean jar.

"I'll speak to him about it," Blythe told her. "A month ago, I would've bet good money Londus Clack is as harmless as they come, but now I don't know. They even think he might've—"

"Might've what?" I asked.

But Blythe had a set look on her face, and I knew she wasn't going to say any more. "Don't forget one of our girls has been killed on this campus. Just be careful," she said.

The crowd was thinning now and some of the booths were closing. Blythe turned away to wade through her basket of names and numbers to determine who would win the big panda. Jo Nell had wandered off earlier to find Idonia, as she was giving her a ride home, and I would bet my next paycheck—all $1.98 of it—the two of them were sitting at her kitchen table this minute putting a big dent in that sour-cream pound cake.

I turned up my collar, stuck my hands in my pockets, and told the girls in our booth to go home. They had sold all the taffy and only a few popcorn balls were left.

"I want to see the Haunted Garden before it's too late," Celeste said, taking down our sign. "Anybody want to go with me?"

Debra, who was helping her, counted their earnings and wrote down the sum. "Not me. It's getting cold out here. Besides, I'm expecting a call."

"Come on, Miss Lucy, it'll be fun, and the proceeds go to the Drama Club." Celeste waited with her head to one side, looking about twelve years old. I shuddered to think of facing Weigelia Jones if I let anything happen to her little sister.

Leslie, I noticed, was helping out with a few stragglers in line for the ring toss game and I waved to let her know I hadn't deserted her. "I've already had one scare tonight. It can't be much worse than that," I said. "Okay, let's go."

I hadn't been on the "haunted" trail since our children were small, and it was fun letting myself be a child again. The college had talked about canceling the Drama Club's project after what happened to D.C., but the students had put so much work into it, they decided to go ahead.

Shrieks and moans against a background of eerie music were being broadcast throughout a thriller obstacle course beginning with the cavelike circle beneath the Tree House. Celeste and I were met by Igor—or was it Quasimodo?—who escorted us past a life-size dummy wearing a Frankenstein monster mask. The gruesome thing hung by its neck with a knife in its chest, but it looked so fake it wasn't even scary.

Dracula swooped out of shadows, ghosts appeared from behind gravestones, and a growling student in a shaggy costume, who I think was supposed to be Wolfman, stalked us along the way. "Look out!" I yelled and Celeste grabbed me around the neck as a witch on a broomstick swooped from behind a tree with a hoarse, rasping cackle that ended in a howling crescendo.

Laughing, we untangled ourselves and had started to walk on when Celeste grabbed my arm and whispered something so low I could barely hear her.

"What?" I found myself whispering too.

"Oh, Lord, there he is again." She nodded slightly to the right.

It was so dark, I could only make out a low wall. "Who?" I said.

"Shh! Not so loud. It's Londus. Watching us. He's been acting real strange lately. Wait and see, he'll be there waiting when we come out."

"Does he do anything? Say anything?" I asked.

"No, he's just *there*—like a bad taste in your mouth that won't go away. And it's always when there's just one or two of us around. I'm afraid of him. If he followed D.C. like this, she would've said something nasty, something that might set him off—and then . . ."

I clawed at a fake spiderweb. (I hope it was a fake spiderweb!) "Sally told me pretty much the same thing."

"Sally Wooten?"

"Right. She was telling Blythe about him just a little while ago."

"Oh. Well, she would," Celeste said.

A tall figure with a jack-o'-lantern for a head stepped up and asked if we had seen her head. I recognized Joy Ellen Harper's voice. Celeste had moved a few steps in front of me, and now she turned and waited.

"What do you mean by that?" I asked.

Celeste managed to look confused, but she knew very well what I meant. "By what?"

"What you said about Sally. She *would* what?"

Celeste looked down as she walked, ignoring Jack the Ripper with a bloody knife. "I shouldn't have said that. There's probably nothing to it, but . . . well, Sally would probably be relieved if somebody else got blamed for D.C.'s murder."

"But everybody says they got along fine. I don't understand."

"They did, or at least they *seemed* to." We stepped carefully over a couple of rubber snakes slithering in our path. "Look," Celeste said, "Sally never mentions this, but D.C. was bad news for her from the first day she set foot on campus."

"How? What did she do?"

"Stole her boyfriend, for starters. Sally had been going with Tommy Jack Evans for almost a year, but we hadn't been back to school two weeks before he gave her the old heave-ho. Next thing we knew, he was dating *guess who?* I saw them together myself,"

Celeste said. "Of course it didn't last long—couple of weeks, maybe—but long enough to make a mess of things."

"How did Sally take that?" I asked.

Celeste shrugged. "Pretended she didn't know what was going on, and maybe she didn't. Tommy Jack never came to the college when he was seeing D.C. He's already finished school. Coaches football at the high school and has his own place here in town, so she must've met him there. Sally was devastated, though. I think she was in love with the jerk—or thought she was. Then, when D.C. started gettin' it on with Professor Hornsby, Tommy Jack Evans was history. Served him right!"

"Do the police know about this?" I asked.

"They should. They questioned everybody in Emma Harris. Wanted to know who D.C. dated—everything about her—which wasn't much. I'm sure somebody must have told them about Tommy Jack."

Our breath came in frosty puffs, and Celeste shoved her hands deep into her pockets and shivered. "She saw him for such a short time, it didn't occur to me to mention it, but now that I think about it I realize I should've said something. It's just that . . . well, this is *murder* we're talking about, and he'd only known the girl a short time."

I could see why Sally Wooten might want to slap her roommate upside the head a couple of times for what she did, but I didn't think she'd have a go at her with a rusty sickle. "So had Sally. So had everybody," I reasoned.

"Maybe so, but she didn't seem all that upset at the service," Celeste said. "Not many of us did."

"Service? What service?"

"They held a memorial service for D.C. here at the college a couple of nights ago. Just about everybody came—felt guilty, I guess. I know I did. It was sad, real sad. I felt just awful, but I couldn't even shed a tear. I wanted to, but the only two people I saw crying were Leslie Monroe and that hypocrite Londus Clack."

"See, there he is! What'd I tell you?" Celeste elbowed me in the side as we left the garden through a gap in the hedge.

Londus stood alone beside a weeping willow, which was appropriate, I thought, considering his forlorn expression. He wore a dark jacket over his work pants and his ears stuck out beneath a visored cap.

The commons area was empty except for a few people packing away their wares. Ed Tillman and his partner Sheila had left, but Kemper Mungo, I noticed, had stayed to help the cleanup committee gather empty cans for recycling. Celeste's co-worker had taken the table and proceeds with her, and Blythe Cornelius was folding her card table. The panda, I noticed, was gone.

Celeste began to walk faster and I glanced over my shoulder to see if Londus was still there. I know I must have appeared surprised to see him approaching us with a determined and slightly disapproving look on his homely face. I paused. This man came and went about the campus freely, and a policeman was in

170

screaming distance. What could he possibly do? I turned to face him, folded my arms, and waited.

He slowed, but kept coming. Out of the corner of my eye I saw Celeste poised for flight, and after what we had discovered in that old shed, I didn't blame her.

Removing his cap, Londus held out a hand. "Miss, I wonder, could I—"

"Aunt Shug!" Celeste yelled louder than all the beasties in theHaunted Garden put together, and Blythe looked up to see who was calling to her.

"Who won the panda?" Celeste ran toward her into the light.

Blythe smiled when she saw her. "One of the cooks from the cafeteria won it for her daughter. Took two people to carry it. I remember my little sister had a bear like that—only not as big, of course. Carried it everywhere she went."

Blythe stood and looked at us as if she were waiting for something to happen. "You know, I sure could use a hand with this table," she said finally.

I glanced back to tell Londus to wait, but the janitor wasn't there.

Usually I don't have trouble sleeping in a strange bed, but that night I kept stumbling over all the clutter in my mind. Augusta had insisted on staying overnight as well—"to get the feel of things," she said, and I knew she was somewhere nearby. Leslie had read for a while after going to bed, but now slept soundly across the room in a cocoon of purple sheets. Her dad was to come for her in the morning and I hoped she would get some much-needed help from her doctor during her stay at home over the next few days. Something was causing her anxieties, and maybe her father did expect too much of her, as Nettie claimed, but I didn't think he was to blame for all of it.

And in spite of the girls' suspicion of Londus Clack, I didn't believe he meant to harm them. After all, can a man who owns a singing teddy bear be all that bad? His very shyness was probably what frightened them, I thought, his reluctance to come out and approach the girls with whatever he wanted to say. Besides, Londus didn't seem the type to read *Alice in Wonderland* or appreciate the Jabberwocky nonsense. I was almost certain he had wanted to tell me something tonight before Celeste frightened him away by shouting to Blythe.

I lay on my back and stared at the window. The curtains were open and a light just outside threw a square of pale silver across Leslie's neat desk and a chair with a sweater draped over it. Sally Wooten across the hall had gone home after the festival and our end of the wing was quiet. I wondered where Augusta had taken up watch. She rests but I've never seen her sleep, so she might be anywhere in the dormitory or even outside. Down the hall a toilet flushed and somebody in the room below was watching a late-night talk show. A car door slammed.

I had forgotten to ask what happened to Riley Herman after his anointment with a chocolate-chip cone. The creep was lucky I had bought ice cream instead of one of those painted pumpkins or a big pot of chrysanthemums from the faculty Garden Club.

I closed my eyes. Tomorrow Ben and I would be hiking up Kings Mountain for a picnic at the top and I tried to think of something good to take along. I flipped over on my stomach and played the alphabet game Charlie and I used to play with Roger and Julie on long car trips. Apples, of course; bread, thick and crusty. Bananas? No, too smushy. Bottle of wine. Cheese. Cake or cookies? I couldn't decide . . .

The door closed so softly I don't know how I heard it, but I woke knowing somebody had stood there silently and then moved on. I sat up in bed. "Augusta?" I whispered, but no one answered.

Outside in the hallway a board creaked. Probably one of the girls had gone to the bathroom, and being half-asleep, opened our door by mistake. Footsteps, slow and cautious, moved away from the door. I sat on the side of the bed and listened. It was almost two in the morning and somebody was opening the door of the room across the hall. Sally's room. Why would she come back to the college at this hour?

The floor was cold to my bare feet as I tiptoed to the door and quietly, carefully turned the knob so the hinges wouldn't squeak. I was just in time to see the door across from me slowly close.

I had slept in an oversized T-shirt. Now, leaving the door slightly ajar, I grabbed the jeans and sweatshirt I had thrown on the foot of the bed and slipped into loafers. Leslie had not moved from her original position and her breathing was deep and even. There was no use waking her and frightening her even more.

Whoever was in Sally's room was making a poor effort to be quiet. A drawer squeaked open, then closed; a closet door banged softly. I stood with my back to the wall as close to the door as possible until I heard someone come out, then listened until footsteps reached about midway down the hall before I risked looking. Somebody in a raincoat—somebody tall—a woman, I thought, with a heavy knitted cap pulled low over her ears crept slowly down the stairs. I snatched my jacket and followed.

I stood listening at the top of the stairs as the prowler moved past Blythe's closed door and down the hall to the lounge, and was working up the courage to follow when someone touched my shoulder from behind.

"Wait for me!" Augusta whispered, falling into step beside me.

"Do you have to do that? You almost gave me a heart attack," I said, although I was relieved to have her there beside me.

It seemed to take forever to reach the bottom of the steps and I looked around for a place to hide. Augusta, of course, didn't have to worry about that. The double doors at the end of the hall stood open and I slinked toward them as quietly as I could. What would anybody want in a room filled with ugly secondhand furniture, old magazines, and sports trophies? And what was I doing at my age snooping after God-knows-who when I could be warm and asleep—maybe even comparatively safe—upstairs, or better still, at home in my own bed?

The intruder rummaged through drawers in the trophy case, looked under sofa cushions, and slowly ran a finger over the titles on the bookshelf. The room had several windows and the security light from outside enabled me to see her plainly at last. For a few seconds she stood with one hand on her hip, apparently stymied in her search. Monica Hornsby.

She looked in my direction but didn't see me as I watched from behind the door, then she turned away to circle the lounge, checking possible hiding places once more. Finally, in a kind of last-ditch effort, she got down on her knees and looked behind the trophy case on the other side of the room. Something must have been shoved in back of it because Monica Hornsby sat on the floor with her back to the wall and slid an arm behind it as far as she could reach. She was drawing out what appeared to be a square boxlike package when a light came on in the hall and Blythe Cornelius charged out of her apartment, banging the door behind her. "Who's in there?" she yelled, clumping down the corridor past the door where I was hiding.

I heard a muffled thump and somebody muttered, "Damn!" Then a runner I guessed to be Monica dashed past me and out the heavy front door, letting it slam behind her.

I stepped out to find Blythe in a pink quilted bathrobe holding on to the back of the sofa and looking thoroughly confused.

"Are you all right?" I asked, and she looked up and nodded.

"I think you'd better call security . . . and would you please keep an eye on Leslie upstairs? I hate to leave her alone," I said before taking off after Monica, who, as far as I knew, still had the package she'd found.

I was just in time to see her disappear around the corner of the building that housed the cafeteria, with Augusta not far behind her. I circled the building from the other side and with my back against the cold brick wall waited until she emerged from the other side. From there I watched her blend with the shadow of a ginkgo tree that sprinkles the ground with leaves like tiny golden fans. She walked quickly but didn't run, and carried the parcel under her arm as if she were on an ordinary errand.

From where I stood, Sarah Bedford by moonlight looked like a print from an old woodcut, all black and white and still. There was no wind, but my ears were freezing, and my bare ankles tingled with cold. I slipped from shadow to shadow, keeping her in my sight until she reached the commons area. And that was when she looked back and saw me.

"Wait!" I called, and realized how ridiculous it sounded. Of course she wasn't going to wait. And she didn't. Immediately Monica Hornsby began to run, and searching for breath, I ran after her. My side felt like it was being stitched by a giant needle and gathered into a knot. Would the woman ever slow down? Clearly she was in better shape than I was, and a whole lot younger.

A dog barked somewhere not too far away and I heard the cold trickle of the fountain. I thought about yelling for help, but it might seem kind of strange since I was the one doing the chasing. Surely Blythe had called campus security by now, but where the hell were they?

And where was Monica Hornsby? Probably far away by now. The silhouette of the Tree House loomed in front of me, and in the darkness I saw the glow of Augusta's hair. I drew closer just in time to see Monica trip and go down; her short cry sounded out over the soft thud of her falling. By the time I reached her she was crawling on her hands and knees, probably searching for the package. When she saw me, Monica swore under her breath and hurried away, favoring her right foot in a limping gait. Near the loose flagstone that had tripped her, Augusta stood smiling, then wiped the soil from her hands before pressing the stone back into place.

A few feet away in the black shadow of the Tree House lay the package Monica had dropped and I scrambled to pick it up. What could be important enough to make the professor's wife go to such lengths to find it?

A gust of wind sent what was left of the leaves on the big oak rustling, and a limb swayed over my head.

I grabbed the box to my chest and stumbled backward when a man's shoes swung past my face. The shoes had feet in them.

Chapter Fifteen

The scream was about halfway between thought and deed when I remembered the Halloween dummy we had encountered in the haunted garden. Whoever had been responsible for cleaning up after the festival had forgotten the stuffed creature hanging there. Thank heavens I hadn't screamed and awakened the whole campus over a fake monster. Poor Frankie. He looked cold and uncomfortable hanging there with his head turned that funny way.

Again the wind parted the foliage above me just long enough to reveal the white socks, the green denim pants . . . *Frankenstein's monster wasn't wearing green denim pants!*

Then the pale light found his face. Londus Clack's face. And he was never going to sing again.

It was a good scream and I didn't waste it.

For some reason, throughout the ordeal that followed, I held on to the package Monica Hornsby had dropped. A couple of people looked at it curiously, and somebody—Blythe, I guess it was—asked me if I didn't want to put it down somewhere. I didn't. Whatever was in that box must have been important for Monica to do what she did and I wanted to find out what it was. But Monica's nocturnal visit was almost forgotten after I discovered Londus Clack hanging around like that.

Later, back at the dormitory, Captain Hardy looked at me with a resigned expression, as though he wasn't too surprised to find me there mixed up in murder again. Good grief! Was I some kind of homicidal Typhoid Mary? I hadn't even known D.C. Hunter, and I had only spoken with Londus Clack that one afternoon in Main Hall. Yet the idea made me feel a little strange.

Leslie was still sleeping soundly when I reluctantly returned to the room to wake her with the grim news of Londus's death, but the captain felt it necessary to speak with all the girls who had spent the night in Emma P. Harris Hall. Huddled in pajamas and robe, Leslie clung to me quietly during the questioning by police. Students were offered counseling of sorts by a yawning school psychologist who then advised them to try and get some sleep, and I felt her body tense beside me.

"I don't want to go back to that room alone," she whispered.

"Why not bunk in with Debra and me?" Celeste offered. "We can push our beds together and sleep three across."

Debra agreed. "Sounds okay to me. Mom always said there was safety in numbers."

"I'll look in on you later," I promised, trying to sound more confident than I was. And as the girls returned to their rooms, I was relieved to see Augusta trailing after.

It was after four and still dark. Ordinarily, I could sleep at that hour on a bed of gravel, but that morning my adrenaline pump was in high gear. Of course I was working on my second cup of Blythe's strong coffee.

Blythe had a bad bruise on her chin where she had collided with Monica earlier in the lounge, and I noticed a raw-looking patch where she'd run into the doorjamb, she said, on the heel of her right hand.

Now the captain pushed aside his half-filled coffee mug, looked at me, and sighed before removing his glasses to rub red-rimmed eyes.

Blythe half-sat, half-lay in the faded green armchair across from him with her eyes closed and her head resting on the back of the chair. The laces of one gray oxford had come undone, and she cradled her bifocals in one hand, gently resting them on her chest. She looked tired and old.

The young sergeant, Duff Acree, stood with his hands on his hips facing the window as though he dared anything else to happen.

"Well," Captain Hardy said to me, readjusting his eyeglasses, "how 'bout telling us what you were doing out in the commons area at two—or whatever—in the morning?"

I glanced at Blythe, who smiled weakly, her gaze falling on the bulky package in my lap. I knew I was going to have to hand it over to the police—but not before I got a look at it first.

"Believe it or not, I was chasing a prowler," I said,

180

"and I'll be glad to give you a play-by-play account . . ." I shifted uncomfortably . . . "but first you'll have to excuse me for a minute." I managed to look a trifle embarrassed. "All that coffee, you know."

Secure in a stall in the first-floor bathroom, I slid the box from its padded envelope. It had obviously been around awhile as it was frayed at the corners, one side was split, and it was held together with string. It had once held typing paper and said so. It still did, only now the paper was filled with text, double-spaced. It was a manuscript typed on a manual machine that was in desperate need of a new ribbon by somebody who had never taken a typing course.

I read for as long as I dared and found it to be a pretty good story. It appeared to be a novel about a botanist named Giles Crenshaw who discovered a lost tribe in the wilderness of the Blue Ridge Mountains. There he fell in love, and into bed, with a spritelike beauty named Ariel who spoke Elizabethan English.

The language was beautiful and melodic, and from the little I read it seemed the writer not only had a sense of adventure but a sharp wit as well. The name "Crockett" had been typed in the top right-hand corner of every page, and on the inside lid of the box I found the title, *High Devongreen*, with the author's name and address written below it:

Amos Crockett
516 Gray Woods Court
Stone's Throw, S.C.

Amos Crockett. Wasn't he the English professor who died midterm, the man Clay Hornsby had replaced? What was his manuscript doing behind the trophy case in Emma P. Harris Hall? I was beginning to get a crazy idea.

I presented the box and its contents to Captain Hardy. "Here. This is what the chase was all about. Careful, it's falling apart."

He frowned, accepting it reluctantly. "What is it?"

"A book manuscript. A novel, by a professor who once taught here. Amos Crockett."

"So it was true!" Blythe came over to look at it. "Everybody suspected he was working on something, but he never talked about it. I thought it was probably some dull scholastic work, he was such a timid little man. A novel, you say?"

I nodded. "And a pretty good one, I think."

Captain Hardy grunted. "You wanna let me in on this?"

I told him how I had heard somebody searching the room across the hall, then followed the prowler down-stairs. "She was looking for something—this manu-script—and she found it behind the trophy case over there."

"She?" The captain popped a couple of Rolaids.

"Monica Hornsby." Blythe and I spoke together and I let her take up the tale.

"I heard somebody in here," she said. "And when I turned on the light and confronted her, she knocked me sprawling and ran . . ."

"With the manuscript," I said. "And I ran after her. She tripped on something out by the Tree House—a loose flagstone, I think—and hurt her ankle, probably sprained it." No use telling about Augusta's part in this, I thought. "Anyway, she dropped the box, and that was when I found him: Londus Clack. The package had landed under the Tree House, and when I went to pick it up I saw the dummy. Only it wasn't a dummy."

I yawned. Even the cracked leather sofa with the cold chrome arms looked tempting. I was ready to go to sleep now.

"And what about the Hornsby woman?" the detective asked.

"I don't know. She didn't stick around, but she was limping, so she can't have gone too far."

"Sergeant," Captain Hardy said, "you and Tillman take the patrol car and pick up Monica Hornsby—No, never mind. We're about finished here. I'd better go with you."

"Thank you, God," I said, letting my eyelids droop.

"Poor Londus," Blythe said. "I know he's been acting strangely lately, but do you think he . . . I just can't believe he would . . ." She clucked softly to herself. "What an awful way to die!"

"Oh, he didn't hang himself, ma'am," the young sergeant said. "At least the coroner didn't seem to think so. He said it looked like somebody'd whacked him over the head real good first."

Captain Hardy groaned as he stood. "Well, fine,

183

Sergeant. Do you have any other announcements you'd like to make, or can we get on with it?"

Blythe Cornelius shook her head numbly. "Another murder. When will it end?" Suddenly she leaned forward and nudged my arm. "Dear God! You don't suppose Riley Herman had anything to do with this?"

The weary captain sighed and sat back down. "Just for the record," he said, "who's Riley Herman when he's at home?"

I told him how Willene's ex had confronted Jo Nell and me and how I had crowned him with a chocolate-chip cone. I thought for a minute he was going to smile, but he didn't.

"He's that man they brought in earlier, sir," Sergeant Acree reminded him.

"As far as either of you know, is there any connection between Londus Clack and this Herman guy?" the captain asked.

Blythe said she didn't know of any unless Londus happened to get in the other man's way. I just shook my head. The two could have been engaged to be married for all I knew—or cared right then.

The captain looked at his watch. "If you ladies don't mind, let us know where you can be reached for the next day or so in case we need to get back to you."

I muttered something in reply as I knelt on the gritty tile floor to retrieve my jacket that had fallen behind the sofa. Ben and I were supposed to go somewhere today. Someplace that required physical exercise and strenuous activity. Kings Mountain. We were supposed to hike to the top of Kings Mountain.

By the clock on the wall it was just after five and I didn't think I could stay awake to drive back home. With my jacket under my arm I groped my way upstairs to the bed I'd vacated in Leslie's room, pausing only to glance in at the sleeping girls down the hall.

Just before sleep came, a troublesome little doubt flitted like a gray moth through my semiconscious thoughts and into some deep dark void where I couldn't follow.

Chapter Sixteen

I'm getting hungry," I said, leaning against a sweet gum tree to rest. "How long before we eat?" I had slept late that morning, then hurried home to change and throw a picnic lunch together. I hadn't had time for breakfast.

Ben turned on the trail to look at me. "We've only been walking half an hour, Lucy Nan. And you ate all those doughnuts on the way."

"Two. I ate two, and they were small ones, at that." I yawned. "Does this seem steeper than usual to you?"

Ben and I stepped aside to make room for a troop of Brownie Scouts chasing one another up the mountain path, and it exhausted me to look at them. The walk up Kings Mountain wasn't a challenge for even an inexperienced hiker and I had climbed to the top more times than I could count, but today the incline seemed straight up and down.

"Look, you're tired. We can go back down," Ben said. "We don't have to do this, you know."

"I know, but I want to—if only it would level off a little." I shoved him ahead of me. "Press on and don't pay any attention to me."

He gave me one of those looks that made me want to run up the mountainside with a big smile on my face. "I think you know better than that," he said. I took a deep breath and chugged along behind him.

As tired as I was after the horrible experience of the night before, being in the woods—even on a well-traveled path like this one—was calming. As a child, when I was upset or worried I would roam the hills above Stone's Throw and let the peace seep in, and I needed that experience today. But Kings Mountain, the scene of a bloody battle during the American Revolution, had not always been a peaceful place.

It was after two by the time we reached the top, where we found a patch of sun-warmed grass and sat on our jackets to eat. Ben unwrapped one of the pimento cheese sandwiches I had made that morning. "Why would anybody want to kill—what did you say his name was?"

"Londus Clack." I swigged tepid water. "I can't imagine unless they thought he knew something. And it would have to have been a man, or else a woman with a lot of strength, to hoist him up there like that. I'm just glad it was dark so I couldn't see any more than I did.

"Wonder how long he'd been there?"

"Couldn't have been too long. He was alive when Celeste and I came out of that Haunted Garden thing, and then we cleared out like everybody else. Must've been about ten." I bit into a pickle and edged away from an inquisitive yellow jacket. "I think he wanted to tell me something. Wish I knew what it was."

He frowned. "What makes you think that?"

I told him what Londus had said and how he had been following the girls. "I don't blame them for being nervous, but I really don't think the poor man meant any harm."

Ben twirled a crimson sweet gum leaf that had drifted into his beard. "Maybe he was trying to protect them," he said.

"Maybe. I don't know. Blythe started to tell us something about Londus last night—something she suspected, I think, but I guess she realized she'd said too much already."

I watched him polish an apple on his sleeve. "Could've been Monica Hornsby," I said. "She's tall enough, and she was prowling about the campus last night." I realized I *wanted* the woman to be Londus Clack's killer because I didn't like what I'd heard about her, but it was hard to imagine her bashing him over the head and stringing him up in the Tree House. Monica would be the type to use poison, maybe, or a ladder with the rungs sawed through.

I crumbled the rest of my bread for the birds and held out a hand to Ben. "Come on, let's walk around some. I don't want to share my chocolate chip cookies with these wasps."

"Thought you were too tired." He took my hand as we walked. "You just wanted to get me off to yourself, didn't you, so you could have your way with me?" He aimed a kiss at my neck.

"Cramp in my leg," I said, laughing, although actually it wasn't a bad idea. We stopped to look at the view. Although it was the last of October, the mountain was still a bright smear of color and the sky an incredible blue that rivaled the brilliance of Ben Maxwell's eyes.

For the last several weeks I had been around college students so much it was a relaxing experience to have a conversation with someone near my own age. Was I mistaking my pleasure in intelligent adult company for something more? Whatever it was, I was enjoying it.

A chill had crept into the air, a gust of wind sent a scurry of leaves around us, and Ben hurried me along. "Guess we'd better be starting back if I'm going to cook you dinner," he said. "It has to simmer awhile."

I had never heard of simmering steaks, which is all I thought he knew how to cook, but I kept my mouth shut.

I was happy to be wrong, and tried not to look astonished on our return when he dumped his collective ingredients on my kitchen table and went about assembling them into a stew almost as good as my mother used to make. Augusta had left a Bundt cake saturated with rum for our dessert and even the smell of it made me dizzy.

Clementine was clamoring to be let out and I noticed the kitchen trash can needed emptying as well, so while Ben was chopping onions I decided to take care of both. The dog usually runs around the yard three times before retiring to do her business behind the summerhouse. I followed her, plastic bag in hand, to add her contribution to the garbage when I noticed an empty cake-mix box in the kitchen trash. First a slow cooker and now cake mix! Augusta was beginning to adapt to modern ways and I couldn't wait to see if she would mention it. The note she had left on my dresser said she had gone to help Ellis with a sewing project but I couldn't imagine what it was. Ellis had shown me the nursery-rhyme cross-stitch she'd completed for the expected new grandson, which was a miracle in itself. I couldn't imagine her starting another project and wondered why she hadn't mentioned it to me. Was Ellis giving Augusta lessons in shortcut cooking? I laughed just thinking about it.

"What's so funny?" Ben wanted to know when I came in smiling.

"Just Clementine," I explained. "She gets carried away and runs so fast she falls all over her big feet. Makes me laugh every time." And that was true enough.

We ate in the sitting room at the small round table that had belonged to my mother. As a child I did my homework there and the surface was nicked and ink-spattered, so I dug out my old wedding linens and we did it up right with candlelight and wine.

The stew was delicious, served with hot crusty French bread and a fruit salad, followed by Augusta's cake and coffee.

"This cake's wonderful, but how did you find time to make it?" Ben asked.

"Oh, Augusta made that," I said. "The woman who rents the room upstairs. She loves to cook."

He finished his last bite as I collected the plates. "I'd like to meet her sometime." I answered with conviction that Augusta would like to meet him, too.

We lingered over coffee catching up on his family and mine. Ben's son is completing his residency in internal medicine at Emory University in Atlanta, and I told him about Julie's new job. As the fire flickered low, we took our second glass of wine to the sofa where we set our glasses on the coffee table. He pulled me closer and kissed my ear. I sighed and turned my face toward his. The phone rang.

"Where've you been?" Weigelia said. "Been tryin' to reach you all day. Heard you found another body last night."

At that particular moment I considered adding a third. Hers. But there was no use trying to put her off. I took a long sip of wine and gave her the rundown. "Celeste is fine," I assured her. "Missed out on some sleep, but not as much as I did. She tell you about it?"

She made an irritated big-sister noise. "Went to Clemson to some kind of goings-on over there, and no tellin' where that girl is now." Weigelia growled again.

"You'd think she'd at least give me a call to let me know she's okay."

I didn't think Weigelia was high on her sister's list of priorities right then, but I was reluctant to say so. "Maybe you can catch her tomorrow," I said. "By the way, they picked up Monica Hornsby. Have you heard any more about it?"

"Kemper says they got her for unlawful entry, but he didn't know how long they could make it stick. What you reckon that woman was doing there?"

I told her briefly about the manuscript that was hidden behind the trophy case, and then I told her good-bye.

"Who do you think hid that box back there?" Ben asked when I got off the phone.

"Had to be D.C. Hunter," I said. "And I think I know when she did it. Must've been that Friday night after Clay Hornsby broke up with her, right before she was killed. I heard she had a key to his office. Probably took the manuscript for security."

He frowned. "Security?"

"Against losing him, I guess, or for blackmail. From what I've heard about his new novel, it sounds like he copied it word for word from Amos Crockett's book."

Ben laced his fingers in mine and drew my hand to his chest. "You'd think he would've gotten rid of it, wouldn't you? Wonder why she hid it there?"

"I guess she thought it would be too easy to find in her room, and didn't have time to look for a better place."

"This isn't looking good for the professor, is it? He had motive enough as the girl's callous lover, but now it seems she might have been threatening to expose him as a plagiarist."

"What I can't understand," I said, "is why Monica Hornsby would go to so much trouble to try and save that jerk's hide. She would've been in real danger if the campus security guards had seen her—especially after all that's been going on. I'd let the turkey steam in his own juice!"

"You're a heartless woman, Lucy Nan Pilgrim." Ben stretched his legs to the glowing coals. "Maybe he offered her a major portion of the royalties, or convinced her he'd never, *never* stray again. This guy has a reputation as a Romeo, you know. He's got to have a certain amount of deceptive charm."

"Huh!" I said. "And speaking of Romeos, I found out last night that Tommy Jack Evans had dated *both* D.C. Hunter and her roommate, Sally Wooten."

"Tommy Jack Evans? Sounds like a stock-car racer."

"Football coach at one of the county schools. Used to play for the university, I think."

"I've heard of roommates sharing things," Ben said, "but that's going a little too far." He shifted my head onto his shoulder. "Of course my grandmama used to tell about this family lived just outside of town. Must've been about ten of them, and they all came down with typhoid or something awful like that at the same time. Didn't have but one pill . . .

I knew he was watching me, so I closed my eyes and tried not to smile.

"So their mama, she tied a string to it, you see—"

"Oh, shut up," I said, and stopped him the best way I knew how.

Chapter Seventeen

"Well, it's been one hell of a weekend," Joy Ellen said when I saw her before class on Monday.

"Tell me about it," I said, and meant it. "Have they found out who killed Londus?"

"They questioned Monica Hornsby, even held her for a while, but I don't think they know any more than they did before. Frankly, I don't think she did it. No motive."

I agreed. I couldn't imagine why anybody would want to hurt the kind-hearted maintenance man. "Londus must have weighed close to two hundred pounds," I said. "It would have to be somebody hefty."

Joy Ellen shook her head. "Not really. Whoever was in charge of the dummy neglected to take it down after the festival the other night, and you know how Londus is—was—or maybe you don't, but he couldn't stand loose ends. Anything out of place or left where it wasn't supposed to be bugged the devil out of him." She slammed a battered satchel crammed with papers onto a tabletop and hung her familiar blue blazer on its hanger. "They think now Londus must've seen the dummy hanging there while he was carting off trash that night. Knowing him, he'd have gone up there to take it down." Joy Ellen looked out at the knot of subdued students hurrying past the window. "That's when he was hit," she said.

"How do you know?"

"The dummy had been thrown to the ground under the Tree House. They found it there not too far from where you saw Londus."

I felt sick remembering the man's body swaying inches from my face. I wasn't sure I would ever be able to handle a Halloween carnival again. "So somebody was up there waiting for him?"

"Probably. It makes sense. Once he was unconscious, all they had to do was put the noose around his neck and drop him over the side." Joy Ellen lowered her voice. "I'm not supposed to know this, but they believe they've found what was used to hit him. It was his own hammer."

I made an effort to appear calmer than I felt as the first students entered the room. "How *do* you know all this?" I asked.

With a slight smile, Joy Ellen shrugged. "My sister-in-law's next-door neighbor works in the County Office Building."

Ellis was right. Stone's Throw didn't need a newspaper.

"Coroner thinks he'd been dead three hours tops by the time he saw him," she added.

I made a face at two girls who had taken seats in the

back of the room and they grinned and moved closer to the front.

"Today, I'd like you to imagine yourselves women in a middle-class home before the beginning of the twentieth century," I said when everyone was seated. "Think about it for a while, make notes if you like, then for the rest of the period, I want you to write a diary entry, or a letter, from that person's point of view, describing how they spent their day."

This was met with a chorus of groans, but after the usual shuffling of papers the class settled down and began quietly scribbling. Other than answering a question now and then I observed them from the side-lines, glad that the activity required less than usual of my energy and enthusiasm because I didn't have much of either.

The students seemed relieved as well, I think, to escape into another period in time and meditate about something other than murder.

I sat at the end of the table at the back of the room where Joy Ellen attempted to compile test questions for her freshman history class, but I could see her mind wasn't on it. Finally she shoved her books aside and put down her pencil. "This is getting to me," she said under her breath. "It's getting to everybody. Lucy, if they don't straighten this shit out soon, Sarah Bedford's going down the tube. I heard three more students withdrew just today.

"R.U. has scheduled one of his rare speeches this afternoon. Required attendance. Calls them 'Earnest

Discussions.'" Joy Ellen shook her head. "Naturally he does all the discussing, but this time he's welcome to it. The girls are scared. *I'm* scared."

"I heard they locked up Riley Herman," I told her.

"Who?"

"Riley Herman, Willene Benson's ex. He nearly scared the daylights out of my cousin and me at the festival Saturday night." I told her what had happened.

Joy Ellen nodded. "I keep forgetting Willene took back her maiden name. Blythe told me they arrested him for stalking, slapped his hand, and sent him on his way. If he shows up here again, they might even make him stand in the corner."

"Then they must not think he had anything to do with what happened to Londus."

"Guess not. He had an alibi."

"What kind of alibi?" I asked.

"The best. He was locked up in jail."

I didn't mention Leslie Monroe's absence or the problems she was experiencing emotionally, although I knew she was in Joy Ellen's freshman class. It wasn't my place to discuss it and I felt Joy Ellen would resent the intrusion, but I wanted to butt in in the worst way. Joy Ellen had admitted earlier that she'd been coerced into heading my class. She was not domestically inclined, she informed me, and didn't give a rat's ass how great-grandma knitted a bedspread out of goat hair and stewed up remedies from weeds.

"No kidding?" I said. "I'd never guess."

She laughed. "Guess I have been a pain in the patootie. But it does give me a chance to grade papers, and that old recipe you gave me for apple butter turned out pretty good."

"*You* made apple butter?"

"Hell no! But my sister did. I'll save you a jar."

I didn't want to risk an uneasy truce by voicing my concerns about Leslie, but the girl could use a break. Her aunt, usually as solid as Mount Rushmore, had cried in my kitchen just the day before.

I had been throwing together a last-minute picnic lunch for the hike with Ben that morning when Nettie came over to borrow Mama's old rug-shampooing machine.

"Leslie's going to be staying with me for a few weeks when she gets back," she said, wiping her feet on that old rag rug on the back porch. "I thought I'd put her in that rose-papered room upstairs, the one she liked when she was a little thing. Remember what a quaint child she was, Lucy Nan? Always making up stories and drawing pictures to go with them. Cute as a June bug—and clever, too—and now . . .

"Anyway, that old rug in there could do with a scrubbing."

She looked so forlorn standing there, I put my arms around her. "How is she, Nettie? Do they think she'll be able to come back to class anytime soon?"

She came inside and sat for a minute at the kitchen table. "We hope so. Maybe next week, but her folks think it would be best if she stays with me for the rest of the term."

Nettie cleared her throat and smoothed her graying hair, patting a stray wisp into place, and I knew she was trying not to cry. I got her a drink of water and a handful of tissues and sat across from her looking so concerned that she laughed. And then she cried. "I'm really worried about her, Lucy Nan. She's not herself anymore. Do you know that Leslie's afraid the other students think she might be involved in that Hunter girl's death? It's no secret she couldn't stand her, and I think the two of them had words a few times."

"True, but I haven't met one person who admits to having liked D.C. Hunter," I said.

She wiped her eyes. "I know, but it's more than that. Something she's not telling us, and it's eating her alive."

"She's seeing a specialist, isn't she?"

"Her family doctor's referring her to a psychiatrist, yes." Nettie sighed as she stood to go. "If he doesn't find out what's wrong with her soon, he'll have to take me on as a patient, too."

I kissed her cheek. "Oh, come on! The man's a doctor, not a magician!" I knew I could make her smile.

"Nettie's already planning what to cook for Leslie," I told Augusta when I got home that day. "Her niece isn't due to move in for several days yet, and she's already making out menus. If anybody can get Leslie to eat, it'll be Nettie McGinnis."

Augusta laid aside the copy of Dorothy L. Sayers's *The Nine Tailors* and made room for Clementine's large head in her lap. "Speaking of food," she said, "wouldn't you like to have some of that good relish to go with those turnip greens Ben brought? That would just strike the area, don't you think?"

First I had to get past "strike the area," which I figured must mean "hit the spot." "Are you talking about chow-chow?"

She nodded. "Why, yes, that's what she called it. Lillian Preston—I was only with her briefly—used to make it every fall. Kept jars and jars of it in her pantry." Augusta smiled. "Had a bit of a zing to it."

"My grandmother made it, too," I said. "Mimmer put horseradish in hers. My brother Joel and I used to ladle on most of the jar to kill the taste of the turnip greens."

"Do you know how to make it?" Augusta reached for her apron.

"Green tomatoes and cabbage, I know, and onions, of course, but I've never made it. It takes all day to grind up all that stuff and then it has to simmer awhile—and you have to have canning jars. Smells up the house something awful." I paused. "I think Bobby Tate Murray sells something like that at the Down Home Store."

"But it wouldn't be the same." Augusta folded her arms. She was standing her ground. "Do you think your grandmother's recipe would be in that cookbook of hers?"

I knew very well it would, as I'd skipped by it often, thanking the good Lord above I didn't have to make it. I sighed. "I'll get it," I said.

"Of course we'll need a food grinder," Augusta said after reading the recipe.

"What's wrong with the food processor?" I asked. After Augusta had learned not to puree everything, she had become quite adept at using it.

"It wouldn't be the same," she said.

And all because Ben Maxwell had brought me a mess of greens.

"You want green tomatoes? Come and get 'em!" Ellis said when I called. "I'll even *pay* you to take them off my hands. Bennett always plants too many and I've pickled them, fried them, and done everything with the bloomin' things except invent a cure for the common cold. I keep hoping a killing frost will come along and do them all in!" Ellis paused. "You have a food processor, don't you?"

"Augusta wants to make it the old-fashioned way—with a *food grinder*," I whispered. "Hardheaded as a mule."

"I heard that!" Augusta said, bustling about the kitchen in her search for the biggest pots she could find.

Ellis laughed. "Where you gonna find that?"

"Jo Nell, of course. She never gets rid of anything—says you never know when *Antiques Roadshow* might come to town."

"Bring a big basket," Ellis said. She had a great big smile in her voice.

With at least a bushel of green tomatoes in the trunk of my car, I turned into my cousin's wide tree-lined street to collect what Augusta considered the necessary equipment for processing the ingredients for chow-chow. And to take my mind off what lay ahead, I listened to the local radio station that plays Elvis and the Beatles and other music that actually has a tune. As I drew closer, I saw Jo Nell picking up rubbish that had blown into her front yard, muttering evil predictions, no doubt, against the trashy people who litter. Her nasty little dog, Bojo, raced to the end of the driveway and began barking as soon as he saw me. The idea of Bojo as a speed bump made me feel almost lighthearted, but I dutifully dodged the little pest and pulled up close to the porch so I could make a dash for it. I was a second away from turning off the engine when the news came over the radio that Claymore Hornsby had been arrested for the murder of D.C. Hunter.

It took Claudia Pharr, looking harried from her day filling in at Stone's Throw Elementary, less than three minutes to hustle over from across the street, and Zee was already there with her contribution of hot peppers she said I'd need for the chow-chow. Idonia, too, appeared from somewhere in the back of the house, but I had no idea what she was doing there.

"Well, I'm not surprised," Zee said, helping herself

to a bunch of grapes from the dining room table. "I thought it was him all along, although I'll have to admit I kind of hoped it would turn out to be Willene's Neanderthal ex, especially after the way he frightened you-all the other night." She shoved a couple of grapes into her mouth and smacked daintily. "You know, I've been craving fruit for almost a week now. Willene gobbles it up as fast as I can bring it home— ate the last banana I was saving for my cereal this morning."

"Willene?" I looked from one to the other of them of them. "Willene Benson?"

My cousin Jo Nell looked kind of sheepish. "Well, she had to go somewhere, and Zee has that perfectly good guest house."

"Did everybody know but me?" I was feeling left out.

"Don't look at me," Claudia said. "I'm always the last to know anything."

"We couldn't tell anybody," Jo Nell explained, "except of course Blythe Cornelius and the person Willene's responsible to at the college—and that was only after she'd moved in with Zee." She shook her head. "Bless her heart, she's had a right hard time of it."

The very thought of that pale creepy-looking man made me furious all over again. "Do you think he'll come back?"

"I doubt it," Jo Nell said. "That judge put the fear of God into him this time. Fined him, too. Hit him in the pocketbook, where it hurts."

"I don't know why she ever married that man," Zee said. "Common as pig tracks and about as ugly as homemade lye soap. 'Course mine weren't anything to brag about either. Married twice and, except for our Melanie, of course, all I have to show for it is a season pass to the Charlotte Knights games and a passable recipe for chicken bog."

Zee searched the fruit bowl for a stray grape. "If Riley Herman does come back," she announced, "Willene swears she'll shoot him—and durned if I don't believe her!"

Jo Nell, who had been searching a top cabinet for the food grinder I needed, almost toppled off the step stool. "Shoot him with what?"

"Why, a gun, of course," Zee told her. "She bought one somewhere and doesn't know a thing about using it. Talk about your loose cannon! I told her as long as she's staying with me she'd have to put that thing where she couldn't get to it. We put it on top of that big old oak wardrobe in the upstairs hall, and that's where it is now—or it better be." Zee slammed her hand on the table. "If I ever get mad enough to kill somebody, I'll just let 'em have it with Mama's old cast-iron skillet."

Idonia looked at Claudia and me and laughed. "You mean by cooking in it or hitting them with it?"

"Go ahead and laugh if you want to," Zee said. "But *poor* Willene's not as spineless as she seems."

"Then I guess she'll be moving back to the campus now," Claudia said.

"Soon as she gets her courage up she says." Zee sighed. "Reckon I better lay in a fresh supply of fruit."

Having found the grinder, Jo Nell joined us at the kitchen table where she patted her lap for Bojo. The little dog jumped into it, then climbed her bosom to lick her face. I turned away.

"You must hear just about everything that goes on over at the campus, Lucy Nan," Zee said. "What's the consensus of opinion? Do they think the professor did it?"

"At one time or another, I think they've suspected just about everybody except the pope," I said. "And they aren't all too sure about him. Now they say D.C. had been dating her roommate's boyfriend."

Claudia frowned. "Who's that?"

"Her roommate? Sally Wooten."

"No, the boyfriend," she said.

"Tommy Jack . . . somebody. Coaches football," I told her.

"Evans," Idonia said. "Tommy Jack Evans. Named after his uncle. You know, Jo Nell, the one who married the—"

"I know who he is, Idonia. We don't need his family history," my cousin told her, "and if memory serves me right he was seeing that other girl, too."

"What other girl? I asked.

"Why, the girl from Florida—the one who drowned in the Old Lake—remember?" Jo Nell scratched Bojo's fat pink stomach. "There was something about him in the paper soon after she was killed."

Claudia massaged her fingers in thought. "I remember that. But he said they'd never dated, didn't he?"

"I don't think he exactly denied it," Jo Nell said. "Claimed they were just casual friends. I think they met at a horse show or something. Both of them liked to ride."

"Sure gets around, doesn't he? I wonder if he's involved in all this." I looked at my watch and stood. I had to make my haul at the grocery store for bell peppers, cabbage, onions, and about a vat of vinegar, and I knew it would take at least five minutes to work my way to the door.

Zee followed me to the living room. "You'd think the police would remember a thing like that, wouldn't you?"

"Maybe they know more than we give them credit for," Jo Nell said, trailing along behind us. "Those two girls were as different as apples and oranges. Now, Rachel Isaacs—I remember reading about her in the paper—seemed like such a nice young woman, smart, too." She drew in her breath. "But that D.C. Hunter— her picture was plastered all over *The Messenger*. Didn't have on enough clothes to pad a crutch."

Zee threw a flaming-pink sweater over her shoulders. "That history teacher you work with—seems she oughtta be able to tell them something," she said.

"Joy Ellen Harper? Why is that?"

"She was adviser to both of them. Willene said Blythe Cornelius looked it up in the records." With a warning look at Bojo, she bolted for the door. "Now don't use too many of those hot peppers!" she said.

What prompted Blythe to do that? I wondered as I searched for a parking place at Harris Teeter. And why hadn't she mentioned it earlier? Odder still, why hadn't Joy Ellen Harper?

Chapter Eighteen

"*Y*es, I was Rachel Isaacs's adviser." Joy Ellen closed the classroom door a little harder than usual and locked it behind her after our hands-on-history session the next day. "What is this, Lucy? You're becoming a regular Nancy Drew."

"Sorry. Just trying to figure out what those two had in common, and somebody said you might remember something—anything." (I wasn't going to tell her who it was.) "Did you know that both Rachel and D.C. dated Tommy Jack Evans?"

Joy Ellen shifted her satchel to her other hand and walked a little faster. "I knew Rachel had gone out with him some, but it wasn't anything serious. She had sort of a steady boyfriend at some college in Florida and asked me if I thought he'd understand if she went riding with Tommy Jack now and then. They were both into horses, and Rachel was shy, plus she didn't know a soul when she came here. Tommy Jack might have wanted it otherwise, but I doubt very seriously if their relationship ever got past the platonic stage."

Joy Ellen spoke to some girls who walked past, then turned back to me. "They say her boyfriend back home was devastated by her death." She paused at the door to her office. "And that's about all I know about it."

I could tell by the icicles dangling from her words that she resented my question, and I didn't blame her. "Go ahead and bop me with that briefcase," I said. "Make me memorize the dates when every pompous government official learned to write capital *I*. I'm a tactless clod and I deserve it, but I didn't mean that the way it sounded. Honest."

Joy Ellen leaned against her door and laughed. "Dammit, Lucy! You do know how to put a person in her place. Okay, I overreacted . . . didn't realize just how uptight I'd become. Gosh, I can't imagine why." She ran a hand through her hair. "Just for the heck of it, though, why *are* you so curious?"

"Do you have a few minutes? Buy you a cup of coffee."

"I'd rather have a beer, but right now I'll settle for anything that doesn't bite back," she said.

We waded through the heavy smell of French fried onion rings to an empty booth in the commons snack shop, and I told her about Nettie and Weigelia and how I'd promised to keep an eye out for Leslie and Celeste. "I'm afraid Leslie's problem is beyond me," I added, "but if anything happened to either of them while I'm here, I'd feel partially responsible."

She stirred artificial sweetener into her coffee and

sipped it slowly. "This is when I miss smoking," she said, leaning back against the scarred pine booth. "You asked about D.C. Hunter . . . Most of our advisement is in an academic capacity, and she was originally assigned to me. I met with her once to make out her schedule, but nothing seemed to suit." Joy Ellen traced a carved initial with her index finger. "I tried to work things out with her, but she missed her next appointment, and the next thing I knew she'd found another adviser. Louise Treadwell—you've met Louise—Drama Department? Said she doubted if God herself could please D.C. Hunter."

I laughed. "What about Tommy Jack? What's he like?"

"Likable enough, seems harmless." She shrugged. "Must have something."

But he didn't have Rachel Isaacs or D.C. Hunter.

My throat had begun to feel a little scratchy earlier in the day and it started to hurt in earnest as I walked to the parking lot after talking with Joy Ellen. My clothing smelled of old grease and I couldn't wait to shower, change into something loose and comfortable, and drink some of Augusta's hot spiced tea.

During class that day two rural black women who kept the craft shop at Bellawood supplied with hand-woven split-oak baskets had brought material to show the girls how it was done. The next day they would return to get them started on their own. Sisters in their seventies, Willie Banks and Annie Carver had entertained us with such wonderful stories while they wove, tucked, and twisted the pliable slats of wood, I almost forgot about my worrisome throat. Now it was back with a vengeance.

Since I was teaching at Sarah Bedford only on a temporary basis, I had been assigned to the student parking lot and I was approaching my car when I saw Sally Wooten and another girl getting out of a blue Mustang a few spaces in front of me with bags from a local mall. Suddenly a red Corvette screeched to a halt beside them and a tanned young man got out and called to Sally.

I could see that she wasn't pleased to see him, but he didn't seem discouraged. "I was hoping you'd show up if I waited long enough," he said, hurrying to catch up with her. His smile was meant to be disarming, but it wasn't working with Sally. She didn't even slow down to accommodate him. "You're wasting your time," she said.

"Look, Sally, I made a mistake. I'm sorry. D.C. never meant anything to me—not like you do, honey. You know that."

The other girl started to leave, but Sally put a hand on her arm. "No, I don't know that, Tommy Jack, and D.C. isn't here to say otherwise, is she?"

Tommy Jack Evans looked like somebody in an ad for aftershave, one with a macho name like Essence of Trail Ride or Eau de Chest Hair. Blond, tan, and good-looking, he exuded sex appeal.

"You're not being fair. At least give me a chance."

He tugged at his hair and looked forlorn. Sally hesitated, and it was all he needed. "Everybody thinks D.C. dumped me when she started seeing that professor, but that's not true." Tommy Jack shook his head and grinned. "How do I put this delicately? Your roommate was the one who came on to me. I was flattered . . . Oh, hell, I enjoyed it! But it was a fling, and it was over almost as soon as it started. Sally, I was the one who stopped seeing her. I swear it!" The coach shrugged. "To be honest, I don't think she cared—guess Hornsby was ready and waiting even then." The man's voice took on an almost childlike quality and he paused. "I've been trying to work up the courage to see you, to try and explain." He smiled and took one step closer. "Look, doll . . ."

That was a mistake. I thought Sally Wooten was going to move back, but she remained where she was, coolly regarding him, and for a minute it looked as if she might even yawn. When she spoke, her voice was low and calm. "Tommy Jack, I really don't give a shit. Bug off!"

When Sally turned and walked away, leaving the bronzed coach standing there with a bewildered look on his face, I wanted to cheer and turn cartwheels. But it was far too cold, and my throat was screaming for tea. Besides, I don't know how.

"My goodness, you look a little beneath the elements," Augusta informed me when I got home.

I rasped in answer that, yes, I did feel somewhat

under the weather, and would dearly love some of her tea. The whole house reeked of vinegar, onions, and horseradish, and my eyes began to water as soon as I stepped inside. Pint jars of chow-chow, glistening and green, marched in a neat row down the center of the table. I knew what I would be giving my friends for Christmas.

Augusta's face was flushed from the heat, but her hand was cool as she touched my forehead. "Spiced lemonade is what you need, and I'll boil up a syrup of thyme and honey. I suppose you have camphorated oil."

"I suppose I don't," I said. I hadn't seen any of that since my grandmother died. "Just let me get a shower and I think I'll live," I told her.

She nodded. "The steam should do you good, and I imagine that menthol rub will work almost as well . . . I'll cut up those old flannel pajamas I found in the rag bag."

I escaped to the shower, leaving her to assemble her antiquated medical supplies. It was a good thing I didn't have appendicitis, I thought, or she'd have me stretched out on the kitchen table while she sterilized the butcher knife.

"It's a shame you can't demonstrate all these herbal cures to my class," I told her later as I sipped hot spiced lemonade while ensconced on the sitting room sofa with pillows at my head and Clementine at my feet. Augusta warmed flannel cloths at the fireplace before placing them on my grease-coated chest, which smelled of menthol and eucalyptus and made me feel sleepy and snug.

The clanking of a spoon against glass woke me about two hours later and I sat up groggily to see Augusta waiting, spoon in hand. I made a face. "What's that?"

"A tonic of thyme, honey, and lemon juice. It will help you feel better and it's pleasant to the taste." She poured the thick liquid into a spoon.

"Augusta, I have decongestants, antihistamines, all that kind of stuff from the drugstore. That isn't going to do me any good."

"You might be surprised. A couple of spoonfuls now and two more at bedtime, and you'll feel better in the morning," Augusta insisted as I begrudgingly opened my mouth. The taste reminded me of a fragrant summer garden and felt so smooth going down she didn't have to convince me to take another.

I was still kind of wobbly when Jessica brought Teddy by in his Batman costume for trick or treat, and for once I didn't encourage them to stay. Later, feeling renewed over homemade chicken soup with celery and rice, I remembered the empty cake-mix box I'd found in the trash. "That rum cake you made the other day was wonderful," I began. "Is that a new recipe?"

Augusta was silent for a minute as she crumbled a cracker into her soup. "As you know, I dislike waste," she said, holding a napkin to her face, "and that box had been in your pantry for months. I made a few changes, of course, but I didn't expect it to taste the same—and it didn't. I believe the rum covered the taste very well, however."

I told her it tasted fine to Ben and me and tried to get a glimpse of her face, which remained averted. Was the angel *crying?* "Augusta? I didn't mean—"

Something that sounded very much like laughter escaped from behind the napkin and I snatched it away to find her attempting to keep it from erupting full-scale. She couldn't, and neither could I. "Did you really like it?" she asked finally as we both gasped for air.

"I really did," I managed to answer. "And so did Ben."

"Well, I hope you won't buy any more," she said, "because I can't remember what else I put in there."

Augusta insisted on washing the dishes and I was glad to let her. She can clean up a kitchen faster than you can say "Jack Robinson," as Mimmer used to say, but I kept her company with another cup of hot spiced lemonade.

"Have they come any closer to finding out who's behind all this evil at the college?" she asked, putting away the leftover soup.

"They arrested that disgusting Hornsby man, but I don't know if he had anything to do with killing Londus, and he wasn't even here when Carla Martinez died," I said. "To tell you the truth, I don't feel a whole lot safer with him locked away."

"I'm uneasy as well. There's someone at Sarah Bedford who is moldering inside, someone who sees the world through tainted eyes." Augusta towel-dried the stock pot until I thought she might wear a hole in it. "And it's not going to end until we find them," she said.

I shuddered in spite of the hot drink. "It must have something to do with that crazy Jabberwocky verse—but what?"

"That's what we have to find out. Do you mind if I sit in on your class tomorrow?"

"Of course not," I said. "And you should feel right at home." I told her about the basket-weaving sisters. "That is, if I'm not too sick to go to class."

But the next morning my sore throat was gone and Augusta—thank goodness—was angelic enough not to say "I told you so!"

The basket-weaving ladies visited with the girls in the classroom while a few of us carried their supplies inside, and Joy Ellen laughed when I told her about Tommy Jack Evans's comeuppance the day before. "Poor Tommy Jack! He really blew it this time, but you know what? He's probably telling the truth."

She leaned closer as we walked. "We had another surprising development last night," she whispered. "When the Drama Club met to assess their festival earnings, Shameka Dawson swore she'd taken that Frankenstein dummy down."

"Down where?" I asked.

Joy Ellen shook her head at me. "From the Tree House. Shameka was in charge of putting it away, but she and her friends were in a huge hurry to get to a party at the university, so she just untied it and left it on the platform. After all, it was only some old stuffed clothes and a mask."

I remembered Augusta's warning of the night before. "Do you think somebody *put it back up?*"

She nodded. "Somebody who knew Londus couldn't stand loose ends. They found a half-filled trash bag on the platform, too. Looks like whoever did it wasn't taking any chances. Probably left a trail of litter on the Tree House steps to lure him up there."

So rested he by the Tumtum tree, and stood awhile in thought . . .

Miriam Platt waited at the door to tell me the same thing. "Do you believe Professor Hornsby killed Londus, Miss Lucy?"

I said I couldn't think of a reason he would, unless the janitor "knew something on him."

"Sounds more like something his wife would do," Miriam said. "She was the one who was sneaking around in the middle of the night." Miriam helped me lift the basket of oak splits to a table. "I heard the police let her go, but they told her not to leave town. Looks like the professor's gonna be in there awhile. Wonder if she'll wait for him. I wouldn't."

And neither would I, but I wouldn't have come looking for that manuscript, either. I still couldn't figure out why she did it.

For the next hour and a half we wove baskets and laughed at stories until our fingers hurt and our sides ached. Annie's specialty was scary tales: witches who shed their skin and flew up the chimney, ghosts that couldn't cross water. I had heard one of her stories from my grandmother. It happened over a hundred years ago, she said, to a girl who one dark night took a dare to stick a knife into a grave. When she bent over to shove it through the dirt, it pierced the hem of her long dress, and the poor girl thought the dead person had reached up and grabbed her. She died of fright right then and there. Both Mimmer and Annie swore it was true.

Annie's sister Willie told funny stories about people she knew, like the old woman who was caught without her teeth when the preacher came to call, and the two neighbor ladies who competed for the same man's affections by cooking him good things to eat until he got so fat neither one of them would have him.

During the time they were there, Augusta had observed closely and laughed at the stories along with the rest of us, and I didn't think anyone had been aware of her until the sisters took their leave.

"I didn't want to say nothin' in front of them girls," Annie whispered as I walked with them to their car, "but I sensed a spirit back there in that room—a good spirit, mind you, so you got no cause to worry; but I'll be John Brown if I didn't hear her laugh . . . and she smelled just like strawberries."

After class Augusta and I went over to Emma P. Harris Hall to collect Leslie's study lamp and some of the other things Nettie thought she might need. Augusta had suggested we take Blythe a jar of the chow-chow, so as soon as I had stowed Leslie's things in my car we dropped in for an impromptu visit.

Blythe's two cats, Miranda and Mabel, tried to wrap themselves around my ankles when I stepped inside, and I had to spend an equal time admiring each. Blythe had been going through her recipe file before we arrived, and I saw what looked like the ingredients for a congealed fruit salad assembled on her kitchen counter.

"I thought I'd have Willene over for dinner tomorrow," she said. "She's moving back into her own place, you know, and I wanted to welcome her home." Blythe frowned at the slightly bent recipe card and held it at arm's length. "See if you can make this darn thing out, will you? This was Aunt Dorothy's Sunday standby, but I haven't made it in ages."

I read the ingredients aloud. "Where are your glasses?"

"I think they're in there on the end table, but they get so steamed up and smudged when I cook, I don't like to wear them." Blythe opened a can of pineapple and measured the juice. "Did you say six or eight ounces of liquid?"

"Eight."

She muttered something under her breath. "Well, drat it, Lucy! I can't even read the measurements. Better bring me the blasted things."

I sneaked a look at Augusta, who seemed to be getting more nearsighted by the day, yet steadfastly refused to admit it. Just last week she had sworn she saw a billy goat in the yard across the street and I had to take her over there to prove it was a planterful of ivy. "Vanity! Vanity!" I mouthed in her direction. Naturally she ignored me.

I finally located the bifocals among an array of quaint relatives on the cluttered end table. Above it on the wall hung a sepia portrait of a family gathering in a carved wooden frame. The house behind them was like many homes of that period, a two-story frame with whirls of Victorian trim; a cedar tree in the side yard reached the top of the gable. The photograph looked a lot like some I'd seen in our own family album: children in blousy white clothing sitting cross-legged on the lawn; small-waisted ladies with hair swept high; solemn men with bad haircuts and bushy mustaches.

I handed Blythe the eyeglasses. "Your old family home looks like the one where my daddy grew up. Do you know when it was taken?"

"Don't you just love it?" Blythe dumped pecans into a bowl. "That was made right around the turn of the last century, I think, and the house was somewhere in Columbia—long gone now, of course." She put on bifocals and studied the recipe. "That's my grandmother on the end. Bet she didn't weigh more than ninety pounds."

I snatched a stray pecan. "Disgusting, isn't it? But then they didn't have pizza."

"Listen! What's that?" Blythe put a warning hand on my arm.

I heard running footsteps in the hall and somebody pounded on the door. "Aunt Shug, come quick! Something awful's happened!"

Debra Hodges stood outside the door looking like she would crumble if you touched her. "Oh, Miss Lucy, am I glad to see you. Hurry—please!" She latched onto my arm and pulled me into the hall. "It's Celeste. She's gotten one of those horrible Jabberwocky poems!"

Chapter Nineteen

"That's it!" Kemper Mungo said to his cousin. "You're coming home."

Again we had collected in the shabby lounge at Emma P. Harris Hall, and Celeste, who sat next to me on the sofa, slowly raised her eyes. "Whatd'ya mean by that?"

"Just what I say. This has gone far enough. You're on somebody's hit list, Celeste, and until we find out who's responsible, you're not safe at Sarah Bedford." The muscles in Kemper Mungo's face were as taut as a banjo string, and the expression in his eyes, just plain scary.

Blythe sat on the other side of Celeste with an arm about her shoulders. "Your cousin's right, but Thanksgiving holidays are less than three weeks away. Maybe we can work something out between now and then." She looked from Kemper to Captain Hardy with an expression that begged for understanding.

"She could commute," I suggested. "Leslie's driving over here every day from Nettie's. Couldn't they come together?" I looked at the frail girl who sat across from us fiddling with her car keys. "What do you think, Leslie?"

She smiled slightly. "I'd be glad of the company."

This was not the best of situations for somebody with Leslie's emotional problems, but the detective had asked her to stay since she had been there when Celeste collected her mail.

Kemper paced the floor, shaking his head. He cast a long shadow. "That's not good enough. What's to stop them from getting to you during the day?"

Captain Hardy said something to Sergeant Acree, then turned to Celeste. "I believe we can come up with a plan to at least allow you to attend classes safely."

Celeste seemed relieved and started to say something, but her cousin still scowled. "When Weigelia hears about this, Vesuvius will sound like a burp in comparison!" he said. "I don't know what we can do unless I go to classes with her myself."

"God forbid he should learn anything," Celeste whispered aside to me.

The captain spoke in a low, calm voice. "This might be the next-best thing," he said. "We'll assign a plain-clothes policewoman to accompany Celeste on campus. Sue Starnes. She's new to the force and looks young enough so that nobody should question it."

"I thought this creep was locked up," Celeste said. "How did he manage to put that in my mailbox?"

"Somebody else could have done it," I said.

"Like Monica Hornsby. She's out and about again, I hear." It was obvious Celeste meant this for the captain.

"When was the last time you collected your mail?" he asked.

Celeste frowned as she thought. "About a week ago, I guess. Probably last Friday. My sister lives here in Stone's Throw and we talk on the phone three or four times a week, and I see my boyfriend on weekends. There really isn't a reason for anybody to write."

"A lost art," Blythe said, looking rather sad about it.

"In that case, Clay Hornsby could've been the one to put it there," Kemper said. "He wasn't arrested until Monday."

"But why? What does he have against me?" Celeste directed this to her cousin, as though he might have the answers. "I mean I understand the problem with the stolen manuscript, or the thing with D.C. getting out of hand. I can even see why he might've killed poor old Londus if he thought he knew something . . . but what have I done? It doesn't make sense."

Her roommate, Debra, had been sitting quietly on the arm of the sofa looking in need of moral support, and I would have given her some if I'd had it to spare. When she spoke, I almost had to strain to hear. "What if they've arrested the wrong person?" she said.

Blythe shook her head and sighed. "Well, at least this should be the end of it."

"What do you mean?" Celeste asked.

"I looked up those verses in the library when all this came about, and if they're taken in order, this should be the last one except for a repeat of the first verse at the end," Blythe explained. "Of course none of them make any sense."

"Amen to that," Kemper said. "Had to read that thing in high school. Went on far too long if you ask me."

"So if you count backward, discounting the first and last verses, Carla Martinez must've gotten the third one—the verse that mentions the Tumtum tree, but there's a verse *before* that one. Could there have been another victim we don't know about?" I asked the captain. "And was the verse Celeste got from the same book as the others? The same typeface and all?"

He hesitated, and I knew he was wrestling with the decision to answer me. Finally he relented. "As far as I can tell it is. A copy like the other two, not an actual page from a book."

Kemper finally sat down—much to my relief, and everyone else's, too, I imagine. "The envelope—did it have your name on it?" he asked Celeste.

She shook her head. "No, it was blank."

"Then how did—who distributes the mail around here?"

"Rosalee Burkhalter," Blythe said.

"How did Rosalee Burkhalter know whose box to put it in?" he asked.

"Apparently she didn't," Blythe told him. "But anybody can get back there. Girls leave messages in each other's boxes all the time. The door's never locked."

Kemper turned to the detective. "Exactly what did this verse say?"

"Sergeant Acree copied it down." Captain Hardy nodded to the young policeman, who flipped through his notepad looking glad for something to do. "Read it," the captain said.

"And hast thou—" The young policeman turned red, then shrugged. "I'm afraid I can't pronounce all this."

"Want me to try?" I held out my hand and he seemed relieved to turn over the notebook.

"And hast thou slain the Jabberwock?
Come to my arms, my beamish boy!
O frabjous day! Callooh! Callay!"
He chortled in his joy.

Kemper glared at me. "You gonna tell me you know what that means?"

I threw up my hands. "Hey, I didn't write it. It's just nonsense verse. It's meant to poke fun."

"Well, whoever's sending them is dead serious," Captain Hardy said.

"I never was a scholar of Lewis Carroll's works," Ellis admitted the following Monday, "but I don't think those verses mean a damn thing except some nutcase has a thing for jumbled verse and killing people."

Nettie wet a finger to knot a thread. "The verses

aren't the only thing that's jumbled. I think there's a twisted logic behind all this. Whoever is responsible is convinced it's for a reason."

"Well, they're smart enough not to leave any prints," I whispered aside to her. "Kemper said the only ones they found on the note were from Celeste and her roommate."

My neighbor had stitched together the squares for our friendship quilt and added the backing. Now we gathered around the quilting frame she had set up in the back of Joy Ellen's classroom, where students sat elbow to elbow talking softly among themselves. Now and then a quilter let go with a muttered swear word when the thread broke or a finger was jabbed, and occasionally, laughter sprang in quiet little bunny hops around those clustered there.

Celeste sat at the far end serenely drawing her needle in and out in tiny straight stitches. Her "bodyguard," Sue Starnes, sat a little apart from the rest of us sewing bright scraps together—for a pillow cover, she said. She was introduced as an interested student who was auditing the class, but I think everybody knew why she was really there.

Celeste had moved back home with Weigelia and her husband, Roy, over the weekend and would be commuting to class with Leslie until the police were convinced of Clay Hornsby's guilt, and her classmates had rallied around her. I saw one student I had considered to be a bit of a self-centered snob glance up at Celeste with a worried frown, then smile when their eyes met. Debra Hodges touched her roommate's arm and whispered something that made her laugh; and Celeste's fellow students surrounded her, I noticed, as they walked from one class to another.

At least one positive thing had come from all this, I thought. We were stitching together more than quilting squares here.

Finally Celeste herself came out and asked what some of us were reluctant to put into words. "Do you think it's an ethnic thing?" She looked around at the quilters, who suddenly became absorbed in their work. "I mean, I'm black, and one of the girls was Jewish."

"If case you haven't noticed, I'm black, too," one of the girls spoke up. "Does that mean I'm next?" She laughed. "With all the sisters here at Sarah Bedford, he's gonna have his work cut out for him!"

"And several of the girls here are Jewish," Miriam Platt said. "But what about D.C.? Where did she fit in?"

The girl next to her made a face. "Do they have a category for pain in the butt?"

"D.C. *was* different, but in another way," Joy Ellen said after the groaning subsided. "She must have been extremely unhappy—or lonely, to say the least."

Celeste smoothed her stitches with a slender brown hand. "Maybe we shouldn't be talking about her. After all, the poor girl *is* dead."

"And she's just as unlikable now as she was when she was alive," Miriam said, snipping off her thread.

• • •

"I wonder if Celeste might have a point," I said to Ellis after class. "Carla Martinez was probably of Hispanic heritage. Maybe there's more here than we realized. Could we be dealing with some kind of kooky white supremacist? Somebody who's pinpointing at random students of different ethnic groups?"

"No way! Think about it, Lucy Nan. D.C. Hunter was as white bread as they come. It all comes down to that confounded Jabberwocky thing."

Nettie was riding home with her niece and Celeste, and Ellis and I had stopped at the campus snack shop to get a sugar fix. In the process of growing up together, the two of us had progressed from jawbreakers and BB Bats to anything chocolate, with or without ice cream on top.

Now Ellis licked chocolate sauce from the back of her spoon. "There are other verses," she reminded me. "You told me yourself it might have started even before that girl fell from the Tree House."

"Probably, but who would know?"

"What about that lady who lives in the dorm? Maybe she would remember," Ellis suggested.

"Blythe? She hasn't been here that long, and she wasn't even in town when Carla Martinez was killed." I polished off my cookies and cream. "Who do we know who goes *way* back . . ."

Ellis hesitated with her spoon in midair. "*What? Who?* You've thought of somebody. Tell me!"

I smiled. "Dean Holland. He spends most of his time

in La-La Land, but Blythe says he can quote "The Thanatopsis" word for word. Remember that thing? It goes on forever. Maybe he can tell us something about the Jabberwocky."

"Do you think we could get Augusta to go with us?" Ellis asked.

"Just try and keep me away," a voice behind us said.

Chapter Twenty

*S*hould we wake him?" Ellis whispered.

Dean Holland slept with his head back against the ancient leather chair in his cluttered office. The dark-paneled walls were covered in framed degrees, certificates, and black-and-white photographs of classes, most of whom had observed at least their twenty-fifth reunion. His snore sounded like a twig caught in the spokes of a bicycle.

"Maybe we should make a noise," I said.

"You could set off fireworks and he wouldn't hear it." Blythe Cornelius, who had ushered us in, stood behind us with her hands on her hips and smiled at the old man.

"We could come back." I glanced at Ellis, who looked at her watch.

"No, no. He'd be upset if he missed you." Blythe lowered her voice. "Likes the attention, you know." She touched him gently on the shoulder. "Company, Dean Holland. Somebody here to see you." She introduced us, which was a good thing because the dean hadn't a clue as to who I was, even though we had spoken on several occasions.

He didn't seem embarrassed to be caught napping, but insisted on standing until Ellis and I were seated. "Now, what can I do for you ladies today?" he asked after Blythe closed the door behind her.

Augusta sat in the wide window seat that over-looked the main campus, now dreary with lengthening shadows as evening approached. She looked almost like a college student herself with her long loose sweater of dusty teal and crinkly broomstick skirt. Her necklace glowed softly with the colors of cranberry and gold as she threaded the stones through her fingers, and I found myself almost hypnotized by the motion until Ellis gave me a rude jab.

"Dean Holland, do you remember a girl named Carla Martinez?" Speaking in a loud voice, I told him what I suspected about the student who was killed by a fall from the Tree House several years before.

He nodded as I spoke. "Saddest thing," he said with an appropriately morose expression. "Music student. Everyone was shocked, but we just assumed that was an accident."

"There doesn't seem to be any account of a note left behind or a verse like the other girls got," I said, "but that doesn't mean she didn't receive one. It might have been thrown away."

The dean tapped the arm of his chair with a gnarly finger. "You phoned today? I'm afraid Mrs. Cornelius neglected to tell me." He smiled. "But I always have time to visit with friends."

Lucy Nan, you must not under any circumstances look at Ellis Saxon! I glanced instead at Augusta, who gave me a "Don't you dare laugh!" look. Leaning forward so the dean might hear me better, I spoke a little louder. "Dean Holland, do you remember if there were any other student deaths that may or may not have taken place before Carla Martinez was killed?"

He cupped a hand over his ear and gave me an apologetic smile.

Ellis nudged me with her elbow. "What about the Jabberwocky verses?" she bellowed in what I call her "green witch" voice. Her early experience as a Girl Scout leader has honed her hollering skills to perfection. "Dean Holland, do you have any idea why anybody would use those particular verses? There must be a reason."

He leaned back and closed his eyes and I prayed he wouldn't doze off again. "Jabberwocky. From *Through the Looking-Glass*, of course. This last girl who died, and the one before . . ." He straightened abruptly and opened his eyes. "There was a group once, if I remember correctly. Yes. Kind of a club—called themselves the Jabberwocks, I think. Something like that." Dean Holland rubbed a white-whiskered chin. "Funny, I'd forgotten that. Wish I could remember . . . I'm trying to picture some of the girls who were in it . . . peculiar little bunch . . ."

"When?" I said, trying not to shout. "The year—do you remember the year?"

The chair squeaked as he rose and walked to the

window, where Augusta stepped deftly aside. "Hazel Godfrey was housemother at Emma Harris at the time. That was back when we still had housemothers. Girls had rules and regulations, had to be in at a certain time. Anyway, I remember Hazel being somewhat vexed by this little group. Dressed in black a lot."

"And when would that be?" Ellis asked.

The dean stepped easily around an obstacle course of stacked books, boxes of papers, and a bronze bust of somebody I didn't recognize. The worn green carpet was spotted with what appeared to be coffee stains and cigarette burns. Blythe had said he wouldn't let her touch a thing in there.

"Had to be sometime in the early or mid-seventies," he said, wheeling about briskly, I thought, for somebody his age. "Hazel retired not long after that. Bought a little place in Chester to be near her daughter."

"Do you know if she's still there?" Ellis asked, and the dean laughed. "Well, if she is," he said, "she's darn near as old as I am!"

But Hazel Godfrey, we learned when we called the city hall in Chester, had died several years before. "Her heart," I was told by the woman who answered the phone in the Records Department. "Her daughter Glenda was secretary at the middle school here for years. I think Glenda bought herself a condo in Charlotte after she retired."

"Too bad we're not looking for information on Hazel's daughter," I told Ellis and Augusta after relating the conversation.

"What about the college annual?" Augusta suggested. "Wouldn't they have some from that period in the library here?"

"Of course! And if that doesn't work, we can try the Alumnae Society," Ellis said. "If only we had a name—just one name! It's a little awkward to call a perfect stranger and ask her if she wore black clothing and acted peculiar in college."

We found a quiet alcove in the library to go through the stack of *Lantern*s, which is what Sarah Bedford calls its yearbooks, starting with the late 1960s, just to be on the safe side. After Ellis and I amused ourselves over the love beads, ironed hair, and ragbag clothing, we moved on to some serious scanning. The first book I examined was dedicated to Miss Henrietta Westfield, the retiring dean of women, beneath whose photograph it read: "Unto the pure all things are pure." And when I looked at her formidable face I didn't doubt it.

"I'm sure she was a fine, upstanding person of great value to the college," Augusta said in regard to our not-so-silent snickering. I noticed, however, that her mouth twitched as she said it.

"Augusta's right," Ellis said. "Will you get on with it, Lucy Nan? We don't have time for this. Besides, the old bat's ghost is probably hanging around somewhere waiting to shove a bookcase on top of us."

I set the heavy book aside. "Nothing here, anyway."

"I think we should look for groups or clubs. They might have been organized." Augusta looked closely at a photograph and turned the page.

We had worked up to 1974 before we found it, and then it was only a snapshot set at an angle on a page of similar informal photographs. The picture showed a black-clad group of seven girls in comical poses by the fountain in the commons. Each had a book balanced on her head; one was blowing a bubble; a cigarette dangled from one girl's lips, and another clenched what looked like a lily in her teeth. The caption gave no names, only the identifying line: "The Mad Jabberwocks."

Augusta sighed. "There they are—at last!"

Ellis shook her head and smiled. "Silly things. Thought they owned the world. Remember that feeling?"

"Vaguely." I examined the black-and-white photograph until my vision blurred. "Does anybody have a magnifying glass? I can't tell a thing about their faces."

Ellis fumbled in her purse. "I've got one somewhere. Have you noticed the print in telephone books keeps getting smaller and smaller—not to mention menus and medicine bottles?"

But even with Ellis's magnifying glass the faces in the snapshot were too small to make out. "Do you think we'd recognize them in a class picture?" I asked.

Ellis flipped through the pages of the yearbook. "For all their trying to be different, they looked pretty much like everybody else—except for the girls with teased hair and preppy clothing. All we can do is copy a few names—like the class president and some of the more involved students who would be more likely to keep in touch." She shrugged. "Guess our next move is the Alumnae Society."

We began with ten names, which Ellis and I divided equally between us. The harried woman who runs the alumnae office was just getting ready to leave for the day when the two of us invaded her domain, leaving Augusta to browse through a few more yearbooks at the library. It took a few minutes of wheedling, but she reluctantly gave us the addresses we wanted.

It was dark by the time we started home, and Ellis stopped by for a glass of wine before going home to start supper. Augusta hadn't had any luck finding more pictures of the Mad Jabberwocks, she said, but a tray of fruit and cheese waited for us by the sitting room fire.

"Here's to the Jabberwocks!" Ellis said, lifting her glass. "We're getting closer now."

"Which means you must be extremely careful, assuming the man the police arrested turns out to be innocent," Augusta reminded us. "Londus Clack's death should prove that the killer isn't going to stop with college students if you get too close to the truth. He would have absolutely no compunction about getting rid of you as well."

"I thought that was your job," I teased. "Aren't you supposed to be looking after us?"

Augusta selected an apple slice and a piece of cheese from the tray. "You know very well I can't intrude in things like that," she said with a slight edge to her voice. "I can only do my best to guide you, as I am doing now."

"I know, I know. Don't get in an angelic flap about it, Augusta," I said. "We'll be careful—I promise."

Augusta considered that as she sipped her wine. "I wish you had promised that sooner. I would be remiss in my duties if I didn't remind you that this killer—whoever that might be—is probably someone you know, and it's likely they're aware of what you're doing."

Ellis stood as she drained her glass. "On that comforting note I'll take my leave," she announced. "And I'm going to start calling the people on my list tonight. The sooner we get to the bottom of this, the better!"

For supper Augusta served roast chicken, fresh asparagus with lemon-herb sauce, and a rice casserole, and I bragged on it so often she told me to stop. She was still miffed, I could tell, over my flippant remarks earlier in the evening.

"Augusta, I'm sorry if I upset you," I told her. "Frankly, I'm frightened every time I set foot on that campus. I suppose that's just my way of putting on a brave front."

"I'm not upset, Lucy Nan, I'm concerned about you—and Ellis as well." She patted my hand. "Sometimes being frightened is not a bad thing."

I put away the supper dishes, and while Augusta mended, phoned the first three people on my list. A man answered at the first number I reached and told me his wife was on a business trip and wouldn't be back until Friday. No one was at home at the second address, and the third woman said she didn't remember any Jabberwocks—mad or otherwise—and did well to remember her own name. I could hear what sounded like about five dogs barking in the background. I had a cup of orange-spice tea and a hot shower, and put the other two on the back burner.

Ellis phoned me at Bellawood the next morning as I was going over the December schedule with Genevieve Ellison, who heads the plantation's volunteers. "I've got one!" she yelled in her megaphone voice.

"One what?"

"One of the class of '74, you batter brain, and she actually remembers the Jabberwocks. I've got a couple of names right here. Want me to give them a call?"

"Without me? Are you kidding? Why don't you come by after I get home tonight? We'll call them together."

"Better still, you come here—and bring Augusta. Bennett's investment club meets tonight—frankly, though, I think they just get together to eat and play poker. Come for dinner. I'll add water to the gruel."

"I can hardly wait," I said.

The chicken stew was better than good, and so were the homemade biscuits and spiced apples Ellis served with it. Oh, sure, she takes shortcuts now and then just like the rest of us, but sometimes I find myself looking at my old friend as she shoves a loaf of bread into the oven with one hand and whips up her elegant apricot pound cake with the other, and I wonder where this domestic person came from. She wasn't in the skinny, flat-chested sixth grader who gave Elroy Rippey, the boy next door, a bloody lip for making fun of her braces. And I don't remember seeing her in the lanky high school freshman who refused to take home economics and planned a career in archaeology. She must've sneaked out when nobody was looking.

And Bennett Saxon couldn't be happier. I watched as he brushed a stray lock of hair from her face and kissed her cheek on his way out the door.

"Hmm . . . you smell like strawberries," he said as he gave me a good-bye hug.

Witnessing the husbandly affection, I'll admit I had an awkward "Charlie moment," when sadness settles like a huge rock in my midriff and I long for my husband of twenty-nine years. But I can't allow it to linger. "Looks like you've outdone yourself on the gruel," I said to my hostess as she poured water in our glasses.

We didn't linger over dessert, as all of us were eager to find out more about the Mad Jabberwocks. "You go first," Ellis said, shoving a notepad in my hand. "I'm too nervous."

My hand shook as I dialed the Greenville number.

Sylvia (Bates) Prater laughed when I reminded her about the snapshot in the *Lantern*. "We were going to change the world! Well, maybe it's not too late." She and another "Jabberwock" had graduated that year, she told me, but they promised to stay in touch with the five who remained at Sarah Bedford. "We did pretty well for a while," she said. "But you know how it is. I married a minister and we've moved from pillar to post. Vera went with a newspaper in Charleston, and the last I heard, she was still there."

"What about the other five?" I asked. "Did they all return to Sarah Bedford the next fall?"

"Oh, yes, and I kept up with them for several years. Eva Jean Eaton married a Philbeck and lives in some little town in North Carolina—Elkin, I think, unless she's moved . . . and I still exchange Christmas cards with Audrey Wallace—Tate her name is now. I'm ashamed to say I haven't seen either of them in almost twenty years."

Eva Philbeck, I remembered, was the other name Ellis had been given to call. "I think I still have Vera Leonard's home phone number if you want it, or you might try her at the newspaper." Sylvia Prater paused. "Are you with the alumnae bulletin? Is this for a feature story or something? I'm surprised anybody even remembers the Mad Jabberwocks."

She sounded so cheerful I hated to give her the bad news, but I thought she should know. I told her about the verses. "Two girls have been murdered in the last few years—maybe more."

"Dear God, I read something about that in the paper but I didn't realize it was anything like that. What can

237

that possibly have to do with us? Seven girls who happened to live in the same dorm! We might've been a bit irreverent, and if we'd come along a few years earlier we might have been hippies, but we were too chicken to rebel."

There was silence on the line, during which time I think Sylvia Prater tried to convince herself the murders had nothing to do with seven girls who, over thirty years ago, longed to defy convention.

"Because of the verses, we believe there's a connection with the group you belonged to," I said, "and it's essential that I get in touch with the rest of them."

"Oh, everybody knows that silly old poem," she told me. But she gave me the names of the members.

Augusta, Ellis, and I sat at the Saxons' kitchen table with the list in front of us. Sylvia and her friend Vera Leonard still lived in South Carolina; unless Eva Philbeck had moved, she was probably in North Carolina, and Audrey Wallace Tate owned a dance studio in upstate New York. That left Irene Friedman, Dorothy Cobb, and Maggie Talbot unaccounted for. Augusta found their class pictures in the yearbook: the two solemn seniors in black drape and pearls; a couple of straight-haired juniors with confident faces, and three sophomores who didn't look old enough to be out of high school.

As students at Sarah Bedford they had thumbed their noses as much as they dared. Now, was one or more of them demanding attention in a shocking and horrifying way?

Chapter Twenty-one

$\mathcal{E}$va Jean Philbeck was on her way out the door when we reached her at her home in Elkin. She still coached drama at the high school there, she explained, and they were rehearsing for their holiday production. I told her I was interested in the Mad Jabberwocks, but I didn't tell her why.

"Oh my goodness . . . you're talking about another time altogether. It's been so long since I've heard from any of those girls: Dorothy, Irene . . . Audrey lives somewhere up north, I think, and Maggie died several years ago."

For a few seconds she didn't speak, and the silence weighed a ton. "Is anything wrong? Why are you asking about the Jabberwocks?"

I suspected that if I told her the truth, that would be the end of it. There was something in her voice that warned me. If only I could see her, talk with her face-to-face. "I'm working with a history class at Sarah Bedford," I told her, "and in looking through some old annuals we came across a photograph of the Jabberwocks. My friend thought it would make an interesting feature for the alumnae bulletin." There, that wasn't lying. Not really. "I've spoken with Sylvia Prater," I said.

"Sylvia *who?* Oh, Sylvia *Bates.* She was a year ahead of me, you know."

And what did that matter? I wondered. But it

seemed important to Eva Jean Philbeck.

Joy Ellen and I had planned a field trip to visit Miss Corrie Walraven, the soap-making lady who lived in the mountains above Elkin. Would it be convenient, I asked, to meet somewhere? I promised not to take more than a few minutes of her time.

"Well . . . this is a busy time of year for me. I can't guarantee you I'll be free."

"Why don't I just call when I'm in the area?" I suggested. "And if you have a few minutes to spare, maybe we can get together."

Ellis stood at my elbow. "Well, what'd she say?" she asked when I hung up the phone. "Is she going to meet with you?"

"She doesn't want to. That's obvious, but I don't think she knew how to avoid it. Seems I shook her up. She wasn't expecting this."

Ellis shrugged. "That's not surprising. After all, it's been over thirty years."

"But don't you think it's strange that as close as these girls seemed to be, they didn't care enough to keep in touch?"

"Maybe there's something they want to forget," Augusta said.

Paula Shoemaker sat demurely at the quilting frame making dainty stitches. "Looks like they'll have to rule out the manuscript motive if they want to get a conviction on Horny Hornsby," she said.

Joy Ellen shook her head and laughed. "Why, Paula!

Whatever would your great-great grandma say if she could hear the way you talk? Do you think your ancestors carried on like that at their quilting bees?"

"Isn't that why they had them?" Debra Hodges spoke up. "I mean, that is where they shared all their gossip, isn't it?"

"What gossip?" Celeste edged nearer. "Did I miss something?"

Paula smoothed a pucker. "Well, you know Ernestine, the cleaning woman who comes to Emma Harris?"

Celeste nodded. "The one who 'threw out' almost half those chocolate chip cookies Weigelia made for me. I know very well she ate 'em. What happened? Hope she got a stomachache!"

"She said the manuscript Monica found behind the trophy case wasn't there when she cleaned in the lounge a couple of days earlier. Told Aunt Shug a pen rolled under there when she was mopping, and it looked like a good one, so she got down on her hands and knees to poke it out and there was nothing back there except dust. That policeman came and questioned her yesterday—that one with the red hair—and Ernestine told him she would've noticed something as big as a box back there."

"So where *did* Monica find it?" Debra asked.

"Brought it herself, I'll bet," Miriam said.

"Why would she pretend to find the manuscript, then let herself get caught taking it?" Debra looked at her classmates' faces and flushed. "Oh. You mean she meant to— She *planned* it that way so it would look like D.C. had hidden it there and that *she, Monica,* was looking for it to save her sorry husband's hide. What a rotten thing to do!"

"Oh, I don't know," Paula said. "I call it sweet revenge. Or it would've been if it had worked. The case against the creep would have been stronger if the police thought D.C. was using that manuscript for blackmail."

"Now they'll probably let him go. Too bad Ernestine had to pick that week to mop under there," Troll said. "But what was Monica doing upstairs in D.C.'s room that night?"

"I suppose she thought if she made enough noise someone would follow her," I said. "And we did."

"He still had a motive," Celeste said, pulling her stitches tight. "And I'll feel a lot safer if that man stays in jail where he belongs."

I thought about the afternoon Ellis and I saw Monica Hornsby in the old shed on back campus. She must have been looking for a place to leave the manuscript then, but since the shed had already been carefully searched, decided on the dormitory.

"Hey! Guess who's back on campus?" Miriam said. "That little mousy nutritionist. The one whose ex-husband was arrested for stalking. I saw her bringing some things into her apartment yesterday, so he must be gone for good."

Debra tugged at her thread. "I heard they warned him not to get within fifty miles of her—but what if he does? She'll always have that hanging over her, won't she? Some night when she least expects it, he might just step out and—"

"Will somebody please pass the thread?" I said. "Is anybody going someplace exciting for Thanksgiving?" I had seen the look on Celeste Mungo's face and it sickened me to know that one person, just by copying a verse from a poem, could be responsible for practically scaring somebody to death.

Jo Nell had asked me to deliver an old end table she'd had in her attic for Willene to refinish for her living room, so I took it by there after class and found her hemming curtains for her kitchen. The curtains were yellow ruffled and not at all like Willene. In fact, Willene didn't even seem like Willene. Maybe it was her chic new hairstyle or soft, flattering blouse. Or maybe it was the gun she kept handy.

"Lucy! I'm so glad you could come by, and thank you for bringing the table. I know just where I'll put it." The radiance from her toothy smile almost made my eyes water, but I was happy to see her more relaxed and less rabbitlike than before. "I thought I'd try a different kind of painting technique," she said. "Sort of a marbled effect—maybe in a muted turquoise. And I've found just the rug for this room.

"I've never been able to do much in the way of decorating," she confided, "since I wasn't sure how long it would be before . . ."

Willene Benson smiled as she took me by the arm.

"Well, let's hope those days are over. Now let me show you the wallpaper I've picked for the kitchen, and I'll need to get some pictures framed, too. These walls look so bare, don't they?" She laughed. "Maybe Blythe will lend me some of her relatives."

I was in a hurry to get to the grocery store before the late-afternoon rush, but Willene seemed so happy to have company, I stayed for a glass of iced tea.

"Tell me about your history class," she said as we sat in her tiny kitchen. "I hear you've been working on a quilt."

I nodded. "Another few sessions should do it, and tomorrow we'll be going to Alleghany County in North Carolina way up in the Blue Ridge Mountains to learn how to make soap. Miss Corrie says it takes a while, so we're prepared to make a day of it." I didn't tell her about the little side trip I had planned.

The unpaved road to Corrie Walraven's house near the little town of Sparta twisted through the Blue Ridge Mountains like a russet apple peeling. We had left in a caravan from Sarah Bedford at a little after nine, stopping in North Wilkesboro for an early lunch.

I had convinced Roger and Jessica that Teddy would benefit as much from our visit with Miss Corrie as he would from a day in the first grade, and fortunately his teacher agreed. Now he sat with Troll and Paula in the backseat, calling out inane jokes until the two students finally gave up on being polite and stopped laughing altogether.

Ellis, who had come along for our hoped-for meeting with Eva Jean Philbeck, sat in front with Augusta and me. I knew Augusta was there, although neither Ellis nor I could see her and I was glad. When you're in close quarters with other people, her presence becomes a bit distracting.

"Watch closely now, Teddy, and maybe you'll see a deer," Ellis suggested.

"Or maybe even a bear," I said, but Teddy was bored with looking out the window and the scenery didn't interest him. I remembered when, at his age, I'd felt the same, but now I saw the landscape in a state of basic beauty, unadorned and waiting for winter.

Most of the hardwoods were bare now, but a few faded amber and burgundy leaves mingled with the brown. Pine, spruce, and cedar greened the surrounding mountains in swirls and patches like a design on a giant quilt.

Teddy kicked the back of my seat. "Are we almost there yet?"

"Just about," I said, "and quit kicking the back of my seat."

"I'm hungry."

"Again? We just ate. Ask Aunt Ellis if she'll give you a cookie." I had come prepared with his favorite peanut butter kisses. I was beginning to wonder, however, if I had made a mistake by bringing along a six-year-old.

"There's a pretty waterfall near here, Teddy," Ellis said, handing him a cookie. "Linville Falls—not too far away. Maybe we can see it on the way home if we have time."

"Where did he fall?" Teddy giggled and repeated his joke. His seatmates ignored him.

"He fell into a dark cave with bears in it because he asked too many silly questions, and nobody's seen him since," I told him. "Now everybody needs to help me look for the wooden sign where we turn. Miss Corrie says it's red and says 'Honey, Apples, and Cider.' Should be coming up soon."

Just ahead of us in a cloud of orange dust I saw Kemper Mungo and his carload turn into a narrow lane, bumping over ruts and stones. The sign was on our right. Since Sue Starnes, Celeste's customary police escort, was off duty that day, Kemper had stepped in with a purpose.

Some people might call Corrie Walraven's house a shack, but it looked snug enough to me, and it was home to Miss Corrie and her brother Henry. The unpainted house with its rust-streaked tin roof had weathered to a rain-washed gray, and it stood in a bare-swept yard between a great gnarled oak and the prettiest blue spruce I've ever seen.

Somebody hollered "Welcome!" as we pulled into the yard, and two barking hounds, three flapping chickens, and Miss Corrie hurried to greet us.

I recognized Corrie Walraven from my childhood storybooks. She was the little old woman who went to market to buy a fat pig. Or maybe she was the one who chased the runaway johnnycake. She wore a knitted shawl over her crisp blue cotton dress, and an apron, made from bleached sacking, I learned later, covered the front of it.

"Lord, it's good of you'uns to come! I don't get much company way up hyare—and lookit you!" She held out her arms to Teddy, who went right into them. "Don't know when I've had a young'un like you to come visit old Corrie."

Corrie Walraven was old. Just how old it was hard to tell because her skin had a crinkled manila-paper look, although her blue eyes were lively and bright. She wore her white hair, streaked with yellow, in a little apple-size knot on top of her head, and when she smiled—which was often—it looked as though about every other tooth was missing.

Augusta took to her at once, as did Teddy, and practically fastened herself to the woman's side, taking in every word. As soon as Joy Ellen and the others arrived, Miss Corrie took us around to the back of the house where she had a fire laid under a black iron pot. The ground had been covered with frost when we started out that morning, but the sun had mellowed the earth so that by the time we got the fire going I felt comfortable in a sweater. Cold-natured Augusta, however, hovered as close to the blaze as she could get.

Kemper, I noticed, seldom let his cousin out of his sight, and Celeste bore it with as much good humor as possible, but I could tell it was wearing on her. When he followed her to the woodpile that afternoon, Celeste stopped in mid-stride. "Will you give me a

247

break, Kemper! The woodpile's only a few feet away, and there's nobody up here but us. I feel like we're stuck together with superglue!"

"At least you can still *feel,*" her cousin said. "That's more than those other girls can do."

The wheels of justice had better grind a lot faster, I thought, if those two were going to remain on speaking terms.

Miss Corrie showed us how to make lye by pouring water over hickory ashes in a crude wooden trough, then collecting the liquid that ran through. She added this to an assortment of fat scraps and boiled the mixture until it thickened. Teddy and the girls took turns stirring it with a wooden paddle, coughing and rubbing their eyes as the smoke searched them out.

With her apron, Miss Corrie fanned the smoke from her face. "It's just me and Henry now, so I don't make lye soap much anymore unless some of them ladies in Elkin or Wilkesboro take a notion to sell some at a church fair or something," she said. Henry, she explained, was her "baby" brother, who worked at the sawmill down the road a piece.

"Now, if it was spring," she told us, "we could make this soap smell real good with some of them wild ginger leaves—that's what Mama Doc used to put in it. That woman knows a purpose for just about everything that grows, but I reckon store-bought spices will do near 'bout as well." Miss Corrie showed Teddy how to tie whole cloves and cinnamon sticks into a piece of cheese cloth, then added it to the pot. When the soap was thick enough she poured some into a square enamel pan to harden overnight. "You-all take this along with you now and you oughtta be able to get a few bars out of it by tomorry." When Joy Ellen and I protested, she laughed and flapped her sooty apron at us. "Lord, I don't need that ol' pan no more! Just keep it. Now you-all come in and have some apple pie afore you go."

We sat at a long table covered in blue-checkered oil-cloth in our hostess's simple kitchen with its white plank walls and worn linoleum. Augusta took delight in inspecting the row of African violets in pink, blue, and lavender that thrived on the windowsill, and a white cat named Aunt Mamie that was as big as Blythe's two put together entertained everyone just by twitching her long tail.

Celeste scraped her plate clean and stared longingly at mine. "Think again," I told her, and she looked at me and laughed. "You know," she said, "I've felt safer here today than I have since this awful Jabberwocky mess began."

Later I would remember what she said.

When we got ready to leave, Miss Corrie insisted on seeing us to our cars, then stood waving as we made our way down the long twisting drive. "You-all come back now!" she called to me. "And bring that pretty lady with you."

"What lady?" I hollered, waving good-bye.

"Why, the one with the long sparkly necklace and candlelight hair!" Her keen blue eyes didn't blink.

Chapter Twenty-two

I phoned Eva Jean Philbeck from a gas station just outside the little town of Elkin and asked her if we could meet somewhere for dinner. "I realize it's late, but we've been making lye soap up near Sparta and it took longer than I thought. We'd like for you to be our guest, of course."

"My goodness, that does sound tempting, but we're babysitting tonight. In fact, my son and his wife are due to drop him off in a few minutes."

"Really? How old is he?"

"Matthew's four months. He's our first, and his parents don't like to leave him often, but some friends are having a dinner party, so we get to have Matthew all to ourselves for a while."

Matthew. She'd said his name twice. Loved saying it, just as I did Teddy's. Sometimes I suffer through entire conversations waiting for somebody to ask me about my grandson, and when they don't, I tell them about him anyway. "Four months!" I said. "Oh, you're in for a treat." And babbled on about crawling and toddling and adorable first words.

"And how old is your grandchild?" There was polite interest in her voice.

"Teddy's six, and he came along with us today. I hoped he would learn something from the experience, but it's been a long drive and I'm afraid we wore him out."

The woman laughed. "Well, he'll grow up fast enough." She paused, waiting for me to go on with it or hang up. It was obvious she wasn't going to invite us over.

"Mrs. Philbeck, I know this is a terribly inconvenient time for you, but this Mad Jabberwock issue is more serious than I led you to believe. My friend Ellis is with me, as well as my grandson, and I give you my word we won't stay long, but if it's at all possible I'd like to see you this afternoon."

She sighed, and I was afraid she was going to say no or hang up on me. "I knew all along something would come of this. All right, come on." The joy in her voice was gone as she gave me directions to a two-story brick on a cul-de-sac called Graylag Drive, which sounded sort of like the way I felt.

Earlier, Paula and Troll, the two girls who had ridden with us, had met their dates at a local McDonald's and would go from there to a fraternity function at nearby Appalachian State, and Teddy, having been treated to a chocolate shake, was currently engrossed in a puzzle book.

"What if she's *the one?*" Ellis whispered when we pulled up in front of the house. I knew what she meant because I'd thought of the same thing. The possibility that one of the Mad Jabberwocks could be responsible for the killings was becoming more and more likely, and Eva Jean Philbeck was the one who lived the closest. How could this loving grandmother be guilty of something so totally evil? But of course she hadn't always been a loving grandmother.

A blue car was parked in the driveway, and as we started up the walk a young couple came out of the front door, then turned and waved to someone who stood behind them. They both smiled and spoke when they saw us, but didn't stop as they cut across the lawn to their car. They looked to be in their mid-twenties, and the man walked with a pronounced limp.

"Our son Ken and his wife, Anne," Eva Jean explained as she ushered us into her living room. "I'd show off my grandson, but he just got to sleep." She introduced me to her husband, Bill, who invited Teddy to watch football with him in the small paneled den. He didn't seem alarmed at our being there, so she must not have told him of her concern. And the woman was definitely nervous. She smiled and said all the proper, polite things, but there was a tense look in her eyes and her hands were never still.

Mrs. Philbeck seated Ellis and me on the sofa and took the wing chair opposite, then thought better of it and stood, offering coffee. Augusta, standing in the doorway, brightened considerably at the prospect but seemed resigned to waiting for her favorite beverage until we got home.

"Thank you, but I know we must be delaying your dinner," I said. "And I really don't want to take any more of your time than necessary." I glanced at Augusta, who gave me a "Get on with it!" look. "I suppose you've been hearing about the murders at Sarah Bedford," I said.

"Yes, the girl they found in the old stone shed. Why, we bought candy and soft drinks there! And if I remember right a few years ago there was a drowning in the lake where we used to swim."

Ellis looked at her face-on. She's good at that. "You know about the verses then?"

The woman picked at a thread in her skirt and nodded. "Of course I do. I just can't understand what it has to do with us. I—I tried, but I can't get in touch with anyone. Irene's in some kind of hospital—nerves, her husband says. I left a message on Audrey's answering machine, but she never returned my call, and I don't even know where Dorothy is." Mrs. Philbeck stood and walked to the window and back. I had never seen anybody actually wring their hands before, but she did.

When she sat again it was as if she had suddenly run out of energy. "Well, I don't care if they like it or not. I can't keep it to myself any longer. This has to be about what happened to Carolyn Steele."

Ellis looked at me and mouthed the words I was thinking: *Who's Carolyn Steele?*

"Carolyn was a freshman in the fall of my junior year," she explained. "A sweet girl—I liked her, but kind of . . . well, I guess you'd call her naive.

"The Mad Jabberwocks, as you may have guessed by the name, were not a serious group. We just liked to have fun—and poke fun, too—probably more than we should've. There were only the five of us left that year and we all lived in the east wing of Emma Harris

Hall." Eva Jean smiled briefly. "Carolyn wanted to join. Heck, there wasn't any joining to it. You either belonged or you didn't, but how do you tell somebody that? She was lonely, I think. Didn't have much family."

She pressed her hands together and looked away. "Dorothy and Irene—oh, what the hell, we were all in on it—we promised her she could join if she'd steal a pair of the housemother's underpants and hang it from the Tree House."

Ellis and I exchanged glances. It sounded like something we might have done ourselves.

"Mother Godfrey—Hazel, her name was . . ." Eva Jean shook her head. "Big as a Mack truck with sort of a bovine face. And strict! We were all scared to death of her. Made fun of her to her back, but never to her face." She shuddered. "No, Lord!"

"And did she?" Ellis asked. "Steal the underwear?"

"Carolyn was such a timid little thing, we never imagined she'd *dare,* but she did. Of course if we had known what would happen, we'd never have suggested it . . . but then you can't go back and change things. Oh, God, how I wish we could!"

Eva Jean Philbeck leaned back in her chair and looked at us. "She fell," she said. "Fell from the railing of the Tree House, they think. They found her the next morning with a broken neck."

"Somebody must remember when that happened," Ben said the next night as we walked home from a

254

local performance of *Arsenic and Old Lace* at the high school auditorium. "Do you know of anyone who might've been at the college during that time?"

It was cold and wind whipped the bare oaks on Heritage Avenue. We walked close together, arm in arm. Ben's big hand closed over mine and tucked it next to his chest, warming more than my hand. "Joy Ellen was probably still in high school then," I said. "And Blythe didn't come until much later."

"What about that peculiar little woman who hid out at your friend Zee's? I'm not too sure about her. Reminds me of Millicent Shackelford."

"Willene Benson? She's fairly new to the campus. Been there three or four years maybe." I waited to see how long it would take him to bait me again about Millicent Shackelford—whoever she was. It didn't take long.

"Couple of years ahead of me in school, Millicent was," Ben went on. "Her daddy ran the picture show and Millicent never missed a one. Claimed she got mixed up at the hospital and went home with the wrong parents." Ben sneaked a look at me. "Looked just like her daddy, though. All those Shackelfords have those big ol' teeth, just like Willene Benson. Acted kinda peculiar, too, she—"

"All right! *All right.* What happened to Millicent Shackelface—or whatever her name was?"

"Nothing much. Married some Yankee stationed at Fort Jackson and lived up north for a while before she brought him back home for a visit. Came home sayin' 'you guys' and 'Jee-a-zuz H. Chriiist!'" Ben laughed as he danced me around a puddle. "Hell, she'd only been up there six weeks!"

We were less than a block from home when Ben decided he needed some pie. The play had made him hungry, he said.

"We can pop some corn," I suggested.

"Don't want popcorn. Want cobbler—blackberry or cherry, maybe. Warm, with a big scoop of vanilla ice cream on top."

"Well, I don't have any," I said, trying not to think of it.

"But The Family Place does." He looked at his watch. "If we hurry, they might still be open."

The first time I ate at The Family Place I expected to find swarthy little men spooning up spaghetti in a dark back room, but it turned out to be exactly what the name implied. They specialized in country cooking, particularly desserts, and you didn't even breathe the air in there if you were on a diet.

I vowed anew to begin one as I pushed my empty plate away and added Equal to my coffee. The walls of the restaurant were filled with old kitchen gadgets, Burma-Shave verses, and faded family photographs that must have come from estate sales. Looking at them reminded me of what Willene had said about borrowing relatives from Blythe.

"I think I'll get Willene a picture frame for a house-warming present," I said. "Her walls look so bare, and she really is trying to make a home for herself. Jo Nell gave her this old end table she'd had for no telling how long and I'm curious to see what she'll do with it."

Ben put down his water glass. "How long has your cousin lived here in Stone's Throw?"

"Born here—just like me. Why?"

"Wouldn't she remember about the girl falling from the Tree House?" he asked. "The first girl, the one who started it all."

"I doubt it," I said. "I barely remember it myself. I think that happened while Jo Nell was working as a receptionist for that doctor's office in Charlotte. I can't imagine why she would've had a connection with the college during that time . . . but . . ."

"But what?"

"Nettie might, or better still, Idonia. In fact, I believe she was working in the registrar's office about then." Over the years Idonia had held an assortment of jobs, among them society editor of *The Messenger*, sales clerk at Mary Lynn's Fashions, and substitute teacher at the high school. She says the reason she didn't stick with one is because she likes variety. I say it's because she's so bossy nobody could put up with her for long.

If Idonia was around when Carolyn Steele was killed, I told Ben, she was sure to know all the details, but I knew better than to call her about it at midnight. Time and tide wait for no man, my granddaddy used to say, but I don't know anybody who would mess with Idonia Mae Culpepper's beauty sleep.

Claudia and Jo Nell were leaving when I dropped by Idonia's after class the next day and Zee's red Honda was in the driveway. Their surprise bordered on the uncomfortable and Zee acted as if she wanted to hide when I walked in. Were The Thursdays holding a secret meeting without me? Maybe I should have called first.

But their awkwardness vanished when I told them the reason I had come.

"Law, yes! I sure do remember when that poor girl fell," Idonia said. "I didn't actually see it, of course, but a student who helped in the office at the time was one of the ones who found her. Said it looked like she either tried to stand on the outside of the railing or leaned over too far.

"That was when you were living out west with what's-his-name, Zee. Your first husband—Walter, wasn't it? Anyway, there were Hazel Godfrey's big old drawers just abillowing from the Tree House, flapping like a great white sail. Trimmed in pink eyelet, somebody said. And that child lay there in the frosty grass all in a crumpled heap." Idonia paused to clear her throat and dabbed at a moistened eye.

I glanced at Zee, who rolled her eyes and smirked. The part about the frosty grass and crumpled heap had been added for our benefit, I thought.

"What about the girl's family?" I asked.

But Idonia didn't know. "Seems she didn't have any, or if she did, I didn't hear of it. It was awful for the college, and embarrassing for that housemother, too. I think she left after that.

"Nobody doubted it was an accident," Idonia said. "Sarah Bedford was just eager to put it all behind them and go on about business."

Until now, I thought.

I didn't have a chance to ask Claudia about her job prospects as she hurried away before I could speak. Did everyone know something I didn't? And if so, what?

"I think you'd better check your telephone messages," Augusta said when I got home. "She's called twice, and I'm afraid the woman is most distraught."

Both messages, I learned, were from Eva Jean Philbeck. I had left my number with her in case she heard from the other Jabberwocks, and the first one was an urgent plea for me to get back to her *soon*.

The second was even more demanding. "Mrs. Pilgrim—Lucy—God, I wish I knew where to reach you! I finally heard from Audrey and told her what you said. Carla, her daughter by her first husband, was killed several years ago in a fall from the Tree House at Sarah Bedford. An accident, they thought. At least they didn't find a note or anything. And I just learned a little while ago that Irene's poor little Rachel was the one who drowned in the lake."

I could hardly understand her last words because she was crying so. "And then there's Ken—our own Ken. Oh my God! Who's next?"

Chapter Twenty-three

*E*va Jean Philbeck had phoned the police, she told me when I returned her call, and they had checked the records at Sarah Bedford to try and locate Carolyn Steele's family. "It's the strangest thing," she said. "Carolyn was listed as a freshman that fall, but there's no record of her relatives or a home address." The woman had calmed down some, but her voice was still shaky. "I wish I could remember where she was from. Seems it was somewhere in the low country of the state—near the coast, I think."

"What about your son?" I asked. "Is he all right?"

"Yes, thank God! They're all here with us—the baby, too." Mrs. Philbeck sighed. "We think Ken has already paid his dues. I just hope whoever's responsible doesn't come back to finish the job."

It happened when Ken was fifteen, his mother told me. He was riding his bike home from school, as he did every day, when he was struck by a car and left bleeding by the side of the road. Neither the vehicle nor its driver was ever found.

"For a while we didn't know if he would live," she said. "And the doctors had little hope Kenneth would ever walk again. It's been a long uphill battle, but you saw him. Except for some scarring and one leg that's a little shorter than the other, you wouldn't know what he's been through." She paused. "I think—I *hope* whoever did this thinks he died."

"What about a note? Did he receive a verse?"

"I never knew about one, but Ken said he did. It came on a postcard a day or so before the accident, and since they were reading that book at school, he thought one of his friends had sent it as a joke. It didn't make any sense at the time, he said, but now that we look back on it, the verse suited well enough."

In what must have been her classroom voice, Eva Jean Philbeck quoted the first two lines:

"Beware the Jabberwock, my son!
The jaws that bite, the claws that catch!"

My son. Because the Philbecks had no daughter. It seemed as if the person behind all this had ignored the first verse and attempted to match the deed to the rhyme. And Kenneth Philbeck must have been first.

"I knew Irene had married an Isaacs but you know how you always remember old classmates by their maiden names, especially if you don't keep in touch," Eva Jean confessed. "She sent me an announcement when Rachel was born, but I never connected that girl's drowning with my old friend from college.

"I spoke with Irene's husband," she said. "He told me she hasn't been the same since it happened—been under a doctor's care. They found a verse, you know, but the police didn't want it publicized. I think Irene must've guessed then it had something to do with what happened to Carolyn. Blames herself for her daughter's death . . . Dear God, no wonder she can't deal with that!"

"After Kenneth, Carla Martinez must have been the second victim," I said, "only no one realized the connection because the verse was never found."

"I'm sure one must have been sent," Eva Jean said, "but it was probably overlooked. I guess nobody thought it was important.

"Audrey wasn't married to Carla's father very long," she said. "Frankly, I'd almost forgotten about him. Her name has been Tate for as long as I can remember."

"Well, that makes three of the Jabberwocks," I reminded her. "What about the others?"

"I don't know what in the world ever happened to Dorothy. The last I heard, she was living somewhere in Virginia. Audrey hasn't heard from her, either—and of course Irene is pretty much out of it. The people at Sarah Bedford are trying to track her down through the alumnae office."

"What was Dorothy's last name?" I asked.

"Cobb. Dorothy Cobb. Can't remember her married name."

Dorothy Cobb. D.C. "If she's who I think she is, she and her husband were killed in an accident several years ago," I said. "And her married name was Hunter."

"Oh, God. Of course! The girl who was killed in the shed." Eva Jean Philbeck began to cry. "I'm sorry. This is all so horrible . . . I didn't know about Dorothy."

"You said the other girl died several years ago.

Didn't you say her name was Maggie? Do you know if she had any children?"

"Maggie Talbot. Yes. There's a daughter. Maggie was the first of us to marry. Left school after her sophomore year, and then her young husband died. Some kind of automobile accident, I think. Maggie didn't have this baby until a few years later, after she married again. We were all so shocked when she died—during a fairly uncomplicated surgery, I believe. Allergic to the anesthetic."

Please, God, don't let this be happening!

"Married a Monroe," Eva Jean went on. "George Monroe. You know, that girl must be close to college age."

If Augusta hadn't been close by, I swear I think I would've fallen flat on the floor. "I can't believe this is happening!" I said, reaching out for her. "If we don't stop this maniac, Leslie's going to be next! Augusta, what can we do?"

The very touch of her infused me with calmness and I rested my head against her shoulder and closed my eyes for a minute. She smelled of fresh laundry dried in the summer sun—and of strawberries, of course.

"I know," she said. "I could tell by your conversation, but it won't help Leslie, or her aunt, either, if you let your emotions run away with you now." Augusta gave me a soothing little pat which I read to mean, "Chin up, shoulders back, and get on with it, Lucy Nan!"

Augusta walked to the window that overlooked the house next door. "The first order of the day is to get that child to a safe place, somewhere no one would even think to look for her."

I picked up the phone to call Nettie, then put it down and took a deep breath. "I'm going over there," I said. "Will you go with me, Augusta?"

"Of course," she said, throwing her cape about her. She was already on her way out the door.

"Is something wrong, Lucy Nan?" I must have looked like an apparition because Nettie seemed alarmed to see me standing in her kitchen doorway.

"Leslie. Nettie, where's Leslie?" The touch of Augusta's hand on my shoulder calmed my racing heart as I stepped inside.

"Why, she's right upstairs working on her term paper. What in the world's the matter with you, Lucy Nan?" Nettie took the top from a pan on the stove and turned crispy pieces of chicken that popped and crackled in deep fat. I probably gained five pounds just smelling it.

"Sit down, honey. There's plenty, and dinner's almost ready." Her voice dropped to a whisper. "*She* hardly eats a thing, you know. Now, what's all this about Leslie?"

"We have to get her out of here—hide her someplace they'll never think to look. Nettie, it's not Celeste they're after. It's Leslie."

She cocked her head to one side and frowned at me. "They? *They who?*"

"Whoever has been killing these girls—the person who left the verses. I don't want to frighten you, Nettie, but Leslie is next on the list."

She acted as though she hadn't heard me and reached for serving dishes in the cupboard, taking care to choose just the right ones, as if it were the most important thing in the world. While my neighbor took up the chicken and spooned butter beans into a yellow bowl, I told her about the Mad Jabberwocks and what had happened to Carolyn Steele. "Your niece Maggie was a member, and an offspring of every Jabberwock who was at Sarah Bedford during that time has been killed, except for the Philbecks' son Kenneth, and he was left for dead. That leaves Leslie."

Nettie pulled her apron over her head and sat, balling it into a wad in her lap. "But Leslie didn't get the verse, Celeste was the one who was sent the warning."

"It was a mistake. Just think about it, Nettie. Their names sound alike: Leslie Monroe, Celeste Mungo. And they live in the same dorm. Somebody put the verse in the wrong box."

Briefly she rested her face in her hands. "I can't let this get to me, Lucy Nan. George, Leslie's daddy, and his wife are on some kind of business trip in Chicago and I don't know how to reach them. I have to think about what to do, where to go."

"Even if they were at home, you couldn't send her there. It would be the first place they'd think to look. In fact, I'd rule out any close relatives," I said. "It has to be someplace where nobody knows her—as far away as you can get without being out of touch. Someplace they wouldn't link to Leslie, or to you."

Augusta stood behind Nettie, her hands on the back of the chair, and when I looked into her face her eyes gave me the answer.

Somebody who lives at the end of nowhere. Somebody with a heart as big as the country that surrounds her. Miss Corrie.

"Believe it," I said to Weigelia, using the telephone in Nettie's back hall. "Celeste is off the hook. It's Leslie Monroe they're after." I told her what I had learned about the Mad Jabberwocks. "I've already made arrangements with Miss Corrie Walraven for Leslie and her aunt to stay there for a while, at least until they find out who's responsible for all this, but they can't be ready to leave until morning. Do you think your cousin Kemper could find somebody to come over and keep an eye on things tonight?"

"Praise God!" Weigelia exclaimed. "Do-law, Lucy Nan, I didn't mean that like it sounded. You know I don't wish any harm to that other girl, but I feel like somebody's just lifted a slab o' marble off my back!"

I assured her that her reaction was perfectly natural and she promised to have Kemper phone me at Nettie's as soon as she could track him down.

It didn't take long. The phone rang less than ten minutes later. "That Weigelia Jones is one stubborn woman," Kemper said. "Just straining at the bit to tell

Celeste the news, and it took me a while to convince her it would be best not let her know of this latest development just yet. And we'll keep Sue Starnes on the job as well . . ." He hesitated. "There's a chance you could be wrong about this, you know . . . if not, we don't want the killer suspecting we know more than he thinks we do. Weigelia has promised she won't say a word about this to anybody, and contrary as she is, she's good for her word."

"I don't doubt that for a minute," I told him.

"And that goes for you and Miss Nettie, too. This can't go any farther until we catch this bas—uh—until we apprehend the perpetrator. Understand?"

I understood, I said. Weigelia was right. Her cousin really was bossy.

As far as the school officials were concerned, Leslie was away being treated for her eating disorder. And Kemper was right, it wouldn't do to let word get out that she was hiding because her life was in danger. I didn't want to frighten Nettie and her niece any more than I already had, but whoever put that verse in Celeste's box must know by now they made a mistake. I didn't think the killer was going to wait too long to make things right.

The phone was ringing when I got home from Nettie's and I hurried to answer, thinking it might be Kemper wanting more information about our plans with Miss Corrie.

"Mama . . ." It was Julie.

Now I can usually tell when my daughter begins

with that word if she's happy, sad, or in between. This time it sounded like the latter. There was a moment of silence on the line. "Buddy won't be staying with me in Cedartown. He moved out last week," Julie said.

If I could remember the words to "The Hallelujah Chorus," I would have burst into song. "He did?" With great difficulty I restrained myself from shouting for joy.

"I thought we could work things out between us," she said, "but I just can't see that happening. He left for Greenville last weekend to go into business with his daddy." My daughter didn't sound unduly distressed.

"I wish him luck," I said, and meant it. "Now tell me all about your new job."

Augusta and I celebrated this bit of good news with orange-cranberry scones and some of her apricot tea, which usually puts me right to sleep, but my thoughts kept wandering next door, where I knew Leslie and her aunt were spending an uneasy night. Kemper had appointed burly Bo Griffin, a rookie policeman who weighed at least two hundred and fifty pounds and was well over six feet tall, to sleep on Nettie's living room sofa. Still, it was after two before I finally nodded off.

"They're on their way," Augusta said the next morning at breakfast, looking as concerned as I felt. Nettie and her niece had planned to leave before light, with Bo riding "shotgun" for good measure, and I looked out the window to find both vehicles gone.

"I'm glad they got an early start," I said. "She'll be safer at Miss Corrie's, and Bo's right behind them . . ." *But he didn't plan to stay. What if something happens after he leaves?*

As usual, Augusta sensed my apprehension. "Would you feel better if I paid Miss Corrie a little visit—just to check things out?"

"That would be wonderful, Augusta! You must be a mind reader."

"Not at all, but I am in tune with the universe, and like you, I'd like to see the child secure in her new surroundings." Augusta poured a second cup of coffee. "Now please pass the strawberry jam."

Leslie had been worried about her class assignments and needed a couple of reference books to complete her term paper, so I promised her I'd take the morning off at Bellawood and get to Sarah Bedford early to take care of those things for her.

On our way home from the mountains a few days before, we'd stopped at one of those knickknack shops where I bought what looked like (but wasn't) an antique frame for Willene Benson. If I had time that morning, I planned to drop by the cafeteria and surprise her with it, but it would seem more like a gift if I wrapped it, so I scrambled in my closet for paper and took the brass scrolled frame from its wrappings. I had been in a hurry when I chose it, and now hoped it wouldn't be disappointing.

"I do hope Willene will like this. What do you think, Augusta?" I held the frame for the angel to see.

She set her coffee cup aside to examine it closely. "I believe I've seen this picture before."

"Probably. They put the same picture in a lot of them." I looked at the frame again. It appeared to be acceptable—even pretty—but the print did seem vaguely familiar. "You're right," I said (although Augusta usually is). "I've seen this photograph some-where else—and recently, too."

Augusta nodded. "Lucy Nan, I believe it's the same one Blythe Cornelius has on her living room wall."

"Why would Blythe hang a print of an old photo-graph in her apartment and tell everybody it's her family?" I asked. But even Augusta had no answer.

I repeated the question to Joy Ellen later as we pre-pared for class. We hoped to finish quilting today, even though Nettie wouldn't be there to help. She had accompanied Leslie to a facility that specialized in eating disorders, I explained.

"Lucy, are you *sure* it's the same one? After all, those old family pictures look pretty much alike."

"Yes, I'm sure. There's that big tree to one side, and a little barefooted boy wearing what looks like a base-ball cap on the front row." I got out the box of sewing supplies and put in on a nearby table. "And if that pic-ture's a commercial print, what about the others? All those relatives she calls by name?" I remembered the family portraits on the walls of the restaurant where

Ben and I had dessert. Did Blythe *purchase* her family at estate sales?

I had spent most of the morning chasing down Leslie's professors and getting her class assignments, reminding them about her eating problems and saying she hoped to be back after Thanksgiving. The reference books were on a shelf in Leslie's dorm room, and as I passed Blythe's apartment, it was all I could do to keep from knocking on her door to see if I could get another peek at the family photograph.

Blythe hurried out a few steps behind me as I left Emma Harris. She was on her way to her office, she said, and I explained to her about the books. "Leslie's had a little bit of a setback," I explained. "But they think she'll be able to come back to class after the holidays. I'm on my way to mail these to her now." I felt almost guilty for lying to her. Why, Blythe Cornelius loved these girls as she would her own. Didn't she?

I looked across at Celeste as we worked on the quilt later that morning. Sue Starnes had moved into the seat beside her and was helping with the stitching. Although neither of them knew about the recent developments concerning Leslie, I thought Sue probably would learn it from Captain Hardy when she finished her shift for the day.

The room grew silent as we sewed, with only an occasional banging of the radiators to remind us of the present. Was Blythe Cornelius pretending to be somebody else? I had been relieved when Sally Wooten produced snapshots proving another person had put

Blythe's thimble and sewing scissors in the pocket of that blood-spattered apron. Now I wondered who would've done such a thing. And why?

Had somebody been trying to tell us something? Someone who might have been too afraid to make an accusation? And I thought of the only recent victim who had no connection with the Mad Jabberwocks. Londus Clack. Shy, hardworking Londus who sang hymns with a recording bear.

I glanced at my watch. Another ten minutes of class. Would I still find it there?

Chapter Twenty-four

Londus Clack had wanted to tell me something the night of the fall festival. The next morning he was dead. If he knew time was running out, there was a chance he might have put something on tape.

I left Joy Ellen to gather up the quilting supplies and hurried across the chilly quad to Main Hall. It was a gray day, and the statue of Thaddeus G. Winterhalter, the school's first president, looked stiff and uncomfortable standing out in the cold with his bald head exposed to the elements. Of course he looked that way in hot weather, too. Students walked all hunched over, bending into the wind, hugging their books in front of them. I was glad for the excuse to rush, so my fast pace wouldn't seem unusual. Dark clouds hung low, and yellow lights shone in the windows of Main Hall as I hurried up the marble steps.

I passed the registrar's office where Violet Ambrose, assistant to the head honcho, sneered over her spectacles at a couple of demanding students. A little farther down the hall a fax machine spit Z's against a background of ringing telephones. Black scuff marks marred the once polished lobby floor, and the bronze bust of John C. Calhoun, one of South Carolina's most famous statesmen, needed dusting. Londus Clack, who only wanted to remain in the background, was noticeable by his absence.

The janitor's cleaning supplies were kept in a closet on a side hall and I prayed that the door wouldn't be locked. Earlier that day I had seen a lackadaisical maid pushing a dirty mop outside the dean's office on the first floor. She didn't look like the type who would be conscientious about securing the tools of her trade.

She wasn't. The key was still in the lock. I stepped inside and felt for the chain on the lightbulb hanging from the ceiling, kicking aside a bucket somebody had left in the middle of the floor. The room smelled like a soured mop. I looked for the bear. It was a big brown bear wearing a red jacket, and Londus might have taken it home, but I was counting on the fact that the janitor considered the closet his secret recording booth. It was far enough away from offices and classrooms so that no one could hear him rehearsing and seemed a logical place to conceal his "singing partner."

The bulb was dim and did little to illuminate the dark corners, and I wished I had brought along a flashlight as I stumbled over a box of what appeared to be containers of hand soap. I dropped my shoulder bag to the floor and edged to the back of the closet, fumbling among cans and bottles that crammed the shelves. The bear sat at the very end, smushed against the wall behind a huge carton of toilet paper. I had my hand on its fuzzy foot when a shadow crossed the open door, and I whirled about just in time to see someone lunge for my handbag and run, slamming the door behind them. The key turned in the lock.

It must have been a full minute before I recovered my senses enough to holler, and then I yelled all those ridiculous things I guess most people yell in situations like that: "Stop! Wait! Come back!" As if the thief were going to turn around and say, "Oh, I'm so very sorry! I'm afraid I've made a mistake. I'll be happy to return your handbag and let you out of the closet." This was getting to be a habit. The thing was, in the brief seconds before the door slammed, I saw the person who took my bag. And it was Blythe Cornelius.

Still, for a minute I thought it might be a joke and waited for her to come back and say, "Fooled you, didn't I?" But Blythe Cornelius didn't seem to be the type for practical jokes. And if she hadn't noticed I was in there, she should certainly know it by now. In addition to the yelling, I had found a metal candle holder which I bashed at regular intervals against the upturned bucket.

Nobody came. The maintenance supply closet was

too far removed from the administrative offices, although there were classrooms—now empty for the day—farther down the corridor. Directly across the hall was the backstage area of the vast auditorium, consisting of dressing rooms, wardrobe, and a couple of small lounges sometimes used as meeting rooms. I leaned against the heavy door and listened to the great organ bellow something that had to be Bach. I could scream and make noise all night, and nobody would hear. Why, oh, why did I insist that Augusta desert me for Miss Corrie's cabin in the Blue Ridge Mountains? And why hadn't I told Joy Ellen or *somebody* where I was going?

Because they probably wouldn't believe me, that's why. Especially if I confided my growing suspicions about Blythe. Yet it was all beginning to make sense. Blythe Cornelius could hardly see past the end of her nose. Without her reading glasses—and sometimes even with them—she had a problem making out letters. I had seen her bend a recipe card in order to read the ingredients, just as my near-blind postman mutilated envelopes. Blythe had misread the name over Celeste's mailbox, thinking it belonged to Leslie Monroe.

The organist across the hall paused and I grabbed the opportunity to get in some serious clanging, but the respite was brief. I had to think of another way to get attention.

I made my way back to the bear. At least Blythe didn't know about the bear! The tape was still inside its stomach and I sat on the bucket with the stuffed animal in my lap and pushed a button to make it play, wondering if Londus's niece really did give it to him, or if he had bought it for himself.

"Hark the herald angels sing, glory to the new born king!" The janitor's sweet but whangy tenor came over the tape and a salty tear oozed down my throat. Oh, Lord, Londus had been getting ready for Christmas!

There was a brief pause, then the sound of a door opening and Blythe's familiar voice.

"Londus, what in the world are you doing in here? What's this?"

"Oh, it's just a toy, ma'am. Got it for my niece for Christmas. Thought I'd hide it in here for a while. Reckon they'd mind?"

"I suppose not. Londus, why did you put my things in that dreadful apron pocket? I know it was you who did it, but for the life of me I can't imagine why."

There was a long silence here and I thought it was the end of the tape, but Londus finally answered.

"I seen you coming outta them woods, ma'am. It was real early that Saturday morning—the day that girl disappeared. And I seen what you did."

"Oh? And what was that?"

"Well . . . you went and put that bloody old apron in the bottom of the hamper there so nobody would think nothing about it when they found it. Only they did. Miz Willene, she knew that wasn't no chicken blood on thar.

"I thought you was a fine lady, Miz Blythe, but all this killin . . . it's wrong, a sin agin the Lord. And them poor little girls . . . well, they don't know what I know, and they won't listen to me, but I'm looking after them the best I can. I don't want nothing else bad happenin' here."

Blythe Cornelius sighed. "Oh, Londus! You know I would never do anything to hurt my girls. I only went for a short walk to clear my mind after sitting up with a sick student all night. I found that apron at the edge of the woods. A dog must've dragged it there." Her voice was sweet now, patronizing. "You do believe me, don't you, Londus . . . well . . . don't you?"

"I don't know, ma'am. I reckon."

"Well, I hope you won't mention this to anyone else. Nobody will believe you, and it will just make you look like a fool. You wouldn't want to lose your job, now, would you? Especially right before the holidays."

"No 'me, I reckon not . . ."

I heard the sound of a door closing and then Londus Clack's mumbled pronouncement: "Just like a time bomb tickin' away . . . that woman is flat-out lyin'."

I turned off the tape after realizing there was nothing more and sat for a minute holding the bear to my chest. The tape was evidence and I had to make sure nothing happened to it. But what if Blythe came back for it—and me?

It was almost five o'clock, and since I wasn't expected anywhere that day, who would know I was missing? Augusta was with Leslie, and Blythe had

277

taken my cell phone along with my purse. How long would it take somebody to get around to looking in a supply closet in the Main Hall at Sarah Bedford? My stomach growled. Although it wasn't close to supper-time, I had lunched hurriedly on cheese and crackers, and just the thought of missing a meal made me feel deprived. I thought hungrily of the package of peanuts in my handbag. Why would Blythe want my purse? Certainly not for the money, of which I had little—so why?

When I thought of it, the realization almost made me sick. Blythe Cornelius wanted to know where to find Leslie, *and her address was in my handbag!* I had as good as given it to her when I told her earlier that I was mailing Leslie her assignments and books. Imme-diately after leaving Blythe, I had gone to a mailing service near the campus and sent the items to Leslie in care of Miss Corrie. *The receipt was in my handbag.*

I had to get out of that closet! If only Augusta were there. Obsessed with her sick mission, Blythe Cor-nelius had locked me in to give her time to reach Leslie. The woman had killed those girls one by one, probably marking them off a list after the deed was done. And then she had killed Londus because he was too naïve and too honest to keep his mouth shut. I remembered Blythe explaining her scraped hand the night I found Londus Clack's body. She had hit it on the doorjamb, she said, yet I had been behind the door when she ran through before colliding with Monica Hornsby and Blythe hadn't come close to the doorjamb. I thought of the shoes she'd been wearing that night, although it hadn't registered with me at the time. The soles of the woman's sturdy gray oxfords had been still damp from the night grass. Blythe had fallen on the flagstone walk in her rush to get away after she'd killed that poor sweet man and left him hanging there. I was almost sure of it.

I took the tape out of the bear's stomach and hid it at the rear of the closet behind a bottle of glass cleaner; I then put the bear back where I had found him. Now the organist was playing something from Handel's *Messiah*. Appropriate. I would probably be in here until Christmas. I screamed a few times—just for the heck of it—and started looking for some other means of making my presence known.

What would Augusta do in my situation? I closed my eyes and pictured her there, sensing her calm presence. I could almost smell her strawberry essence, hear her humming her favorite song, "Coming in on a Wing and a Prayer"—always slightly out of tune.

The people who worked in the offices would be leaving soon if they weren't already gone. The student at the organ would finish her repertoire and go to dinner, and the maid had ditched her smelly mop and bucket for the day. Earlier I had tried to poke the key out of the door and slide it inside on a piece of paper, but Blythe had taken it with her. So . . . if making noise wouldn't get me rescued, I'd have to try another way.

Use your senses, Lucy Nan. Augusta's serene voice beside me was so convincing I looked around to see if she was there. She wasn't, but her message was clear. *Senses*.

Looking about, I found several bottles of bleach, but I didn't dare take a chance on breathing the fumes in a small enclosed place. The cleaning solution had a brisk, antiseptic odor, but it wasn't strong enough for my purposes. Finally I settled on a large two-gallon jug of oily red furniture polish that contained pine tar and smelled like the nastiest kind of cough medicine. Londus must have used it on wooden floors and furniture as well because I had noticed the odor in the halls at Emma Harris. There was at least a half-inch crack beneath the door and I poured the polish through the opening in a steady trickle, using a dust pan to divert the flow and keep it from coming back inside. The smell was overpowering, and I found a pile of relatively clean rags Londus had probably meant for dust cloths and tied one over my mouth and nose.

Kneeling, I poured the polish at an angle, hoping there would be enough slant in the floor so that it would drain into the front hall. God! Did all these people have clogged sinuses? The people in the next block should be able to get a good whiff of this stuff! I looked at my watch. Blythe had been gone almost an hour. She could be halfway to Miss Corrie's by now, and I couldn't do a thing to stop her! I drained the last of the polish and looked around for something else to pour.

I was on the third bottle of hand soap when I heard voices in the hall.

Chapter Twenty-five

"What *is* that god-awful smell?"

"Watch out, it's oily—don't step in it!"

"Looks like somebody turned over a vat of crankcase grease. How did it get way over here?"

"Where's it coming from?"

"*HERE!*" I screamed. "It's coming from *here!* Somebody please let me out of this closet—and hurry!"

I had to wait while one of them went back and looked for a key, which seemed to take forever. Meanwhile, one of the students who worked in the office stayed behind, to reassure me, I guess. "Ms. Harper was in here looking for you," she said. "Must've been about half an hour ago. Said it was real important."

"Do you know what she wanted?" The pine-tar fumes were getting to me and I tried to fan them away with the top of a cardboard box.

"Didn't say, just that it was real important. Are you all right, Ms. Pilgrim? You haven't been . . . well, hurt or anything, have you?"

"Look, don't worry about me. I'll be okay. But I want you to hurry now and call the police—and keep them on the line until I can talk with them. Tell them it's an emergency." Maybe it wasn't too late to stop Blythe Cornelius.

A few minutes later I heard Violet Ambrose rattling keys in the lock. "What in the world is this vile stuff you've poured on my floor?" she said. "I almost broke my neck trying to straddle it—and God only knows what it's doing to the marble. I just hope it's not going to stain."

I heard the blessed sound of the latch clicking and the door opened a little at a time, as if Violet were afraid to let me out all at once. "What on earth were you doing in there?" she said, stepping aside as I skidded into freedom.

"Contemplating my navel." *You autocratic, clabber-faced old moth. Damn!* What was I going to do for car keys if Blythe had taken my purse? "Has anybody seen a brown shoulder bag?" I asked.

They hadn't, but after a hurried search somebody found it in the trash can just outside the front door, complete with everything but my cell phone *and the receipt for Leslie's package!*

Captain Hardy had left for the day, the police dispatcher said, so I told Ed Tillman what had happened. I've known Ed since he and my son, Roger, played together as children and I knew he had a level head on his shoulders, but I doubted if he thought the same of me.

"You've got to stop her," I said. "She's probably over halfway to Miss Corrie's by now. Somebody has to warn them!"

"Now slow down, Miss Lucy Nan, and start over," Ed told me. And so I did, but I don't think he believed me . . . until I told him about the tape—my proof, of sorts. While Violet was trying keys in the door, I had taken it from its hiding place and I wasn't letting it out of my hands.

"Stay there, I'll be right over," Ed told me. "And I'm putting in a call now to the sheriff up there— Alleghany County, isn't it? Meanwhile, why don't you get in touch with this woman, Corrie, and let them know what's going on? You have her number, don't you?"

I did. It was in the little notebook where I kept names of resource people for my history class and for activities at Bellawood, only the little notebook was in my office at the plantation. While Violet scurried about trying to find somebody to clean the floor, I got Corrie Walraven's number from the information operator and hoped I would reach her in time.

The line was busy. With Ed's help, I persuaded the operator to interrupt the call and found myself talking to somebody named Gladys who was on Miss Corrie's party line. "Oh, Lord, yes, I'll free the line, honey! Is anything wrong? Corrie's not sick, is she? Anything I can do?"

Just hang up, I told her, and give me a chance to call. And she did. I had a strong suspicion Gladys would listen in, but it didn't matter because nobody answered the telephone at the little gray house on the mountain.

I called again. And again. Fear and frustration rose like boiling water inside me until I thought I might explode. And that was how Joy Ellen found me. I hadn't had a chance to call her, but somebody else had, and now she came running in looking bleached but unironed, so I guessed she'd heard all the details.

"What's all this about Blythe?" she asked after she saw I was still in one piece. "Leslie Monroe called looking for you and left a crazy message with my student assistant."

"Leslie? When? What did she say?"

Joy Ellen looked at her watch. "Oh, about two hours ago, I guess. I didn't see it until I got back to my office after class, and she didn't leave a number. I've been looking all over town for you—knew you couldn't have gone far since your car's still here. What in hell's going on, Lucy?"

I told her as much as I knew. "What did Leslie say? Blythe couldn't have reached her that soon. That was before she knew where to find her."

Joy Ellen plunked herself on a bench outside the dean's office and shrugged out of her jacket. "Said she remembered something about Blythe . . . the night before D.C. was killed."

I paced in front of her, too antsy to sit. "Well, what about her?"

"Leslie said she remembered seeing Blythe knocking at D.C.'s door that night. It was kind of hot, she said, and she was lying in bed with her door open trying to get to sleep when she heard somebody walk past."

"How did she know it was Blythe?"

"Not much doubt about it. Leslie had left a note on Blythe's door asking her to check on D.C. because she was in such an emotional state, then D.C.'s door opened and Blythe went on inside. Didn't stay long, but Leslie said she could hear them talking. After a few minutes, Blythe went on back downstairs."

"Then later Blythe claimed she hadn't seen D.C. that night, so Leslie must have known she was lying," I said. "That must have been when Blythe gave D.C. the fictitious message that her lover would meet her in the old shed.

"But why didn't Leslie say something about this before?" I asked, listening to Miss Corrie's telephone ringing on and on.

"D.C. had been gone for at least a couple of days before anybody became concerned," Joy Ellen said. "And then we didn't know what had happened until the girls came upon her there in that old stone shed, remember?"

"Remember? How could I ever forget?"

"Blythe told the police she'd only left the infirmary to get that sick girl some pajamas," Joy Ellen continued. "Claimed she didn't see D.C. that morning at all." She shrugged. "Maybe Leslie thought she'd just imagined seeing her—dreamed it or something."

Leslie couldn't let herself believe their beloved Aunt Shug could possibly have had anything to do with D.C.'s death, and no doubt did her best to block the idea out of her mind—yet her mind had trouble accepting it. Soon after that happened, Leslie began having a recurrence of her emotional problems. Now the fear for her life, the awful threat hanging over her must have jarred her back to rationality. *Leslie*

Monroe saw what she saw, heard what she heard, and now she knew the truth.

I sat with my hand on the telephone. There was no use calling anymore. Miss Corrie wasn't there. Maybe she and Nettie had taken Leslie somewhere for safety's sake. And Augusta would be nearby. Oh, God, I hoped so!

I stayed long enough to give my story and Londus Clack's taped conversation to Ed Tillman. He had contacted the Alleghany County Sheriff, he told me, and Captain Hardy was on his way over, but Ed already knew everything I had to say and the tape would tell the rest. Nettie McGinnis had been like a second mother to me since we moved into the house next door over twenty years before, and I was responsible for sending Nettie and her niece to Miss Corrie's. If anything happened to either of them, I didn't think I could bear it.

"I need your cell phone," I whispered, taking Joy Ellen aside.

"Why? What for?" she bellowed.

I explained, as quietly as I could, what I planned to do. "It may be too late to warn them, but I have to try. I want you to tell Ed I'm in the rest room," I said. "Tell him I'm not feeling well . . . tell him I have a galloping gallbladder—I don't care, but try to stall him as long as you can."

Joy Ellen gave my shoulder a squeeze as she put the phone into my hand. "Good luck—and be careful!" she said under her breath.

I had no idea what kind of car Blythe drove, so I made a quick stop at Willene Benson's before leaving town. She met me at the door with a puzzled smile. "Lucy! Come in and see what I'm going to put in that lovely frame you gave me."

I didn't have time to pad the blow. I told her what Blythe had done, and what I *thought* she had done as quickly as I could. "What kind of car does she drive, Willene? I want to be on the lookout for her."

She stammered the description so I had to ask her to repeat it. If I had slapped the woman I don't think she would have been more stunned. "It's a Buick—tan, I believe. I'm afraid I don't know the year. Why, it hasn't been much more than an hour since she phoned me, Lucy. Asked me if I'd feed her cats for a day or so. Seemed sort of abrupt, I thought, but then Blythe has been acting a little strange lately . . . and did you notice that print in the frame you gave me? It's the very same one she has in her living room . . ."

I gave her Joy Ellen's cell phone number so she could call me if she happened to hear from Blythe again, and she was still rambling as she followed me out the door. ". . . still, I can't believe Blythe could be capable of killing anyone! Are you sure about this, Lucy? That has to be a mistake."

"Lock your doors!" I called to her as I hurried to the car. If Blythe were to phone her I wondered if Willene would tell her she had seen me.

Although Joy Ellen had given me her word she would try to stall the local police as long as possible,

I stiffened whenever a car approached, prepared for sirens and blinking lights. I had promised Ed Tillman I would wait for him, and neither he nor Captain Hardy were going to be happy about me taking things into my own hands. It was dark when I drove past the turnoff to Kings Mountain where Ben and I had picnicked days before. How different it was from the last trip to Miss Corrie's for our afternoon of soap-making, when it had seemed more like a family outing than a class field trip. Now, as I sped through sleeping farmland, I felt a gray chill inside and out. Tonight I was alone, and I was frightened. "What am I going to find when I get there?" I asked aloud.

"I can't answer that, but whatever it is, we'll face it together," a voice spoke beside me. Augusta!

"Am I glad to see you! But what made you come back?" If I hadn't been driving, I would have hugged her. "And is Leslie all right? I haven't been able to reach them."

"They reached their destination safely, and I lingered long enough to see that they weren't in any immediate danger. Corrie Walraven is a capable woman and a kind one as well. When I left they were picking out nut meats for an applesauce cake." Augusta rolled down her window and let the wind blow her autumn-gold hair.

"But Blythe Cornelius is on her way there," I said. "Augusta, she means to kill Leslie! Leslie needs your protection more than I do right now."

The angel nodded. "I'm aware of that, Lucy Nan,

but you are my first priority, and I sensed that something was dreadfully amiss back at the college."

"That would be putting it mildly," I said, and told her about being locked in the closet in Sarah Bedford's Main Hall. "You must have heard me hollering," I joked.

"I try to keep my nose to the ground and my ear to the grindstone," she said, adjusting the mirror on the car's visor.

That sounded extremely painful to me, but I was currently concentrating on the turnoff for Interstate 40 in Hickory, North Carolina, and so I let it pass. I had thought briefly of phoning Eva Jean Philbeck to ask if she remembered Blythe Cornelius, but I didn't want to take the time. I hoped that her family was safe, and was glad I hadn't told anyone there remained another living victim of Blythe's deranged scheme.

We drove past farmhouses set back from the road and framed by dark silhouettes of trees. The lights from their windows looked warm and inviting and I couldn't help but feel a bit envious. "I suppose families are gathered around their supper tables—safe and together," I pointed out, "and here we are driving blindly into only God knows what."

"That assumption is correct," Augusta said, closing her window against the chilly night. "You do, however, possess the power and intelligence to make wise choices, Lucy Nan . . . and, of course, you have me."

I thought about my children, Roger and Julie, and of how important they were in my life, and of how I looked forward to watching Teddy grow up. "Well, if anything happens to me, I'm going to really be pissed to miss out on the rest of my life," I replied.

"That's exactly why I'm here, but you must be aware that you're responsible for your own decisions," Augusta said. "And using vulgar language doesn't add to your advantage."

"Huh!" I said, and glanced over to find her smiling. "I don't suppose you told anyone where you were going," she added.

"Then you suppose wrong. Every police department between Stone's Throw and Alleghany County probably knows where I am by now. I just hope no one has mentioned it to Roger." My son was the more protective of our two children and I didn't have the time or the inclination to explain my actions on a daily basis. And Ben wasn't going to be thrilled about it, either, I thought. Well, what he didn't know wouldn't hurt him. He would be there if I needed him. And that was enough.

Near Statesville we merged into the main highway, Interstate 77, which would take us closer to where both Virginia and Tennessee border North Carolina before we turned off on Highway 21. There the road became steeper, climbing past stubbled fields and into woodlands.

Augusta had been silent for most of the drive, and from time to time I noticed her studying the dark landscape beyond her window. "From what you've told me, there doesn't seem to be any particular order in the way Blythe Cornelius chose her victims," she said finally. "The first, Kenneth Philbeck, had been only fifteen and the youngest. Then some time passed before Carla Martinez was killed, and later, Rachel Isaacs and D.C. Hunter. Now she seems to be intent on finding Leslie. Why now?"

I remembered Nettie's visit to her niece's dormitory after her first quilting class at Sarah Bedford. Ellis and I had found her having tea in Blythe's apartment, and she had told Blythe Cornelius about Leslie's mother living there.

I lurched to avoid a possum in the road, wondering if that particular species had made a suicide pact to throw themselves in front of vehicles, and frowned, carefully watching the road ahead as I thought of that afternoon. "Blythe had been interested in Leslie's mother's name," I said, relating the incident to Augusta. "She even encouraged the girl to point her out in an old yearbook. Maggie Talbot didn't have any living children by her first husband, Doug Dixon, so Blythe was probably not aware that she had remarried and produced a daughter *until Nettie told her!*

"And now it seems like Leslie's health might prevent her from returning to school for a while—"

"And so Blythe feels compelled to accomplish her bizarre mission at all costs," Augusta added.

And that was what frightened me the most. This woman didn't care about her own future; she didn't care about the people who got in her way. She meant to find the last of the Jabberwock children, and she meant to kill her.

Chapter Twenty-six

The closer we got to Miss Corrie's, the heavier the lump in my stomach became, until it felt like I'd swallowed one of those "fallen rocks" by the side of the road. With any luck, I thought, the sheriff had already apprehended Blythe Cornelius and she was safely locked away. But luck doesn't always jump in my lap, so I wasn't going to be surprised at anything we found.

Earlier I had turned off my car heater. Even as cold as it was—and it was close to freezing here in the mountains—my forehead was clammy with perspiration, while Augusta, wrapped in a blanket, shivered beside me. I held onto the steering wheel the way a drowning person must grip a lifeline and searched for landmarks on the narrow gravel road.

"There's a small white church in the bend of the road just before we turn off," I said to Augusta. "Help me keep an eye out for it."

"I think we just passed it on the right," she said, pulling the blanket closer about her.

"Then the road to her house should be just up ahead." Concentrating on the dark shapes of rocks and underbrush on either side of the road, I went right past the faded red sign that marked Miss Corrie's turnoff. "Now's the time to start praying," I said, searching for a place to turn around in the narrow winding road. "If we meet another car out here, we're dead meat—or at least I am!"

Minutes later, having accomplished this, I swerved left at the wooden sign, hoping I wouldn't go into the ditch on either side. In the darkness it was almost impossible to see the rugged weed-grown trail that wound up the hillside. "If Blythe Cornelius found Corrie Walraven's house on her first try—and at night, to boot—she must be kin to Daniel Boone," I said.

Augusta must have noticed the anxiety in my voice because she reached out and touched my arm. "We're almost there," she said in her soothing lullaby voice.

Still, it seemed we should have been there by now and I was beginning to wonder if we had taken a wrong turn when I saw the welcoming beam of a flashlight approaching and a familiar voice called my name. Nettie!

"I've never been as glad to see anybody in all my life!" I yelled as the two of us hugged each other in the wavering yellow light. The man who held it was in uniform and looked as though he'd like for us to quit dancing around in the road and get inside where it was warm. He had a point.

Augusta, I noticed, had already gone ahead and Nettie rode with me while the man with the light led the way. Ed Tillman had called the sheriff's department there, my neighbor told me, and they told her I was on my way. "Where is she?" I asked as we bumped to a stop in Miss Corrie's slate-and-clay yard. "Is Leslie all right?" When I opened my door, I saw Nettie was crying.

"Oh, Lucy Nan, I wish I knew! We left home so

quickly this morning, we forgot to pack a lot of things we needed, so early this afternoon I drove back to Sparta to do a little emergency shopping. Couldn't have been gone more than an hour or so, but when I got back here they were both gone . . . and oh, dear God, I don't know what to think!"

The door was unlocked, Nettie said, and she thought Miss Corrie might have taken Leslie for a walk, but when they didn't return after an hour, she telephoned the county police. Not long after that, Ed Tillman contacted the sheriff there about Blythe Cornelius.

"And you haven't heard anything since?" I asked as we walked inside together.

"Nothing, except for Henry. That's Miss Corrie's 'baby' brother—funny old man—he told me not to worry, that his sister wouldn't let any harm come to Leslie, and not to answer the phone. And then he left, just took off in that old beat-up truck of his, and he hasn't come back. The sheriff's been out here off and on all night, and they've put out an ABC—or whatever—on Blythe Cornelius." Nettie took my arm as we warmed ourselves by Miss Corrie's wood-burning stove where, I noticed, Augusta was already established. "Lucy Nan, do you really believe Blythe is behind all this? She seemed genuinely fond of those girls. And to think Leslie was *right there in the building* with her all that time!"

"Yes, I believe it," I said, and told her about Leslie's phone call to Joy Ellen. "She must have called while you were out shopping—when she realized Blythe had been lying about seeing D.C. Hunter the night before she disappeared."

Nettie frowned. "Do you suppose that's why Corrie took her away?"

"Probably," I said, to reassure myself as well as Nettie, "and maybe it's just as well that she did." I told her about Blythe locking me in the closet, but I didn't tell her how she learned about Leslie's identity. I never would. "Blythe took only two things from my handbag—Corrie's address and my cell phone. I'm surprised she hasn't tried to call."

"I expect she has," Nettie said. "Corrie's phone has rung several times, but Henry told me not to answer it, so I didn't." She nodded toward the lanky policeman. "James here stays in touch with everyone through his radio."

James had taken up residence in the kitchen, where he cracked and ate pecans and stayed in contact with his partner at the county sheriff's department. He was there for the night, he assured us, and later, when Nettie was out of hearing range, confided that Blythe's tan Buick had been sighted in the area.

"Where?" I whispered. "How long ago was this?"

He concentrated on picking a nut meat from its shell, then got up and loped to the window, squinting into the darkness. "Couple of times, 'bout ten minutes apart, but by the time we got there she was gone. Must know we're on her tail, though. Last sighting was less than an hour ago."

"Then Leslie and Miss Corrie couldn't be with her.

295

They disappeared long before Blythe had time to get up here." But where were they? And if they were safe, why didn't they let us know?

"You don't think she's found them, do you?" I spoke softly so Nettie wouldn't hear. "I mean, Blythe doesn't know the area, except maybe how to get here, and she must know you're watching the house."

He nodded, and I could see he was avoiding my gaze. "Well, I reckon she could've called the girl on her cell phone—looks like she took it with her—told her some story or other to get her to meet her somewhere."

But knowing what Leslie did, I didn't think she would agree to that. In the darkness outside the window a cold wind rattled the bare branches of a sourwood tree by the back porch. Surely the two women had taken shelter from the bone-chilling weather.

"Does Miss Corrie have a car?" I asked.

"No," James said, "but her brother Henry does, and it's not here."

And neither was Henry.

Later, when Nettie disappeared into the kitchen to make hot chocolate to go with our "supper" of applesauce cake, Augusta reminded me that I hadn't yet spoken with Eva Jean Philbeck to warn her about Blythe Cornelius.

I was relieved to find her at home. "Blythe Cornelius . . . Blythe Cornelius . . ." I could almost hear the whirring of her mind. Then a gasp. "No, it can't be! There was a woman by that name—I think it was Cornelius—in one of my classes when I took a few courses in summer school back in . . ."

"When? When was it?"

"It was the summer before Ken's accident. Blythe and I took a computer course together. I'd been wanting to learn and she was working on a business degree. She seemed lonely. She was a widow, she said, and sometimes we'd have lunch together, or go for coffee or something. She told me she didn't have any family, and I think she just wanted somebody to talk to." Eva Jean's voice quivered. "I think I must have talked too much."

"Why?" I asked. "What do you mean?"

"I told her about the Mad Jabberwocks. Oh, Lucy, I must have started it all!"

After she had composed herself Eva Jean told me how the subject had come about. "We were talking about college," she said. "Blythe was putting herself through school and I told her how I admired her for it, and how we had kind of taken things for granted at Sarah Bedford. She seemed interested—asked me about going to school there, when I was there, things like that. Of course I thought she was just being polite. Her sister went to school at Sarah Bedford, she said. And I suppose I must have been feeling guilty because I told her about our silly little club and how I was afraid we were to blame for a girl's death. That always bothered me, you know—bothered me a lot—and

Blythe was easy to talk to. You've met her, you know how she is."

What willpower it must have taken for Blythe Cornelius to appear calm and friendly after Eva Jean's confession, I thought. A few months later she began her campaign of revenge, and the next year came to Sarah Bedford as Dean Holland's secretary and took rooms in Emma P. Harris Hall. I felt a flulike chill just thinking of it.

"How could she be sure these girls would be coming to Sarah Bedford?" I asked.

"There was no way she could be positive, but I must have mentioned that Audrey and Irene had planned to send their daughters there. A lot of alums send their children to Sarah Bedford. Ken would probably have gone there, too, if he'd been a girl. It *is* a good little school, you know, for all our bad-mouthing it."

Or was. I hoped it could survive.

Later I dozed in the old cane-back rocking chair in Miss Corrie's tiny front parlor with one of her colorful handmade afghans over my lap. I had insisted that Nettie stretch out on the daybed, and although she swore she'd never sleep a wink, now and then I heard a soft little snore coming from beneath the faded patchwork quilt. The old house was cooling now, and once in a while a coal popped in the stove on the hearth. I was glad when the Walravens' big white cat, Aunt Mamie, leaped into my lap and curled up like a warm muff.

Captain Hardy had called earlier to get a report from

James, and to tell me he was trying to come up with a law I was breaking so he could lock me away. "If we'd known what was on your mind," he said, "we would've let you *stay* in that closet! If Blythe Cornelius hadn't been in such a hurry she would have silenced you the way she did Londus Clack. There's no telling what the woman might do if your paths cross again.

"Thought I'd better warn you," he added. "We got a call a little while ago from Willene Benson—says her gun is missing. She got to worrying after you left there today and thought she'd better check. Thinks Blythe Cornelius must've taken it sometime before she got home this afternoon. Blythe has a key to her place, she said."

When the young patrolman went outside to check the grounds, I told Augusta what I had learned. "The captain said they were keeping in close contact with the sheriff here, but it looks like Blythe has gone underground for the night."

"Of course she might be anywhere," Augusta reminded me. "There are plenty of places to hide in the mountains."

"Thank you for that comforting thought," I said.

Augusta warmed her hands at the stove. "What manner of person could hide her wickedness so well that she won not only the trust, but in some cases, the love of her intended victims?" Her eyes darkened to the same smoky twilight blue as the necklace she wore. "Poisoned with bitterness," she said. "What a sad waste."

After a good bit of backtracking, I told her, Captain Hardy said they had dredged up enough information on Blythe Cornelius to explain the reasons for her mad behavior. Carolyn Steele, the girl who fell while attempting what she thought was an initiation requirement, was Blythe's younger sister and only living relative. The two girls were orphaned at an early age, he said, and lived on a farm outside Columbia with an elderly aunt. After she died when Carolyn was ten, and Blythe, twenty, Blythe raised the child herself and saved for her education. Carolyn was all the family she had and she devoted herself to her.

"But she must have married," Augusta whispered with a glance at my sleeping neighbor, "since the sisters didn't share the same last name."

Several years after Carolyn's death, I explained, Blythe fell in love with Jack Cornelius, a carpenter, but they had been married only a short time when he was killed in an accident on a construction site. Lonely and bitter, when Blythe learned the truth about her sister's death, the canker of vengeance grew until it blotted out everything else.

"I suppose her pathetic need for a family led Blythe to invent one with other people's old photographs," Augusta said.

I nodded. "Probably the only *real* family picture the woman owned was the one on her living room table, the photograph of the two sisters as children."

And now she had a gun. There was no verse about firearms in the "Jabberwocky" poem, but now that she was this close to the end, I didn't think Blythe Cornelius would be a stickler for details.

I shifted in my chair, waking the cat. The contours of the rocker had been molded to somebody with a much bigger bottom than Miss Corrie's skinny little fanny, and the cushion underneath me did little to fill the hollow. I was on the edge of sleep when a car pulled up outside and a low exchange of male voices came from the kitchen. A few minutes later I heard the groaning of footsteps in the small back room and a light shone under the door. Henry must be home. Had he found Miss Corrie and Leslie? I threw off my lap robe to ask James, but he must have anticipated my question because he came to the door and whispered, "Go on back to sleep. I'll wake you if we hear anything, but there's not much we can do until morning."

The next thing I knew I was looking up at Santa Claus in earflaps, and Augusta was nowhere around.

Toto, I don't think we're in Kansas anymore, I thought as I squinted past the not-so-little round belly and into his broad bearded face. He wore an ancient leather jacket over bib overalls and smelled of fresh sawdust. "It's time," Henry Walraven said.

I yawned and pulled the coverlet up to my chin. "Time for what?"

"If you want to see Corrie and the girl, we'd best be leavin' now." I heard a noise behind me and saw that Nettie was already dressed for the outdoors and had even found a pair of Leslie's socks and walking shoes

301

for me. I dug my gloves out of my jacket pocket, pulled the warm hood over my head, and started after them. The three of us left quietly out the front way because James was asleep with his head on the kitchen table and his feet sprawled on either side of his chair. The old Seth Thomas clock on Miss Corrie's mantel that probably had ticked away at least a century said twelve minutes past six, and it was still dark outside.

A current of warm air had descended on the mountain during the night and thick fog clung to the landscape. I could hardly see two feet in front of me, but Henry seemed to know where he was going, so Nettie and I followed along behind him, wading through tall wet grass and shoving aside branches. At one point the old man held apart rusty strands of barbed wire so that we could step through into what once must have been a pasture. On the other side he helped us over a clear stream that gurgled past smooth brown rocks.

Still we climbed. Twigs snapped underfoot and we fought our way through loops of snakelike kudzu vines, dormant and brown for the winter. I smelled wood smoke from somebody's fire, and a couple of squirrels scampered past, but other than our noisy passage they were the only signs of activity. I glanced at Nettie, puffing as she walked, but with a determined look on her round face. That treadmill she'd invested in last year must be paying off, as she didn't seem as out of breath as I was.

Henry had not spoken since we left the house and I had no idea what had happened to Augusta. Were we crazy to trust this strange old man without waking the sleeping policeman? Nettie pointed out that he had even pinned up the two dogs to keep them from following us. Now we seemed to be wandering aimlessly, following no path that I could see, and I had no idea where we were going.

Finally we stopped, and through filmy patches of fog I saw the tops of trees below. It seemed we had been walking for at least an hour, but when I looked at my watch I saw that it had only been about thirty-five minutes.

"Do-law, these old bones are about to give out on me!" Nettie said, taking advantage of a convenient rock to sit and rest. I was glad to join her.

Henry shoved his cap in his pocket and smiled at us. "Oughtta be there right soon now."

"Where?" I asked. "Where are we going?"

"Goin' to Mama Doc's up on the ridge a piece."

Nettie wiped moisture from her face with what she once jokingly called her "dew rag." "Mama Doc's. Is that where they are? Leslie and Miss Corrie?" Her tone said, *You'd better not mess with me, man!*

Henry nodded. "Used to be the 'yarb' woman, Mama Doc did. Still does a little doctorin', I reckon, but she's gettin' on close to ninety. Ain't nobody knows whar she lives 'cept we'uns that growed up here. Nobody goin' find her there."

After Henry started talking, seems like he didn't want to stop. He told us how Blythe had called the day before and Leslie recognized her voice when she answered the phone. "Scared that young'un plumb to death, and Corrie knew she had to get her away from there afore dark." He had driven his pickup all over the county the night before, he said, to see if he could catch a glimpse of Blythe's car. "Got good eyesight," he bragged. "Just as good as when I was a young'un, but I never seen it."

It wasn't long afterward that I began to feel uneasy. I felt exposed, vulnerable, and longed for a nice safe hole to hide in. I could tell Henry sensed it, too. The two of us walked in silence, with me looking over my shoulder now and then to be sure no one was behind us, but Nettie kept up a constant chatter. Now that she knew Leslie was safe, she expressed her admiration for just about everything in sight: the size of the trees, the view from the hillside, the trickle of water over mossy stones.

Finally, with a shake of his head, Henry laid a finger aside of his nose, making him look even more like an old Coca-Cola ad. Nettie looked at me and shrugged, but plodded on in silence. The land had leveled off some, so the climb wasn't as steep now, but fog had settled even closer in the higher regions, almost obscuring the ground.

"Now, right hyare's where the way branches off," Henry said in a louder-than-usual voice. "The left leads back down toward the main road, but we want to keep straight. Mama Doc's is jest a little ways ahead." And he shot out his stout arms like a crossing guard, forcing

Nettie and me behind him onto the path to the left, then signaled us to continue quietly up the hillside.

One look at Nettie McGinnis told me she suspected the same thing I did. *Someone—possibly Blythe Cornelius—was following us up the mountain,* and yet I wasn't afraid. Augusta was near. I could sense her reassuring presence, and I silently took my neighbor's hand, hoping to pass along my new-found confidence. At this point it was essential that we remain calm—or "think blue," as Augusta says. And Nettie must have gotten the message because she gave me a stiff little smile and squeezed my fingers.

Draped in fog and with Henry in the lead, we inched a few steps farther until he directed us to crouch behind a large outcropping of rock. Nettie's knees popped as she stooped and I held my breath as I heard the crunch of footsteps coming closer. Leaning against the rock, Nettie stiffened and held a hand to her mouth as though to silence her breathing. We knew who it would be.

I heard her breathing before the mist parted briefly and we saw her pass below us. A green plaid shawl covered her short graying curls and she wore the collar of her navy jacket turned up against the weather, but I recognized Blythe Cornelius. And she was carrying a gun. She must have hidden close by in her car all night waiting for us to lead her to Leslie, and if any of us made the slightest noise she wouldn't have to be a crack shot to bring one of us down.

I was getting a cramp in my foot when Henry

silently prodded us onward. What if Blythe heard us here? What if she hadn't fallen for Henry's deception and was quietly stalking our footsteps? Then suddenly there was the cabin: Mama Doc's cabin, snug against the mountain with the clouds for a coverlet and the hillside for a lap. And there on the stoop stood Miss Corrie with a big smile on her face, and Leslie, waving, was running to meet us.

I wanted to call out to her, to warn her not to shout, but Henry shook his head and smiled. "Ain't no need to worry now," he said, plopping down on Mama Doc's big rock doorstep. "The way she was agoin', and with this fog thick as it is, won't be long afore that woman takes to flyin'."

"Flying?" I felt all weepy watching Leslie and her aunt hugging each other.

"Yep. Nothing out there but a sheer drop-off. Straight down for at least three hundred feet."

And that was when I heard Blythe Cornelius scream.

Epilogue

"I heard some of the students who left Sarah Bedford have already returned," Zee announced as The Thursdays gathered in my sitting room to work on our annual project for children who would be spending the holidays at the local hospital. This year, instead of the customary sock dolls, we were making rag dolls from a pattern Claudia had found in a craft magazine. It was too soon to be sure, but the idea seemed like an improvement of sorts.

"Blythe Cornelius always seemed like such a nice person," Jo Nell declared. "For the life of me, I just can't imagine her being behind a cold-blooded plan like that. Did the woman have no conscience at all?"

"Crazy," Ellis said. "Pure-T crazy! When people get like that they lose all ability to reason."

"Blythe was wonderfully patient with Dean Holland, though," I pointed out. "I think she was genuinely fond of him. You're going to have your work cut out for you, Claudia."

Our friend would soon be taking over as the dean's assistant as well as various other duties and could hardly wait to begin.

Ellis smiled. "Oh, he's such a teddy bear! You'll get along just fine." She glanced at my efforts at stuffing. "Lucy Nan, I don't want to start a rumor here, but you might want to keep a closer eye on your little Daisy Marguerite. She looks a little bit pregnant to me."

"There's no such thing as a little bit pregnant," I said, examining the lumpy creation I had named Daisy Marguerite because the doll resembled a girl I disliked back in the second grade.

Idonia reached for the fiberfill. "I'm just relieved to know Blythe Cornelius won't ever hurt anybody again. Must've bounced off every rock going down—"

"It was kind of Willene to take in her cats," Nettie said quickly.

"They should be good company for her," Zee added, "but if I had an ex like Willene's, I'd rather have a great big guard dog."

"I think that judge shook him up pretty good," I said. "And besides, Willene's a lot tougher than we gave her credit for."

"Sure is. I heard she was toting a piece," Zee said. "And even wears white after Labor Day," Idonia added.

Ellis giggled. "Chews gum in church, too—bless her heart."

Jo Nell tossed a sofa pillow in her direction. "Oh, hush! You're bad—all of you! Nettie, you and Lucy Nan must have been terrified up on that mountain, knowing that woman was lurking somewhere close by."

My cousin has become fond of the verb *lurk,* I've noticed, and uses it as often as possible. "What's done is done," Nettie said, biting off a thread. "I just hope Leslie can put it behind her. Under the circumstances her parents have persuaded her to transfer to another school when she finishes with her treatment.

"I'll never forget Corrie's brother, Henry, though. What a peculiar little fellow he was! I asked him how he knew what to do when Blythe was so close to finding us, and do you know what he said? Told me an angel warned him—said he saw her plain as day! Can you believe that—*an angel?*"

Ellis concentrated on her sewing. "Yes, I can believe it," she said. "Well, frankly, I've slept sound as a baby ever since," Nettie vowed. "What about you, Lucy Nan . . . Lucy Nan?"

"Earth to Lucy Nan Pilgrim, come in, come in!" Ellis said, and I realized I had let bits of the conversation sail right past.

"Sorry, I was just thinking about what to serve Jessica for Thanksgiving dinner since she won't eat turkey," I explained, although, to be honest, I was a little miffed at my friends' recent secretive activities and wasn't in much of a mood to chat. They had tried to gloss over their little get-togethers, explaining them away with flimsy excuses, such as, *Nettie wanted to show me that old photo of my mother when they were in school together . . . Zee needed a fourth for bridge . . . Idonia asked for help refinishing a table . . . Jo Nell promised she'd teach me how to make ambrosia . . .* I was beginning to get that "cold left-out feeling," and frankly, I was sick of it. It was on the tip of my tongue to say just that when Ellis stepped up with a smile.

"Shall we let her in on it, ladies?"

"Let me in on what?" I asked, immediately suspicious.

"We know your birthday isn't until January, but since Julie will be here for the holidays, we thought you might like your present early," Jo Nell said, producing a large brown bundle she'd stuffed into the hall closet.

"What present?" We usually didn't give birthday gifts, but the year I turned fifty they had all chipped in for a box of denture cleaner and a membership to the AARP, so I was understandably leery.

"It's something you've always wanted," Nettie said.

Claudia took the misshapen doll from my hands. "Why don't you just open it and find out?"

I glanced up to see Augusta standing by the fireplace with what can only be described as an impish smile on her face, and tugged at the yarn bow. Folded inside the paper was a quilted coverlet of multiple colors and designs. "You've made me a quilt!" I couldn't say another word because the tears were on the spillway and I hate it when people cry over things like that.

"Well, not a quilt, exactly," Zee said. "We didn't have time for a quilt, so it's more of a throw, but if you feed it vitamins, maybe it'll grow into one."

"Why, this is from that dress you made to wear to Roger's wedding," I said to Nettie, recognizing a square of turquoise silk. "And you've embroidered your name on it, too!"

"We all did," Claudia told me. "That's why it took us so long. I hope you can read mine."

"It's wonderful! Beautiful!" I held the coverlet to the window light to better see a square of tiny red and white stripes. "Mama made me a dress like that when I was in the fifth grade, remember?" I looked at Ellis. "Where did you find the scraps?"

She shrugged, exchanging smiles with Augusta. "I just had to know where to look."

Idonia fingered the throw, lingering over a lavender iridescent square in the center. "How lovely! Why, it seems to change colors. Where on earth did this one come from?"

But nobody answered, because nobody knew that most likely it didn't come from earth at all. Except for Ellis and me. And Augusta, of course.

Augusta's Savory Fish Stew

4 cups mild fish
3 strips bacon
1 lb. can diced tomatoes
1 8 oz. can tomato sauce
1 28 oz. can vegetable juice
½ lemon, sliced
1 large onion, chopped
5 or 6 small potatoes, peeled and diced
2 teaspoons salt (or to taste)
1 tablespoon hot sauce
2 tablespoons Worcestershire sauce
½ teaspoon black pepper
½ teaspoon curry powder (optional)

Precook fish. Fry bacon in large pot. Remove bacon and save. Combine all ingredients except fish and bacon, bring to a boil, and simmer, uncovered, for 1 hour. Scoop out lemon and add crumbled precooked fish. Cover and simmer for an hour or more, topping servings with crumbled bacon. May be served over rice. Serves 6-8.

Orange Cranberry Scones

2 cups flour
½ teaspoon baking soda
¼ teaspoon salt
¼ cup sugar
grated rind of one orange (can use dried variety)
½ cup butter, chilled
½ cup buttermilk
½ cup dried cranberries

Preheat oven to 350 degrees.

Stir together flour, baking soda, salt, sugar, and orange rind. Cut in butter until mixture resembles coarse meal. Gradually stir in buttermilk until all ingredients are moistened and a dough forms. Turn out onto a floured surface and knead in cranberries. Roll out dough to ½-inch thickness and cut in rounds. Bake for about 15 minutes, or until golden brown, on a lightly greased cookie sheet. Makes about a dozen.

Grated Sweet Potato Pudding

2 fairly large raw sweet potatoes, peeled and
  grated (about 2 cups)
1 cup sugar
¾ cup milk
2 eggs, beaten
¼ cup melted butter
½ teaspoon cinnamon
¼ teaspoon nutmeg
¼ teaspoon cloves
¼ teaspoon allspice
¼ teaspoon ginger
½ teaspoon vanilla extract

Preheat oven to 350 degrees.

Combine all ingredients and pour into a greased baking dish (better in a cast-iron pan). Bake for 1 hour, stirring several times during cooking. Good served with cream. (Or even without!) Serves 6.

Lemon Mystery

2 tablespoons butter
1 cup sugar
4 tablespoons flour
juice and grated rind of one lemon
3 eggs, yolks and whites beaten separately
1½ cups milk

Preheat oven to 350 degrees.

Cream butter and sugar together. Add flour, salt, lemon rind and juice. Stir in egg yolks mixed with the milk, then add beaten whites. Pour into a greased baking dish and set the dish in a pan of hot water. Bake for 45 minutes. Good just plain or served with whipped cream. Serves 6.

Lemon Chess Pie

1 tablespoon plain flour, sifted
1 tablespoon plain cornmeal, sifted
2 cups sugar
4 eggs
¼ cup milk
¼ cup melted butter
¼ cup lemon juice
1 teaspoon grated lemon rind
1 deep dish unbaked pie shell

Preheat oven to 350 degrees.

Toss together flour and cornmeal and add sugar. Cream in eggs, milk, butter, lemon juice, and grated rind. Pour into pie shell and bake until set (about 40–45 minutes). Cover crust with foil for part of the baking time to keep it from burning. You can get two pies from this recipe, but I find they are a little shallow. I sometimes use this filling for tarts. Serves 6.

Mimmer's Squash Casserole

1½ pounds small summer squash (about 2 cups, cooked)

1 medium onion, chopped (save half for casserole)

3 tablespoons butter

½ cup milk (canned is good)

2 eggs, beaten

1 cup toasted bread crumbs or soda-cracker crumbs

¾–1 cup grated cheddar cheese (optional)

¾ teaspoon salt

¼ teaspoon pepper

extra bread crumbs and a little extra butter

paprika

Preheat oven to 350 degrees.

Cook squash and ½ onion in salted water until tender; drain well and mash coarsely with fork. Add butter, milk, eggs, crumbs, cheese, ½ onion, and salt and pepper. Pour into greased casserole dish and sprinkle with extra crumbs. Dot with about a tablespoon butter and sprinkle with paprika. Bake for 45 minutes, uncovered. Serves 6-8.

Cheese Olive Balls

2 cups sharp cheddar cheese, grated
½ cup butter, softened
1 cup sifted flour
½ teaspoon salt
½ teaspoon paprika
dash of hot sauce
dash of Worcestershire sauce, if desired
48 small pimento-stuffed olives, drained

Preheat oven to 400 degrees.

Cream butter and cheese and stir in other ingredients, except the olives. Mix well.

Wrap a little over a teaspoon of dough around each olive, covering it completely. Bake on ungreased baking sheet for about 15 minutes, or until done. (Watch closely, as ovens vary.) These can be frozen on a cookie sheet and transferred to a freezer bag, to be baked later if you want to make them ahead of time. Makes 48.

Center Point Publishing
600 Brooks Road ● PO Box 1
Thorndike ME 04986-0001 USA

(207) 568-3717

US & Canada:
1 800 929-9108